Lilith

BOOKS BY ERIC RICKSTAD

Lilith

a novel

ERIC RICKSTAD

**BLACK
STONE**
PUBLISHING

Printed in the United States of America

First edition: 2024
ISBN 978-1-0940-0074-9
Fiction / Crime

Version 1

Blackstone Publishing
31 Mistletoe Rd.
Ashland, OR 97520

www.BlackstonePublishing.com

For my wife, daughter, and son. Always.

Book I

"I don't wanna go to school."

Lydan tugs his Snoopy sheet over his head and curls up, his back to me.

I wish I could keep him home. I do. I wish I could crawl into bed with him and snuggle him, tell him silly riddles, and help him organize his Pokémon cards all day.

But I can't.

He's my son. I am his mother. But I can't.

He's not sick. I can hear it in his voice, see it in his eyes. A mother knows. My mama always knew. Once, as a child, in a bid to stay home from school, I ran hot tap water on a washcloth, then pressed the cloth to my forehead, and I opened a can of hash and scooped the hash into the toilet and told Mama to feel how hot my forehead was and to look at my vomit in the toilet, and she felt my forehead and looked in the toilet, and she said, "You must be dead, because you have a fever of a hundred and twelve degrees and you're throwing up food you never ate. Now listen. Listen good, child. There are people in this world, people who are truly sick, people who truly suffer, and you are not sick, you do not suffer, and you don't ever want to be one of them or make light of others' trials. And don't waste food like that. Show respect. You can go without dinner tonight. But"—and Mama smiled her smile that could melt the sun—"I give you an A for creativity. It will serve you one day, you will see, that imagination of yours, that *mind*. You are special, my special one. Chosen to use your gifts."

"You have to go to school," I tell Lydan. It's not true. He doesn't *have* to go. A son does not have to be sick to stay home with his mama, does he? No. I could call in. That's why we have PTO. I could spend my time with my boy today. All we have is time. More than that: We *are* time. We are physical markers of time, no more and no less than the mountain wearing down over epochs or the mayfly fluttering away its few ephemeral moments. He is time and I am time and right now our times align, and I know that this will not always be; already our times are diverging, and he does not always want to spend his time with his mama, with my time. And one day, both an eternity into the future and in a single beat of my heart, it will be all I can do to have my son visit the older me and ask how I am doing, if I need anything, before he shoves off again to his life he's made, or spare me a brief video chat the day after my birthday apologizing for forgetting it—he got busy, but *happy birthday and I love you, Ma. Gotta run. My own life beckons.* I know he will do this because this is the way of things. It was this way with me and my mama and her with her mama and on and back and back. But now. Right now. He, my boy, my son, he is saying, *Spend time with me, Mama. Stay home with me. Be with me. Just for today. Before it is too late.* Right now, he is offering me a gift. And I, the responsible one with the job, with other children who need me today of all days, am going to refuse that gift and say no and regret it until the mountains and the mayfly are forever vanished from this earth.

"Please," he says.

I feel unwarranted resentment at his plea. It's not easy, holding another life in one's hands. Mama knew. She who raised me alone, me with no memory at all of the man I would have called Papa.

"You have to go to school," I tell Lydan.

"I got an icky feeling," Lydan says.

I worm a hand beneath his bedsheets and press a palm to his forehead.

"You aren't warm," I say.

I press a fingertip to his neck.

"Your glands aren't swollen."

Yet I do sense something troubling him.

I wonder if there's some conflict with a classmate. Already, even at his tender age, Lydan faces social struggles—a private life with his friends and those who are not friends—that he no longer shares as freely with me as he did just a couple of months ago but that I hear about from other teachers and kids. It's the natural order of things, but that doesn't mean it doesn't shatter me.

"Are you having trouble with a friend?" I say.

Monastic silence.

"With a bully?" I say.

Silence.

"I just got an icky feeling," he says.

"You can't stay home if you're not really sick." I loathe each syllable I speak, each cell of myself. Because I can feel it. Something is wrong. This is not the same day as all the other days before it. This is the start of something, yet I cannot know what that something is. I can only feel its edges, as if I am in a deep, dark cave, trying to find my way with my fingertips out to the sunshine.

All I can muster is a cliché response, as if I am reading a line from a play written for me by someone else, but I have no free will to go off script. "You'll get to see your friends after being stuck here with boring Mama all weekend."

"I won't go."

"You have to. I can't just play hooky." A lie. To soften it, I say, "It stinks to go to school on *any* Monday, let alone *this* Monday. I'd like to get in my pj's and snuggle in with my buddy, eat doughnuts, tell each other riddles, organize your Pokémon cards."

"I won't *go.*"

I snatch a bowl crusted with dried cereal from his nightstand.

"Get up," I say. "We leave in fifteen minutes."

I park my car in the empty teachers' lot and get out and open Lydan's door, wait for Lydan to unbuckle his seat belt, lug on his backpack, and trudge out of the car. His face is glum, his shoulders slack. He didn't speak on the drive, just stared out the window as if there were nothing out there to see, as if our world were no longer out there.

"Go play on the playground. Your friends will be there soon," I say.

"Can we go home? *Please?*"

I lift his chin with two fingers to meet his eyes with my own. "What's going on?" I say.

Lydan seems about to speak. No, not speak: confess. I want him to tell me what is happening. Explain it to me. Give me a reason to go home. If he can, I will take him home so we can tell each other ridiculous riddles.

But time ticks a second too long.

"Liiee-duuun!"

A boy beckons Lydan from the playground swing set.

Lydan looks at me with a face of torment.

"Liiie-duuun!"

"Lydan, what is it?" I say.

Lydan waves at his friend. "Coming!" He adjusts his backpack and heads off toward the playground without a goodbye.

If Red or Blue Lights Are Flashing DO NOT Enter SCHOOL!

I press the call button outside the main entrance and stare up at the CCTV camera.

The lock buzzes and clacks as if I'm entering the Pentagon.

I am cold with dread.

The lobby is empty.

The tile floors gleam from their weekend polishing.

I walk the desolate hall, its yellow cinder-block walls decorated with colorful construction-paper leaves cut so lovingly and earnestly by the first graders.

At my classroom door, I try to still my heart, but my heart won't be stilled.

I am early. I am always early the third Monday of the month. I require time to settle my nerves before my kids arrive. I could have spent more time at home with Lydan, not rushed him. No harm would have been done. Still, I need time to myself here in my classroom this morning.

What has become of this world? I wonder for the thousandth time. The millionth. What went so wrong that the morning's task before me has grown so rote that teachers and children alike perform it without qualm or question, as if it is normal?

It is not normal.

It is a tear in the fabric.

A societal psychosis.

It claws my heart ragged, drowns me in helplessness, as if I am the one failing the children, as if I am the one responsible for this godless state of affairs.

I sit at my desk. My temple flutters.

I stare at the nap mats stacked in the corner of the room.

Goldfish swim in endless circles in their fishbowl perched on the window ledge.

The two hamsters scurry on their wheels, getting nowhere for all their effort.

The second hand of the analog wall clock ticks.

tick tick tick

     tick

        tick

           tick

              tick

tick

tick

tick

I wish the clock would stop.

I wish time would stop.

I wish I could go back in time to before all this began.

Back to when?

When *did* it begin?

Colorado?

Oklahoma City?

Hiroshima?

Cain and Abel?

Eden?

The primordial swamp?

Has it always existed, this vulgar compulsion for destruction, germinating, populating and repopulating, until now it is an insidious, noxious weed, its roots too deep and fixed and stubborn to rip out from the hardened earth of so-called humanity, its thorny stems too tough for the axe, its fruit poisoned?

Is this the fruit of the nation?

Of humankind?

Is this what must be accepted?

I cannot accept it.

Will not.

Ever.

Is there any going back, or is there only ever marching forward toward the end?

Is there no hope?

Is there no one who will rise up and do what is—

A muffled scream startles me.

Outside the window, on the playground, Lydan cries out as he and two friends clown around on the monkey bars. I feel compelled to go get him and bring him home and spend the day as he wanted. It's not too late.

"Ms. Ross?"

A student, Jennifer Pettibone, stands in the doorway, clutching her My Little Pony lunch box to her puny chest and gazing at me with her cosmic green eyes. "Ms. Ross?" Jennifer says again. "Is today Lockdown Monday?"

I nod.

"I *knew* it. You always cry on Lockdown Monday."

I touch a fingertip to my damp cheek.

"Do you want me to crawl under the sand table now?" Jennifer says.

"Wait until the rest of the class is here."

I stare out the window at Lydan.

I must get him home.

"Ms. Ross?"

I blink.

Jennifer is staring at me.

"My brother says hiding under a sand table is like hiding under a piece of paper," she says. "He says it's stupid, that I'll just be blasted to raw hamburger. Is that true? Will I be blasted to raw hamburger? Or is he just trying to scare me?"

"He's—"

"Did you have Lockdown Mondays when you were in kindergarten?" Jennifer says.

I tell her no, we didn't.

"How come?"

"I . . . Things were different then."

I must get Lydan.

"*How?*" Jennifer says.

"They. We. The people. Were different. Somehow," I say. I don't know if this is true or not. Maybe I am remembering wrong. But something along the way *happened*, and if somebody doesn't *do* something soon—

Jennifer watches the goldfish swim in circles.

She taps a fingertip on the glass bowl, panicking the fish.

"Don't," I say.

"I wish things were like when you grew up," Jennifer says.

I need to get Lydan.

"Look at *me!*" Jennifer has crawled under the sand table. She knocks on its plastic bottom with a serious, calculating face.

"Don't," I plead. "Please."

"My brother's right," Jennifer says. "I am going to be blasted to raw hamburger."

I turn to the window.

Lydan is gone.

The kids and I are singing "The Wheels on the Bus."

I try to sing in a cheery, floating voice as they follow in unison:

> *The wheels on the bus go round and round,*
> *round and round,*
> *round and round.*
> *The wheels on the bus go round and round,*
> *aaalll through the town.*
> *The babies on the bus go—*

Pop pop pop.

Out in the hall.

Pop pop pop.

Muted, dissonant. Popcorn in the microwave.

Pop. Pop pop.

Silence.

Wails.

"Under your desks!" I scream, breaking rule number one: *Do not scream. Remain calm for the kids.*

Pop.

Crack

crack

crack crack crack

Lydan.
Down the hall. An ocean between us, and I cannot swim.
pop

                   pop

                                   pop

Pop pop pop popopopopopopopopopopopopop

I fight against my soul to remain here, desperate to go to my son.
My son, who did not want to be here.
I lock the classroom door, an unpardonable sin against my own flesh.
I stare at the kids.
They stare back.
Fear rampages in their eyes.
They know.
They've always known.
This is the horror of it.
To know.
One day.
Out, a voice demands. *Out.*
I look around as if someone spoke beside me. But there is no one here except me and my students, and Mama, who I carry in my heart and speak to in my dreams. I know this voice but don't know this voice. I've heard it all my life, yet I have never heard it. It is my voice, yet it is a revelation, an ancient voice, as if I myself am a stranger, speaking to myself, across all of time.
We are supposed to stay here and hide under desks, the sand table, and . . . wait.
Wait for what?
Death.

No. I will not wait for it.

"Out." I point at the door that leads out to the playground.

"We're supposed to get under," Jennifer says.

"Out."

I unlock the door and throw it open.

"Stay calm," I say. "It's probably someone with firecrackers."

"That's not firecrackers," a boy says; I can't remember his name.

I cup the back of the boy's head and herd him and the others outside. Once out, I say, "We're going to race across the field to the town library. Anyone who beats me gets ten dollars. Run!"

The kids run their hearts out.

The librarian looks up from her circulation desk at us. She knows.

She hurries to lock the library's steel door behind us, tells the few patrons sitting in the periodicals, "Upstairs. Now." She leads the kids up to a room whose door is blocked by a paperback carousel rack. "Inside." I push the carousel out of the way. The librarian and the others hide inside.

"Give me the keys to the library," I say. The librarian gives me the keys.

I shut the door, drag the carousel back into place.

Outside, I lock the steel library door behind me and look out across the field toward the school.

Lydan is in there. Somewhere.

I race to the back of the school, to the door nearest Lydan's classroom, and press my back to the brick wall. Blood hurricanes in my head.

A door next to me is propped open a crack with a folding chair.

Someone from maintenance must have put it there while they lugged equipment in or out.

I grab the door handle. Behind me, a man's voice commands: "Stop!"

I throw open the door and lunge inside, knocking the folding chair to the floor as I fall to my knees in the hall.

The door shuts behind me and locks.

The corridor is foul with the acrid odor of gunpowder.

A fog of gun smoke crawls along the ceiling.

Around the corner, toward Lydan's classroom, gunshots echo off the cinder-block walls.

Silence.

My body pulses with adrenalized fear.

I run for Lydan's classroom. The door is open, splintered from gunfire. I lurch inside, shut and lock the door behind me.

Silence floods me.

Breaks my bones.

Horror.

Everywhere.

Horror.

My mind is a shorted electrical wire, my vision a fractured kaleidoscope.

I grip a child's desk to keep from collapsing.

My hand is sopped with blood.

My mind disbelieves what my eyes see.

I vomit down the front of my shirt.

Time fractures.

I am here but not here.

I am me but not me.

I have never existed and never will exist.

I have existed for eternity.

This is real and not real.

I force myself to look among the ruined bodies for Lydan.

Vomit again.

Lydan. Where *is* he?

A whimper behind me, behind a closed closet door.

Blood seeps from beneath.

Pop. Pop pop.

In the hall.

A shriek, cut short.

I want to run out into the hall. My life be damned. Rake his eyes out. Rip his heart from his chest.

Remember this rage. Remember it.

A moan from the closet.

I slip in blood, slide toward the closet, ease open the door.

A boy. Fetal. Wedged against the far rack of art supplies, hands and arms cradling his head, painted with blood, face turned away.

Lydan?

What was he wearing this morning? I can't remember. Can't remember what his face looks like. My own son's face. My mind is bleached. Terror howls in my head.

I crouch. My fingers touch his shoulder. He recoils and whimpers, an abused animal. So much blood.

"Not again," he whimpers. "Please. Not again."

It is Lydan.

A sob heaves out of me.

His life. Our life. It is gone. Obliterated.

I shut the closet door. Darkness claims us.

"Shhh. It's me." I shake so violently I can barely speak. I feel I will break apart. "It's okay," I say in the dangerous darkness, as I have said so many nights in the safe darkness of Lydan's bedroom when he has awakened from a bad dream. "Shhh. It's Mama. Shhhhhhh. Now. Baby. Mama is here. Right here. Shhhhhh."

Crack.

Just outside the classroom door.

Lydan's chest makes deep, wet sucking sounds. He moans, too loudly.

"Shhh. Please, shhh." I hold him close. I do not want to hurt him more than he's already hurt, but I must hold him, cradle him as I did those first few short years when he sought it, needed it. He needs it again now. I do not dare let him go. Oh God, if I let him go.

Rage ruptures me. Hatred incinerates my heart.

I kiss my boy's face, his cold clay cheeks.

"Mama is here," I say. I am no longer sobbing. I am a rock as I rock my baby boy.

If we stay, we die.

We. Will. Die.

I crack open the closet door and peek out.

A shadow passes by on the other side of the classroom door's window.

I heft Lydan up, sling his arm around my shoulder; his blood, wet and warm, drenches me. I nudge the closet door open wider with my hip.

The figure passes by the door's window again.

There is no door to the outside in this classroom. Just a window that cranks open a few inches.

Lydan's ribs rise and fall, shallow and weak, with the sound of a balloon leaking air. I don't dare put him down.

Carrying Lydan, I step toward the body of a man slumped in a chair at the teacher's desk. He's been shot in the head. Stan Taylor. He started his teaching career three weeks ago. Garrulous, creative, a teacher adored by students and teachers and parents alike. A natural. What *was* he, twenty-three years old?

"Close your eyes," I say to Lydan, even though his eyes are rolled so far to the back of his head that only the whites show. I don't know if he hears me or not. I rest him as gently as I can on a desk, beneath which lie two destroyed children.

The classroom doorknob rattles.

It knows someone is alive in here because I locked the door behind me.

I pick up a wooden chair and smash it against the window. The glass spiderwebs.

Poppoppop.

Wood splinters around the classroom door's knob.

I slam the chair against the window again. The glass shatters.

Pop pop. The doorknob blasts from the door.

I lift Lydan in my arms, unable to be gentle any longer as he bellows in pain. I push out the window, shoving Lydan in front of me, my body between him and what is behind us.

My face is gashed and arms sliced on ragged glass teeth that rim the window frame as we escape out of the mouth of the beast.

Crack crack.

A ferocious, cauterizing heat rips at my side, sears my flesh.

I fall next to Lydan as he howls.

His howl is music.

The music of life.

He's alive. For now.

Two men in black riot gear charge past us, toward the smashed window.

I look back and see a man standing in the classroom looking out the smashed window, his face as pale as the moon.

Dark, bleak, bottomless time. I sit a sleepless vigil beside Lydan's ICU bed, sob until I am emptied, numbed, and dead. It terrifies me, this deadness, as if it is I and not Lydan suspended in the pentobarbital coma.

Ethereal specters—Doctors and nurses? Police or friends? Who knows? Who cares?—orbit in and out of my peripheral vision, speaking fleeting comforts that evaporate in the air.

Hours on hours, days on days, ocean-trench-black nights on nights, I sit. I wait. I watch. Lydan's sealed, plum-swollen eyelids twitch. The air is sour, medicinal, and ill with the monotonous suck and wheeze and beep and gasp of monitors and tubes and pumps that both violate and assist Lydan's brutalized body. My torso's shredded, puckered flesh numb, zippered with sutures black and crusted beneath a bandage. No memory of it. Dead. What I suffered is a skinned knee to what Lydan suffered. I remember nothing of my days here, save the details told to me of my son's injuries. These are carved into my heart.

Nine hours of surgery to salvage his bladder so it might work half as well as it did, if infections do not consume him. His prostate cut from his thin boy body, seminal vesicles too, rendering him unable to know a certain intimacy but familiar with the incontinence of the old man he probably will never be, his injuries likely to shorten his life by at least two decades. If he survives the next breath. If he ever wakes. And this surgery came only after another that was more vital.

Seventeen hours of delicate, intensive surgery on his lower spine, two cracked vertebrae fused together using bone from his hip, the shrapnel from a bullet lodged too close to his spinal cord to risk removal. His gallbladder gone, as well as a lymph node. Feet of small intestine excised, the lower lobe of his right lung damaged, leaving him with such diminished capacity that playing on the jungle gym will be tantamount to summiting Everest. My boy's body parts incinerated somewhere in the bowels of the hospital. All this just his bodily damage. Who can know the damage to his soul and mind?

For what?

My phone lights up and vibrates and pings and jangles in a cascade of texts and calls and emails from friends and scavengers, profiteers, and leeches.

I let each message plummet into the void. None of it means anything.

I am beyond condolence.

I am beyond the reach of my fellow human beings.

Beyond God.

Adrift in isolation, cracked wide open, flayed by grief and rage.

I shut off the phone.

Someone has left a newspaper here.

I read only enough to have the names and faces of the wounded and dead branded in my memory.

I hear the newspaper flutter down the thousand years to the floor.

A voice.

But no one is here.

It comes from a tiny TV perched in a high corner of the room.

I didn't know the TV was here. Someone must have turned it on.

Or perhaps it has been on all along. I don't remember.

I don't care.

A pale flicker plays on the walls in my shadowed nighttime hour.

A man on the TV is talking to a blond woman.

The man is broad and bulked. He sports a double-breasted navy blazer that fits square on his frame. His mane of hair, mantled above his immense forehead, is the same deep shoe-polish black as his handlebar mustache.

His unbuttoned blazer reveals a silver dress shirt that shimmers like shark skin and a tie as red as blood embroidered in white thread with the words THE 2ND AMENDMENT IS MY GUN PERMIT.

I gnaw the inside of my cheek. Taste blood.

The ticker below the man: *Maximillian Akers: Founder of More Guns Less Crime.*

The anchor says: "Maximillian Akers. You're a regular we speak with here, as our loyal viewers know, after terrible events like yesterday's at the Bristol High School in Indiana."

Indiana.

Another one.

Already.

"These events are such a tragedy, Suze," this Akers says.

Events.

Tragedy.

"We invite you because you *are* the leading expert on the Second Amendment," Suze says. "And you believe that the Second Amendment is under siege and events like yesterday's, and last month's at Franklin Elementary in Franklin, Michigan, are being weaponized to take away your rights. You believe more guns is the answer to stop these sad events?"

More guns.

Akers winks at Suze. "Suze. Suze. Suze. I believe that with every drop of my red, white, and blue blood. That's why More Guns Less Crime pushes for all students and teachers to legally carry firearms on campuses and in schools nationwide, as is their God-given right."

God.

"Think, Suze. If teachers and students, good, God-loving citizens, are armed and trained—and More Guns Less Crime trains folks; you can sign up for a reasonable fee to get training at any of our five franchised schools across this great land—do you think someone is going to try to shoot up a class if they know classmates and teachers and even the damn janitor are armed and trained to kill?"

Suze nods for him to continue.

"That's why, Suze, that's why for ten years of owning my gun shop here in Jessup, the leading gun shop in all these great United States, I haven't had a security system. I don't need one. I got iron bars in the windows for nighttime security. And from the second I step foot out of the house in the morning, I have a Beretta M9 strapped to my hip to defend myself in any and all situations against the evils of this world. I don't need anything else."

"Opponents call you the Profiteer of Paranoia," Suze says, "say you play off people's fears to make an obscene profit of blood money. They say the Rolex you wear is an example of a fortune amassed by body count—"

With a practiced vigor, Akers snaps his arm out, his French cuff riding up to reveal a fat gold Rolex that hulks on his hairy wrist.

"My followers embrace my success as a *legal* gun dealer. They'd love to be in my shoes. Who doesn't want a Rolex? None of my gun sales have ever been proved to be linked to a shooting or to illegal provenance."

Proved to be.

"They point to your vast amounts of holdings in arms manufacturers," Suze says.

"*Not* illegal. It's my God-given right to make money. Frankly, I am sick and tired of being slandered and victimized. We all are," Akers says. "I speak for millions of good people. And I profit off *reality*. And *the reality is* that the fear my followers have of their guns and rights being stripped away is real because the threat is real. And these events, they're used against those who love their country and, yes, their guns the most. What is wrong with loving what keeps you safe and free from tyranny? Some even say these events at schools are staged."

Nausea bubbles in me.

"Do you believe this?" Suze says.

"I'm no expert. But . . . who am I to say otherwise?" he says. "My opponents can't attack facts, so they attack success. That's what losers do, Suze: attack winners."

"They say you lack empathy for the children."

"As a father, I *pray* for the children. No one prays harder for them than I do."

His voice slurs, degenerates to a guttural demonic growl. His face distorts; flesh melts from the bone to reveal the skull of a bloodless fiend beneath.

"It kills me," Akers says, "*literally* kills me, to see these sad events exploited to take our guns based on emotions. Not facts." His voice is normal again, appearance human.

My exhaustion must have me seeing things.

"I'm famous for saying, 'Save our students; arm our teachers!' Someone's got to *fight* to see those kids don't die in vain. God has chosen me as his general in this war to save America."

God, again.

I know God; I've studied the book. Despite my protests, I was made to attend Sunday school, receive Communion, achieve confirmation. I never went back after I did, but I can still attest I do not recognize this God Akers touts.

"Maximillian Akers," Suze says, "founder of More Guns Less Crime and owner of the world-famous Max Gun Shop in Jessup, Iowa. As always, it's an honor to have you speak with us."

"God bless you, Suze, and God bless these United States of America."

Who is this man?

"Who are you?" I say.

A voice speaks behind me, and I wheel around to see a nurse changing an IV bag on the other side of Lydan's bed.

"What?" I say, not sure of the words the woman spoke. I don't know how she came into the room without my knowing.

She is an older woman with resplendent gray dreadlocks partly concealed beneath a purple-and-lime headband. Yellow smiley faces adorn her scrubs, which are the same shade of baby blue as her Crocs.

"What?" I say.

"You said, 'Who are you?' I thought you were asking me who I am, hon. I said, 'I'm Ella.' I'm on nights this week."

"I didn't know you were here."

"I rapped before entering, and when I saw you, I tried to be quiet. You were entranced by that fiend on the TV."

"Fiend," I say, my voice monotone, as if I'm in a trance. "Yes."

"Someone needs to do something," Ella says.

"Yes," I say.

I am bleary. Vanquished by exhaustion. Too tired for sleep.

"Sleep is hard in your state," Ella says, and it seems she knows my thoughts, my feelings, or maybe she has seen enough mothers like me to know sleep is a foreign land to our broken kind. "You can go on home if you like, hon. I know you can't imagine leaving your boy, but we're here for him, and your sleep, your self-care, is vital for what awaits you. Without it, our minds slip. We'll call you if we need you. But rest assured, Lydan's been medicated into his state so his body can put all its energy into recovery. I will make sure he's comfortable. You go do what it is you need to do."

It does not sound like she's talking about sleep.

Ella finishes swapping out IV bags and opens the door to the hallway. She looks back at me. Her face is solemn, but in the hallway light, it also radiates ageless kindness and wisdom.

"What you did was so heroic," Ella says. "I admire you. So many of us do."

"'Us'?"

"Women. Girls. My grandbaby girl says you're as badass as Monica Rambeau. Can't say I know who that is, but my grandbaby sure does. And apparently, Ms. Rambeau is something. I'm saying too much. I ought to tend to my rounds," Ella says. "Don't feel guilty if you want to go home to sleep or eat, plan for your time ahead."

"Plan what?"

"You're in a new world now," Ella says. "It is the same world. The old world. Old as time. But it is a new world too. For you. For all of us. There will be much to do that you have never had to do before. Never even contemplated."

Yes. There are rough weeks and years, a rough life, ahead for Lydan. Yet it seems Ella means something else. Something more.

"I might get some fresh air," I say. "Maybe I could go home. Just for a bit. Just to try to rest. Change my clothes. Shower."

"Do what you need to do," Ella says. "Lydan will be fine here."

Ella is wrong. Lydan will never be "fine" again.

The hospital corridor's bright light hurts my eyes.

I close my eyes against it and try to breathe. I cannot bear to leave Lydan. I cannot leave him. In my absence, I fear something bad will befall him or he'll awaken alone, terrified and needing me.

I press my palm flat to his door, press my cheek to it. The door is cold.

It is all I can do to pry myself away. I stand there awhile longer, then head down the hall to take the elevator to the lobby.

Night drizzles. A cold wind snags at my sweatshirt. I have no idea where the sweatshirt came from, or the sweatpants, whose they are or who gave them to me. Who dressed me. I don't recall putting them on. I reek. I tug the hood up to shield my face from the wind and rain.

The fresh air feels good in my lungs, but a pain stabs at my sutured torso and buckles my knees. I sit on a bench, dead with fatigue, no ease in the pain. I lift the sweatshirt and look at the homely zigzag of black stitches in my jaundiced and purpled flesh.

Even if I wanted to go home, I don't have a car to do so. I was brought here by ambulance, I imagine. I don't know where my car is.

I don't care.

Akers. His face and voice raid my mind.

I take out my phone and search his name.

I find dozens of video interviews.

I click on the link to his website: GunsGunsGuns.com.

His grotesque mug dominates the page.

The company's motto—*More Guns Less Crime*—is emblazoned above his headshot. Another line claims: *The World's Most Famous Gun Shop! Located in Jessup, Iowa. 10,000 guns! Ten times more guns than citizens of Jessup!*

There's a shop that hawks bumper stickers and T-shirts and trucker caps and beer cozies with one-liners that read:

KNOW GUNS, KNOW PEACE. NO GUNS, NO PEACE.

I scroll down.

SHOOT ON SITE IN OUR STATE-OF-THE-ART FIRING RANGE!

SPECIALIZING IN PROTECTING YOUR CONSTITUTIONAL RIGHT!

I want to close out, but the site is a car wreck from which I cannot look away.

I scroll through images of sinister black rifles displayed in rack after rack. Each gun is named in a parade of acronyms: *AR-15, AR-10, M4, DPMS, AP4, M16A2, Stag-15L Model 4L, C15 M4, SR-25, P415, REC7, CAR A4.*

Home-protection shotguns carry names such as the Persuader and the Punisher.

We've got pink rifles and handguns for the ladies who like their barrels hot!

Above these racks of guns are displayed two signs:

THIEVES WILL BE SHOT. SURVIVORS WILL BE SHOT AGAIN.

MY SECURITY SYSTEM IS MY GUN.

An ambulance swings into the nearby ER entrance, red lights strobing, siren silent.

I hunch my shoulders against the wind and yank my hood tighter around my face.

I look back at Akers's website. *More than 500 handguns!*

The offerings dizzy: a double-action Colt M1877 "named for its first year in production, 1877. Made for 32 years in .32-, .38-, and .41-caliber chambers: the Rainmaker, Lightning, and Thunderer." Oddities and gimmicks. A double-barreled .45 ACP 1911; a SIG P226 chambered in 19 mm Parabellum; a Czech Republic CZ 75; a Remington 1911 WWII service pistol. Ruger, Beretta, Smith & Wesson, Taurus, SIG Sauer, Accu-Tek, Browning, Chiappa, Colt, Glock, HK, MAC, Phoenix.

On and on and on.

I click on a tab to the chat room.

Scroll down the thread topics.

LOSE 2A RIGHTS LOSE ALL RIGHTS!!!!!

THIS IS WAR!!!

I click on the first thread.

THE DANVILLE MEMORIAL GRADE SCHOOL "SHOOTING" ON 10/23/2020 NEVER HAPPENED!!! LEARN THE TRUTH! SEE PROOF! FIGHT!

I click out of the chat room.

I'm collecting myself to go back inside when a young woman with long red hair charges at me from the dark, brandishing a black object. A gun.

I shrink, covering my head with my arms.

"What do you have to say?" the woman shouts. "Ms. Ross! Elisabeth!"

It's not a gun. It's a microphone. A man trails behind the woman, wielding a klieg light whose white-hot glare blinds me. How long have they been out here, lying in wait? Weeks?

"What do you have to say?" the reporter says.

I shield my eyes from the light. I wonder if this is being recorded or if it's live. "About what?" I say.

The reporter is agog. "About what you *did*. Saving the lives of seventeen students and your son."

I want to get back to Lydan. I should never have left him. "What I have to say doesn't matter," I say.

"It *does*. Going back into that school, *unarmed*, to save your son. You're a hero."

"I did what anyone would do. Any mother at least."

"Many might say they would. But they might be too afraid to die themselves."

"Not for their own child. I wasn't thinking about death; I was thinking about the love for my child. You will die for that love," I say.

"That's a beautiful sentiment in that moment."

"That's not all I was thinking."

The woman holds the microphone closer to me. "What else were you thinking?"

"'I hope we don't die here, like this.'" It's true, but it's not what I want to tell the reporter. I want to tell her that if I'd listened to Lydan and stayed home, we'd both be at home eating dinner right now, before settling in to watch TV on the couch. We'd still be in the old normal world, not in this new horrific one.

Lydan would have been spared, but kids in my classroom would surely have died.

There is nothing in this life that can be done without a cost.

"What do you make of the person who did this?" the reporter is saying.

"I don't want to talk about it," I say. "I want to have my son heal. That's what matters, not my words, not my thoughts."

I flee the glare of the klieg for the cruel lights of the hospital lobby.

I sit beside Lydan.

I place a palm on his chest, feeling its weak rise and fall. I cannot look at the ventilator tube shoved into his mouth to snake down his open throat, the oxygen tubes violating his nostrils, his slack, gray, blood-less body.

Suze. Suze. Suze. Frankly, I am sick and tired of being slandered and victimized.

Victimized.

What does Akers know about being a victim?

Nothing.

This is why he believes what he believes.

I awake with a start in my chair, drool pasted to my cheek, neck stiff and sore.

The room is a splash of bright sunlight, and someone is standing above me and looking down at me. A doctor, I gather. Except he isn't wearing a white coat. He's wearing chinos and Dockers and an orange polo shirt snug at his taut biceps. I don't recognize him but think somehow I should, as if he is from my faded dreams. He seems winded; maybe he's just come off the front nine of a private golf course and stepped in to check on Lydan on his way to the clubhouse for his usual pint of IPA and some blustering with his fraternity of MDs before hitting the back nine.

He's tan. Too tan. From time spent outdoors. A lot of time. I wonder how he has such leisure time while the lives and well-being of his patients hang in the balance.

He should appear pallid, drained. He should be losing his hair from worry, not coiffed like Ken.

He is young. Younger than I am by ten years. I imagine him at the end of the day striding to his reserved parking spot behind the hospital and tucking himself in behind the wheel of a Tesla, checking his jawline in the rearview mirror.

I expect him to smile, to bare impossibly straight white teeth in a manner meant to reassure me yet also simply to display his winning smile. He can't help himself.

"Mrs. Ross," he says. "I'm Dr. Randall. I'm the head surgeon here." He pauses as if he expects me to respond, a pause he's cultivated to elicit widened eyes at the impressiveness of his station. When he was a resident, did he practice this line and its companion pause in the mirror each morning to find the balance between a blasé statement and a declaration of stature to the patients who submitted to him in matters of life and death?

When he looks at Lydan, does he see a destroyed boy, or does he see a new cottage on a Caribbean beach, a month in Amalfi with his latest redheaded conquest?

Does he look down on me, perceive himself to be the savior of this mother's son, this grade-school teacher, this single mother, this woman he likely assumes "settled" for teaching because she can't or doesn't aspire to some "greater" post in life, like being the head surgeon here: *those who can, do; those who can't, teach.* This woman who graduated summa cum laude with a psychology major from Yale and a master's from Stanford. Is my accomplishment diminished because I went on a need-base scholarship, the poor but bright girl, that interloper into the ranks of his hermetic privileged class? This woman who could have practiced as a psychologist anywhere she desired, catered to and enriched herself off the neuroses of the moneyed in Cambridge or Forest Hills or Westchester. This woman who *chose* to teach public grade school, turned her back on his kind, rejected the circles of the white-collar acronym elites, the MDs and JDs and PhDs and PsyDs in their 6,500-square-foot pristine homes with vaulted ceilings in gated neighborhoods with their Range Rovers parked in their heated attached garages. This woman who chose to live in a 750-square-foot rented ranch, living paycheck to paycheck, but never once regretted her decision, because she awoke one day after completing her master's and asked just what she was going to do in this world that was worthwhile. Worthy of her existence. *You're a gift. Special. Chosen.* Mama's words. *Do good and you will do well.*

And until that day, I did.

That day that left *my* boy in *this* bed.

All my decisions, each one of them was a link in the chain leading to the single day of doom.

"Mrs. Ross."

The young doctor, the head surgeon, is standing closer to me now, looking down from above.

"Ms.," I say.

"Excuse me?"

"Not *Mrs.*, *Ms.*"

"Of course. As I was saying, I'm the head surgeon." His pause is shorter this time, but it's there. "We didn't meet yet because you were in your own surgery at the time and then recovering yourself for some time. But I believe you met others on the staff charged with follow-up. But. Now. I wanted to inform you that your son's team, as led by the hospitalist and myself, believe we can begin to bring him to consciousness. The reduction of IV-fed medications will begin later today. It will be very gradual and monitored closely, minutely, but we expect in four days he will awaken."

Awaken. He says it as if Lydan will awaken from the dead.

"I see," I say.

"It is highly likely he will be confused about where he is, how he got here, perhaps even who he is or who you are. He will most likely not recall the events that brought him here, not at first, anyway."

Events.

"He will be logy—that is, groggy."

"I know what *logy* means."

"Yes. Right," the head surgeon says. "As your son fully comes to, he might be terribly confused and agitated, highly emotional. Distraught. Or perhaps elated."

Your son. I wonder if he even knows Lydan's name, this head surgeon.

"Your son might also be placid and detached, uncaring and without emotion, upon awakening. I just want you to be prepared, really, for any and all sorts of erratic and heightened behavior from him that might swing wildly moment to moment. It can be jarring and quite distressing for everyone."

"Will he be able to . . ." I don't know what to say or how to say it. "Function? To walk? Or—"

"It is my responsibility to be direct," he says. "Your son is never going to be the boy you once knew, ever again. He will have to regain motor skills, fine and gross, to the best he can, but it will never be what it was. He will likely always have a pronounced limp. He will likely always be in some sort of pain and discomfort. He likely will endure years of debilitating PTSD, I am told by my colleagues versed in the psychological aspects of such cases, and they will speak to you directly. But bouts of volatile behavior as well as chronic depression are common and might grow more dramatic and acute as he goes through adolescence and his teens. The trauma will manifest itself manifold. I can't speak to the specific physical prognosis other than to say he suffered no permanent spinal damage and should recover most sensation, though ambulatory mobility is not dependent on an intact spinal cord alone. Muscular, other nerve, bone, and ligament and tendon damage play a role, and he has endured traumatic injuries to many of these systems. But the specifics are the territory for physical and occupational therapists, his neurologist, and many others. This is a team effort. He has a long road ahead. He won't be off medication or anesthetics or painkillers entirely for some time, and he'll always need some sort of medication or another. He'll need to be on a drip for many more days to come, postawakening, to manage pain. And while he'll sleep a lot on his own, he will need periodic daily sedation for some time yet. Overall, his progress is astounding. He is alive and he is not paralyzed. And if I may be blunt—" His tone takes a turn now to one of surprising compassion and empathy. He rests a hand lightly on the back of my hand, and I do not pull away. It is the first time I've been touched during this entire ordeal. It is a human touch, a humane touch. "Lydan had minutes to live," he says now, using Lydan's name. Knowing it. "When the EMTs got to him, he was seconds from death. I am told this is literal. He was seconds from death. You alone saved him. You saved your son

Lydan's life. Not any of us here at this hospital, certainly not me. You. And you saved an entire classroom of kids. I want you to know that. I think it's important you know just what a good and brave thing it is that you did. The type of person you are. Not many of us have such mettle. I don't know that I have it."

I have been petty.

I have misjudged this man.

"Lydan?"

Lydan's eyelids flutter open to reveal dark, blank, unseeing eyes, then close.

"Lydan."

His eyes open again and stare at me unblinking for an age, as if he dares not ever close them again.

"Who . . ." he says, his voice as fragile as that of a terminally ill old man. I sob to hear it, my heart wrenched open as if it's a vault that's been sealed for a thousand years.

I take a cup of water on the bedside table and put it to his chapped lips.

Ella and two doctors, a woman and a man, stand behind me. The man is the anesthesiologist. The woman is Lydan's assigned physician. I was told their names but can't recall them.

I tilt the cup, and water dribbles down Lydan's chin.

"Who—" He gulps air.

"It's Mama," I say.

"What's . . . Mama?"

I don't know what to say or what to do.

"Me. I'm your mama." I lift his limp, skeletal wrist, mindful of the IV needle jammed in the back of his bruised hand, and kiss his fingertips. He pulls free, as if I might bite his fingers.

A wheezing, leaking sound escapes from his throat. "Heeeeeee."

I can barely hear what he's saying. It is scarcely more than a breath on my cheek. I lean in, my ear to his mouth.

"Heeeee."

"'He'?"

Lydan's chin sags in a phantom nod.

"He what?" I say.

"Heee . . . saaid."

"Who said what?"

"The man."

"What man?"

"Who killed me."

"Don't say that," I say. "He's dead. Not you. He's gone. You're here."

"I'm . . . not . . . here. The man said." Lydan's eyes shut. "I needed to die. He was here to kill me. So he killed me."

Terror shears through me.

"That's not true," I say. "You are right here. With me."

"He said . . . I *had* . . . to die. It was my purpose. He was sent. To . . . write . . . his part of . . . of . . ."

"We should let him rest," a male voice says behind me.

"Part of what?" I say.

"The . . . scrit."

"Script," I say.

Lydan's voice is a faded whisper, and I lean in closer. "His scrit is done. I'm not here. Not anywheres."

"Shhh now. Let's not say that. Okay?" I cradle Lydan's face in my hands and kiss his cheeks, the tip of his nose, his eyelids, his forehead, the top of his head.

"I'm dead and I don't know you," he says.

"Please," I say.

A finger taps my shoulder.

"Mrs. Ross," the anesthesiologist says.

He stoops over me, his face leaning down into my face, too close, the medicinal, minty reek of mouthwash unable to mask his halitosis.

His pores are cavernous. The red capillaries in the yolks of his eyes seemingly about to burst.

"Ms. Ross," I say. "*Ms.* Or Elisabeth. Not *Mrs.*"

"Of course. We should allow Lydan to rest. He's fragile. And out of sorts. Let's let him rest." His hands hook onto my arm as he tries to extract my son from my embrace. "The head of surgery prepared you for this, yes?" the anesthesiologist continues. "About what to expect, about alarming and troubling behavior. Wild swings. Disconcerting behavior. It's expected, even if not so readily accepted."

"My son says he doesn't know me," I say. "He thinks that he's dead and—"

"He needs to sleep. You do too. It's for the best."

The anesthesiologist grips my elbow and wrangles me to my feet. "There," he says, his voice sounding as if he's speaking from the far end of a long, barren culvert. The ceiling breathes.

Ella steps around me and injects a clear liquid into Lydan's IV.

Lydan's eyes glaze.

"What did you give him?" I ask.

"Mama," Lydan whispers, his voice quailing as if he's fighting to remain conscious.

"Lydan?" I take his hand.

"Elisabeth," the physician says.

Lydan's eyes open and lock on mine. "I see it," he says. "All of it."

"I should have listened when you said you were feeling icky," I whisper.

"I . . . didn't say . . . 'feel icky.'" Lydan closes his eyes and grinds his teeth in pain. "Said, 'I have a icky feeling.' A *bad* feeling."

I have an icky feeling. Not *I feel icky.*

"Mrs. Ross, please," the anesthesiologist says again. "This is detrimental."

"I knew . . ." Lydan thrashes, his eyes wide with panic. Monitors beep. Frantic. The sound of a dozen smoke alarms going off.

"Stop," I say and grab his wrists. "You'll hurt yourself."

The anesthesiologist seizes my shoulder. "Mrs. Ross. I insist—"

"Elisabeth, please," I hear Ella say.

"Breathe, Lydan," I say. "Slow down and breathe."

Ella rests a palm on Lydan's shoulder. "Sit back, hon." Lydan heaves until finally he wilts back onto the pillow, eyelids twitching.

Ella presses a button on the monitor. The beeping stops.

"I tried," Lydan whispers, his voice a ghost. "I'm dead. You are too. We're dead."

His eyes close and he's deep asleep.

The physician, a Dr. Downing, I see now, going by her name tag, says, "He's confused. Conflating his imagination with reality. It's common."

"He's not imagining it," I say. "He did tell me he had an icky feeling."

"He also said he's dead. And you're dead. Neither of you are dead. Are you? Was he distraught? When he had this bad feeling?"

"He was . . . insistent," I say. "He *really* didn't want to go to school."

"More insistent than any other time he wanted to get out of going to school?"

"Probably not," I admit. Still.

I got an icky feeling. I won't go! And later, in the parking lot: *Can we go home? Please?*

"This is part of the recovery," Dr. Downing says. "The things I could tell you about what patients have said or done or believed when they've been brought back to consciousness. He is undergoing his own highly traumatic experience in his own way. As does everyone. And clearly you are both alive. Right?"

I catch my image in a window that's been transformed into a mirror by the outside nighttime blackness.

I do not recognize the face. Drawn and pale. Aged. Eyes opaque. Dead.

"What happened is an atrocity," Dr. Downing says. "But there are many fine people and resources available to both of you. I will be tracking his recovery and well-being for the foreseeable future with the entire team. You'll be sent a letter and an email with links to all these resources and to a patient portal. Use them. Take advantage of it, for your health. Your well-being. And for your sanity."

Hollowed by hunger, I wander to the hospital cafeteria. The place is desolate save a weedy man in short-sleeved scrubs who wheels a squeaky mop bucket in front of a coffee station. The man's sharp elbows, pink and scaled with rashes, jut out as he swashes the wet mop back and forth.

I trundle a plastic tray along steel rails, selecting a yogurt and a banana and a ham sandwich.

In a far corner, I sit alone at a round table. As I peel back the foil from the top of my yogurt, I look up at a TV on the wall to see Max Akers. He is waving to an adoring crowd from a podium set up in front of a helicopter. He smiles a toad's smile, closes his eyes dramatically, as if in prayer, and extends his arms out far to either side, palms open to bask in the raucous greeting of his followers.

"Enough." He waves the crowd off, opens his eyes, and smirks again. He cannot help himself. "Okay. A bit more never hurt."

The crowd roars, manic, hoists signs: STAND STRONG! FIGHT!

"All right. Okay," Akers says, holding up both palms. "I'm the one that's supposed to be talking here. *You* are here to listen." The crowd settles to a simmer. "Let me tell you," Akers barks. "Today is a dark day. Very dark. Very sad. Now first, let me say I send thoughts and prayers to the bereaved. I am the first one to pray. I care. That is why I am here today. Because I care. And to end the craziness. Children have died in

now three horrible events these past weeks, and it is a god-awful tragedy." He adjusts his red tie, tightening the knot at his meaty throat.
"But *they*. You know who I mean. *They* want to make even more out of
it than there is."

More out of it than there is?

"*They* want to politicize it," Aker says. "*They* want to use these awful
events to attack your God-given rights!" He can't even bring himself to
say the word *shootings*, to say the word *gun*.

"Hang them!" a man shouts from the crowd.

Akers jabs his finger at the man. "Now that's a man who shoots
straight!"

The crowd erupts with laughter.

"I kid," Akers says. "*I* would never condone hanging. But I do admire
the moxie! Let me tell you. We are at war. I am outraged at how they
want to bastardize these events and weaponize them in a loathsome attempt to disarm you because they know *you* have power when armed.
They want to disarm you so they can take your power. *Own* you! Enslave you! When you are armed, no one can enslave you! *No one* can
harm you! You have the power! You are the power!"

"Damn straight!" the crowd exults.

"No one is angrier than I am. I am the angriest man in America. A
man in China just stabbed thirty people with a knife. True. You saw it.
Should China ban knives?"

"*No!*" the crowd chants.

"Hell no!" Akers crows. "Well, maybe Ginsu knives. *Oh.* The media
will make hay out of that one. That racist Akers joked about *Ginsu* knives!
Seriously, folks. What's happened to this world?"

You *are what's* happened.

You and others like you.

You don't know pain.

If you felt what I felt.

"We can't let these terrorists take our guns because of a few odd
events enacted by mentally ill people or individuals on drugs. We don't
back down!" he rails. "What do we do?!"

"Fight!" the crowd screams.

"That's right! Fight!" He gives that toad's grin again, eyes squinting to slits, as if his face might split in two with the glee derived from inciting the crowd.

I walk to the TV, look at it from so close I can feel the heat of it on my face. The screen is so pixelated it renders Akers as no more than thousands of colored dots.

"And that is why, on this gorgeous day, in the same town where Abraham Lincoln announced his candidacy, I, Maximillian Stanford Akers the Third, announce my candidacy for president of the United States of America! And the first thing I am going to do is sign an executive order ridding this land of background checks and state laws requiring guns be locked away at home, made useless with trigger locks, even in your own car's glove box—how can you defend yourself or home or loved ones when your guns are locked up? I will make it legal across the land to open carry everywhere, on federal grounds or national parks, without the unconstitutional red tape of permits, and strike down all the other laws foisted on us that impinge on our right to bear arms!"

The crowd roars.

Dizzy, I collapse in the nearest chair.

Akers unknots his tie and yanks it from around his neck with a flourish, tosses it offstage as the crowd cheers and some followers weep, reaching out their arms, clutching and grabbing at the tie.

Reveling in the mayhem and adoration, Akers stands back, feet wide apart like a gunslinger, grabs each side of his button-down shirt, and rips it open to reveal a red, white, and blue T-shirt touting: *FIGHT FOR AMERICA!*

He stands with his head thrown back, basking in the rapture of the crowd.

At his hips, tucked into each side of the waistband of his trousers, is a twin pair of revolvers, their pearl handles iridescent in the brilliant sunlight.

With cinematic swagger, he quick draws the revolvers and aims them toward the sky, his arms in a V. He fires two shots. Crack crack.

I bristle at them, every cell in me tensing at the sound.

I can smell blood. See it seeping from beneath the closet door.

I am in the darkness with Lydan.

I am jolted back to the present by the crowd's rhapsodic cheers of glee.

Akers seats the revolvers back into his waistband.

"Their current so-called *president*," he bellows, "surrounds himself with *armed* Secret Service! Twenty-four seven! The so-called *important* people get *armed* guards. The *important* people who want to take your guns are surrounded by and kept safe with, guess what?" He cups a hand to his ear and leans in, that smirk cracking his face.

"Guns!" the crowd shouts.

"That's right! Good ole guns! Well, I for one believe that you are just as important as that 'president' of theirs. You are more important than him. That's for damn sure. Maybe not as important as me but—I kid, I joke. But. *They* want to make you feel small. Unimportant. What do those elitists call you? 'The everyman. The common man.' That's what you are to them. Common. Just because you work hard and play hard and live the right way, just because you are decent, God-fearing, Jesus-loving people. Well, I don't think you're common. I think you're exceptional, more important than that president, and you should be able to protect yourself like the president is protected. We need more guns more than ever. *You* need them. Because, damn it, you are under attack! This is war! Be tough. Stand strong. Fight!"

"Fight!" The crowd explodes, jubilant and raucous and rancorous with a venomous glee.

"That's why I am going to be your next president of the United States. I will always tell you the hard truth, the whole truth, and nothing but the truth, so help me, Jesus Christ! And the truth is, and you and I know it in our bones, that this is war, and I am here to fight!"

"Fight!"

Akers brandishes his pistols in the air, his teeth bared now in a wolfish grin as he bathes in the crowd's refrain: *"FIGHT! FIGHT! FIGHT!"*

Stop him.

The thought is a white-hot comet sizzling across the dark recess of my mind, scorching it.

Stop him.

I can't. It's unthinkable.

Yet I thought it.

Once a seed of thought is planted in the mind, the imagination waters it, and reason cannot kill it.

No. Someone else can stop him. And how would I anyway?

I must forget about Akers, live my life with my son, raise him, nurture and comfort him. Turn off the TV and ignore it. What does Akers have to do with me?

Everything.

I can't do nothing. Live life blind and dumb. Expect someone else to make the sacrifice. That is what it takes. Sacrifice.

The news show is now replaying "highlights" of Akers's event, talking heads commenting on it, giving Akers free airtime, his firestorm more oxygen. Again, he thrusts his arms up in a V, firing the pistols into the air like some tin-pot dictator as a talking head says, "Join us tonight as we speak to the man himself, the man of the hour, of the millennium, who says he will fight to save America, Maximillian Akers."

This is war!

Fight!

I cannot think here.

The lights are too bright.

The halls too barren.

The silence too loud.

I need to be home.

To think.

To truly be alone and think.

No one will fault me.

No one will miss me.

In the hall, I see Ella. "I think I'll finally take your advice and go home for a spell. Rest, if I can," I say.

"Good, hon," Ella says, touching my wrist. Her skin is soft, but her grip is true. "To take care of others, we must first take care of ourselves."

"I'll try to be back as soon as I can."

"You take all the time you need for you. We'll take care of him. If he wakes up at all, he won't be up for longer than a few minutes. His body is still recovering, and he'll sleep almost around the clock on his own for the next week at least. And frankly, for your peace of mind, when he does wake up, he likely won't remember whether you were here or not afterward."

"If anything happens, if he does wake up and starts to say things or—"

"There is nothing we're not prepared for. We'll call. We have your number."

"Use my landline number," I say. I give it to her since I don't know if it's on file. "I can't keep my cell phone on. It's too much."

"Go on and rest. For as long as you can. You deserve it."

I take an Uber home, not speaking the entire way. I feel as if I am in another realm, sitting here in a strange car with a strange man driving.

My Subaru is in the driveway when I get there.

I exit the Uber and step into a light rain.

Walking toward my front porch in the dark, I stop midstride, dumbstruck by what I see in front of me. It takes a moment for me to understand. On the steps, on the porch, overflowing onto the lawn and walk, is a pageant of flowers, bouquet heaped upon bouquet, arrangement beside arrangement of roses and carnations, lilies and irises and gerbera daisies, all wilted now and rusted. They bloom mold in the drizzle, but their sorrowful state does not matter. The gestures of the people, the notes propped in tiny plastic tridents, the ink on the mini envelopes blurred by the rain, stun and touch me—as do the Tupperware tubs, casserole dishes, and tinfoil-covered baking pans of food set out by my front door.

I take a moment to absorb the scene.

Stepping past the spoiled offerings, I see an envelope atop a sheaf of letters, wrapped in a red postal rubber band. The envelope is addressed to me in a hand I know well; in the one hand I welcome.

I put the envelope in my pocket and unlock my door.

In the kitchen, I turn on the oven vent's light. Even this pale light is too bright, assailing, accusatory. I hold the envelope in my hand.

It is addressed in my great-uncle Homer's handwriting.

He is my only family, besides Lydan. Mama was an only child herself, as I am and Lydan is. My father was never spoken of by Mama, and Lydan's father is a moldered memory of a man who left when I would not do what he insisted I do, as if a choice between him and my expected child might be difficult for me.

I don't know how Homer learned of what happened to me and Lydan.

Last I knew, he lived and, evidenced by his return address, still lives his hermit's life in the UP, with nothing for entertainment and news but the used books he buys at Goodwill on his monthly drive into town thirty-five miles away and an AM radio set to Detroit's WXYT sports station to keep up on his Lions and Tigers, Pistons and Red Wings. Homer finding out what happened to me and Lydan seems as unlikely as his moving to a Detroit high-rise.

I have not seen him in person since Mama's funeral. Mostly, I hear from him via the cards he sends on my and Lydan's birthdays and around the holidays.

It is he who taught me what little I know of guns.

I recall that summer Mama took me to visit Homer. He lived in a camper, an old rounded number, silver as a dime with a certain charm, set off a rutted dirt road that cleaves through many lonely miles of deep Michigan pine wilds. The camper's metal exterior was raked by the claws of black bears trying to get at food inside. The sight of the scars made me shiver.

To ward off the bears, Homer wore a black revolver at his hip, one with a long barrel. He kept shotguns and rifles locked in a steel safe at the back of the camper; the shotguns he used to hunt grouse and hares, the rifles for hunting deer. He stored the ammunition separately, in metal boxes secured with padlocks. "My firearms are hunting tools, each with its own purpose; they are not toys," he said. He planted his wiry hands on his knees where he sat in the kitchen chair and looked me in the eye and said, "I have one very rare, very special rifle meant for a special purpose one day in the future."

"What special rifle, what purpose?" I asked, drawn by his mysterious tone.

"A very important one, for someone very special," Homer said. He glanced at Mama, then winked at me.

That day, he taught me how to shoot his .22 rifle, plinking tin cans he set on a stump.

Before he unlocked the safe, he told me his four rules for gun safety that had to be understood and respected if I was to be entrusted with handling the rifle.

1. *Never* point the muzzle, accidentally or not, at another person.

2. *Always* keep the muzzle pointed in a safe direction.

3. *Always* make certain of your target before putting your finger on the trigger.

4. *Always* treat your weapon as if it is loaded.

"Guns are dangerous," he stressed. "They don't allow a single mistake. So never make one. You don't ever want to see the damage they can do to a human being."

Only when he was certain I understood the gravity of the rules did he show me how to load the .22. How to rest my cheek against its stock and settle its butt comfortably against my shoulder, line up the front post site in the rear V site's notch. How to calm my breath and to squeeze the trigger, never pull it.

Shooting the cans caused a brief thrill of having done something well to impress my cherished uncle, but I soon grew bored of it. Sensing my boredom, Homer said, "Let's go pick us some wild blueberries instead. They're just ripe."

Until now, I'd never thought about shooting the rifle but often recalled my joy at picking more blueberries than Mama and Homer did and baking a blueberry pie with Homer, complete with homemade crust and hand-cranked vanilla ice cream.

I wonder now about Homer's very special gun meant for a very special purpose.

I tear the envelope open and read his letter. It is written in black pen on a piece of unlined paper.

I AM HERE FOR YOU, MY SPECIAL ONE.
FOR ANYTHING.

The letter is not signed. He never signed any of his cards over the years. I once asked Mama why, and she said, "Because you know who it's from and you know he loves you. Some things are difficult for him."

I think of Homer up there in his camper, and I feel, somehow, bidden.

This is war, and I am here to fight!

I have one very rare, very special rifle meant for a special purpose one day in the future.

The future is here.

In the cellar, I root around in moldering boxes of Mama's old belong-ings. The fustiness of the contents makes my eyes water and throat itch. I find what I need. An old road map with the route to Homer's place marked on it in red pen. My 2005 Subaru doesn't have GPS, Blue-tooth, or digital interfaces of any sort, so it can't be tracked if I stay off toll roads. I hope.

I tuck the folded map into my jacket pocket.

In the kitchen, I set my phone on the counter.

I want to take it. It's my only lifeline to the hospital.

You can't take it, a voice says. My voice, yet not mine. Someone else's. Mama's.

I need to get another phone. A new phone with a new number. A phone that can't be traced to me. I'm struck by terror as I realize I searched Akers's website on my phone outside the hospital. It can be traced. There is nothing I can do about it now.

For a moment, I pause, thinking: *Go back to the hospital. Go back to your son. Forget this.*

But I cannot go back. There is only forward.

From the back of my bedroom closet, I drag out a trunk of old Halloween costumes and rummage until I find a black wig, à la Snow White. It doesn't look that real, but I can't do anything about it. I take out a case with blue contact lenses and a pair of glasses, both without prescriptions in them, both parts of costumes of years past.

At the bathroom mirror, I bobby pin my hair and situate the wig on my head, fidgeting with it. It makes my scalp itch. I put on the eyeglasses. I do my eyelids up smoky with shadow, lengthen and thicken my lashes with mascara, brush blush onto my cheeks, all of which I never do. The mascara is clumped, it's in such disuse. But it will do. On the way out, I grab a Lions ball cap from Lydan's room, adjust the strap in the back to fit my head.

From a sock in the back of my bedroom bureau, I take a wad of cash. A hundred and ninety dollars. Emergency money.

When I start up the Subaru, I'm relieved to see the gas tank is full. I won't have to fill up here in town.

Two hours north, I pull off the highway, following signs for food and gas. After five minutes of driving along a dark road, I wonder if I've gone the wrong way. But soon the glow of signs for restaurants and stores beckons ahead. At the first convenience store, I park across the street in front of a town library, dark and closed. The night is cool and drizzly. I adjust the wig in the rearview, don the ball cap, and hurry toward the door. I wait as an eighteen-wheeler thunders past, and then I sprint across the road.

Entering the store, I'm greeted with a sour, yeasty stench of warm beer gone foul and the blare of crowd noise from a Lions game somehow being aired on an old tube TV displayed in the corner above the register. A middle-aged bald man posted on a stool at the register sports a green visor as if he's working a 1940s racetrack window. He peers at me over wire-rimmed glasses, returns his attention to the football game.

Down an aisle of soup cans and potato chips, I pause and feign interest in various products, feeling conspicuous, as if I'm about to shoplift.

Get what you need and go, I tell myself.

I know what I need is here, somewhere. Likely at the front of the store, on the other end of the register. I grab a bag of potato chips and walk back to the front. The crowd on TV is booing.

I survey a display of batteries, phone chargers, and . . . there they are. Phones in plastic shell packages offered for thirty-nine dollars.

I try to take a packaged phone from its rack, but it's locked on its metal rod. I don't want to ask the cashier, but I need to. My temples throb as I approach him.

The man lifts a finger to hold me off, his focus on the game.

Even in a neglected store like this, there must be a security camera trained on me, so I don't look up or around. I keep my eyes on the man's profile, waiting.

Boos from the football stadium crescendo and die.

"Damn it," the man says and slams a fist on the counter, startling me. He tears his eyes away from the screen. "No wonder they're cellar dwellers," he says. "Lions haven't been worth watching since Sanders retired. That poor son of a bitch, best running back to ever play the game and he was stuck with a loser franchise. No wonder he retired in his prime. Calvin Johnson too."

The man glares at me, but he doesn't see me.

"Yeah?" he says. "What?"

"I'd like to get a phone," I say, my voice coming out with a slight southern twang without my meaning to do it. It just comes out that way. A southern drawl I've never had, a disguised voice to match my physical disguise.

"Phone," the man says. His nostrils flare and his eyes squint.

He snatches a ring of keys that would make a prison guard blush, twirls it around a finger, and heads around the far end of the counter.

I point to the phone I want—the cheapest—and he unlocks it. "Which card do you want?" He sweeps a hand at a rack of cards as if he's Vanna White.

I pick one for twenty dollars.

When I pay in cash, he hardly notices. His eyes are back on the game as he reflexively rings me up and counts back change, his fist pumping in the air as he shouts, "Yes, ya bunch of bums. Yes!"

Three hours later, I drive on 41 West. I miss Lydan and am consumed with the urge to go back, to end this now. The compulsion is so strong, a magnetic pull, that I make a U-turn and start back.

I don't make it a half mile before I am overcome with an even stronger impulse to turn around again.

Forward, my deep inner voice says, as if I have no say in the matter, no control over myself, my mind battling my body, my heart. I pull another U-turn in the middle of Route 41. An oncoming car blares its horn at me, its headlights flooding my car, blinding me. My car careers toward the woods, shuddering on the shoulder. I yank the steering wheel hard and right the car, my heart galloping.

I continue, drawn like a compass needle to north, unable to resist the magnetic pull of my future.

I wonder if the man at Franklin Elementary that day felt as I do now, that once the idea formed in its brain, he had no say in the matter; he was tugged forward by an unseen force. He was the actor performing in a script written by someone, something, else.

Am I any different?

I believe I am.

But I do not know.

In the dark heart of night, jack pines crowd the edges of the road, the car's bright headlight beams illuminating their scaled trunks. I am dog tired, but my heart races from adrenaline. My fingertips buzz on the steering wheel as I drive in the silence toward L'Anse, a small township at, as the locals say, "the bottom" of Lake Superior's Keweenaw Bay.

I recall Homer telling me something about the jack pines. They grow readily in the sandy soil of the UP. They're nicknamed *fire pines*, or *flame pines*. Their needles and bark are dry as tinder and their cones tacky with pitch, so one single spark can ignite them into a roaring tornado of napalm fire that engulfs everything in its path, the winds off Lake Superior a "Bellows of the Devil." In the 1800s, a wildfire burned nearly every building in L'Anse to the ground. The area was home to the largest Native American reservation in Michigan. Chippewa, Ojibwa, I think.

Homer took me fishing along the shore of the bay once, and we walked among what looked like tiny houses erected among the trees, an old burial ground from a battle 350 years ago.

Twenty miles out from L'Anse, I pull over and check the map. Another five miles up, I hang a left down a single lane of dirt so choked with jack pines that the trees' lowest branches scrape the sides of my car.

In the dark, I know I'm passing sandy clearings in the pines, dunes formed eons ago by retreating glaciers.

I drive miles of the extensive web of old dirt roads used primarily by logging trucks. I stop again to check the map and take a left, check the map again and take a right, then another right and another left as I wind deeper into this labyrinth. It all looks the same at the edge of my headlights. The hard-packed sand of the one-lane track of road. The black night. The foreboding pines. The drive seems preposterously, impossibly long. At times I wonder if I'm driving in a circle. Is it possible? A tree leaning out over the road looks like one I passed a while back. I slow the car. No, it isn't the same tree. Is it?

I creep the car around a dark corner, and there it is. A glimmer of silver in the headlight beams up in the woods.

I pull onto the sandy track that serves as a rutted driveway.

The camper squats in its small clearing in the forest.

It's 4:13 a.m.

I get out of the car. A light blinks on inside the camper.

The door to the camper opens, and silhouetted in the wash of light stands Homer.

"Lizzy," Homer's voice cracks.

The camper is far smaller and more cramped than it is in my memories. It's no surprise; everything is smaller and paler and duller for adults when the electric fizz of youth has gone flat. Still, it unnerves me.

Homer does not seem smaller. Or that much older. His black hair has turned pewter, and his face has wizened some, but he's not lost any of his hair and his skin is tanned and his eyes are bright. He's still wiry and tall, the sort of man whose legs and upper body are of equal length. He looks of two pieces when he walks, as if the upper half and lower half are joined precariously with a weak hinge that might snap at any moment. His shoulders are slighter and more rounded, perhaps, his posture less commanding, but he moves about making a pot of coffee with the same smooth agility as I recall.

He hands me a mug of coffee as I sit at the same old little tabletop that folds down from the camper wall.

He sits and reaches his hands across the table to hold mine. The backs of his hands are mottled with amoebic age spots, but his knuckles betray no sign of the disfigurement of arthritis. Behind him, sitting on the narrow countertop by the sink, is a framed photo of me and Mama and him, taken on our wild-blueberry-picking excursion. The three of us hold up our fingers to show how stained they are. I recall how Homer tinkered with his old camera for several minutes to take a photo on a timer. All these years melted and gone, and he's kept a photo of that day right in sight of where he enjoys his morning coffee and eats each meal, alone.

"I'm sorry," he says. He squeezes my hand.

"How did you *know*?" I say.

"A friend visits. She told me. I called you, several times."

"I keep my phone off. I have to shut it all out, be left alone."

"I see." He nods at me, and I realize I am still wearing the wig and have on ridiculous makeup. I take the wig and glasses off and pluck out the bobby pins.

"I didn't leave a message," Homer says. "It didn't seem right to just leave a message, not for this sort of thing. But. I knew you'd find your way here. I've been expecting you."

I'm not sure what he means by this. He said nothing explicit in the letter about my coming to visit. Did he think he'd implied it? Even so, why would he expect that I'd drive this far up here to see him, with Lydan in the state he is in? I myself do not fully believe I am here. Yet I know now I am supposed to be here. Homer was not at all surprised to see me in his yard at 4:15 a.m.

Homer releases my hand. "What do you need?" he says. "You came because you need something."

I'm taken aback by his bluntness and feel ashamed that my motives are so transparent and selfish. Yet every simple act we perform each and every day is about needing or wanting something. "That's not the only reason I came," I say. "I came to see you, too."

"If I can help, I will."

"I need to learn all I can from you," I say. "About guns."

Homer leans back in his chair.

I see in his eyes the questions he wants to ask, but they remain unasked.

"Do you still have the old books and magazines on firearms, for collectors?" I say.

"In a box."

"You mentioned, the day we picked blueberries"—I glance at the photo of him and me and Mama—"that you had a certain special rare gun that was for a special purpose. Was that true or . . ."

He smiles as he stands. Stooping, he sneaks to the back of the camper and works a padlock on the closet door to reveal the steel gun vault inside it. His fingers tap out a code on a digital keypad. From the vault, he takes a long black metal case, brings it to the table, and sets it down.

At each end of the case is a cleated latch secured with a padlock. Homer picks up a glass saltshaker on the small counter and unscrews its lid, spills the salt out into the palm of his hand and from that salt plucks a tiny brass key. He wipes the key on his pant leg.

He unlocks each padlock and unsnaps the latches.

Slowly, he lifts the lid.

The black metal of the weapon gleams on a bed of gray egg-carton foam.

"What made you think of it?" he says.

"I was hoping to go to a journalist friend. I'd have her write up a piece, with me as an anonymous source, about how easy it is for anyone to get even the rarest of guns. It is rare, right?"

"This," Homer says and slips his fingertips under the rifle and lifts it out, standing it on the butt end of its stock on the table, "is the Belgium-made, 7.62-millimeter self-loading rifle. The LAR. Light Automatic Rifle. A masterwork of a firearm. There are seven million of them, used by every NATO country other than the US. So many its nickname is the Right Arm of the Free World."

"That doesn't sound rare."

"An object isn't rare just because its numbers are few," Homer says. "The word for that is 'scarce.' An object is rare when it's coveted yet nearly unattainable, even despite its numbers. There might be two million of these rifles in military use, but they're illegal to own for the world's civilian population. It's all but impossible for a US citizen to possess this rifle. For collectors, this rifle is as rare as it gets."

"Yet you have one."

"After my final tour in 1975, before coming home, I traveled Asia at the urging of a friend. I bought the LAR on a lark from an old man in a market on the steppes of the Himalayas. It was a different world then. Another world. I brought it back in my GI trunk on a military plane. I didn't understand what I had. Only much later did I realize if I were caught with it, I'd be in serious trouble."

"I don't want to get you in trouble," I say. "I wouldn't want to risk it getting traced back to you—"

"It can't be traced to me," Homer says. "It's not possible. But if you did get caught, I wouldn't want to get you in trouble. I'd *insist* you admit where you got it. I'd insist you had no idea it was illegal. How could you possibly know?"

"Just *look* at how menacing it is," I say, staring at the sinister rifle, as black and gleaming as polished onyx. It chills me.

"The AR-15 is just as menacing," Homer says. "I'd testify on a stack of Bibles that I told you it *is* legal but rare. You wouldn't stand a chance against me."

I nod at the LAR. "Tell me about it."

"I can do better." Homer grabs a book from a shelf at the back of the camper and hands it to me. *The Bible of European Military Arms, 1900–1945*, volume twelve.

I settle in with the book. Read and reread the pages dedicated to the LAR, taking notes, committing facts to memory. I scour the illustrations that depict how the LAR works, how it is made, details and names and functions of each part of a disassembled LAR.

LAR: Light Automatic Rifle, a.k.a. the FAL, Fusil Automatique Léger. A black gun designed by Dieudonné Saive and first manufactured by FN Herstal in 1953. Produced in both full automatic and semiautomatic. Smooth gas-operated action run by a short-stroke, spring-loaded piston affixed atop the barrel. In full auto it fires seven hundred rounds a minute.

Seven hundred rounds.

In sixty seconds.

Twelve bullets fired in a hair over *one second.*

"One thousand one," I whisper.

Twelve bullets.

I read on. The Fusil Automatique Léger boasts a fore-end regula-
tor—whatever that is—which gives the rifle a soft recoil to make it easier
for the shooter to fire the weapon accurately. The recoil is so smooth a
skilled triggerman can squeeze off nearly as many rounds in the semiautomatic model as in the fully auto model, especially with a bump stock.

I look at the rifle, then at Homer, who is sipping a cup of tea and
chewing on a stick of red licorice he plucked from an old tobacco can-
ister sitting on the small counter.

"May I?" I say.

Homer sweeps a hand at the rifle. "It's yours," he says. He looks me
in the eye. "In a way it always has been."

Yes, I think. It has.

I slip my hands under the rifle, pick it up.

It's light, far lighter than I even imagined. And balanced. It is a
marvel how slight and *perfect* it feels in my hands. I expected it to be
much heavier. Solid. A dead weight. This feels alive.

I examine the stock.

"This one's got a folding stock," Homer says and reaches out for
the rifle. I hand it to him, muzzle pointed to the ceiling. Homer works
the folding stock, demonstrating the ease with which it can be locked
in place and unlocked and folded. "It's got a tilting breechblock. See
this." He shows me. "The recoil spring is set in a modified receiver cover.
You don't need to know what that means unless you want to impress
your friend." The way he says *friend*, I sense he doesn't believe a word
I've said. So why doesn't he call me out? Why doesn't he ask me what
I am really up to?

Because he knows.

The LAR takes clips with a capacity of thirty rounds. Three loaded
clips sit in the case.

"Do you have more ammunition for it?" I say.

"Why?"

"It would make a big statement in my friend's story if I have a lot
of ammo for it too," I say, another lie. "'Anonymous woman gets hands
on a rare automatic rifle and hundreds of rounds of ammo.'"

"I've got fifteen hundred rounds in a metal ammo box," Homer says and juts an elbow toward the closet.

"If I can arrange for a high-profile collector to meet my friend, to vouch for the rifle being what I say it is, a collector would welcome the opportunity?"

"It's a Van Gogh of black guns. Any collector would cut his ear off to see it in person. Do you want to shoot it?" Homer asks.

"I'd rather die," I say. "But it will help to get to know it." I need to get to know it. "Do you have any handguns?" I ask. "Not for the article. For me. For protection. With everything that happened."

He does have a handgun. Several. Most aren't registered and can't be traced. "I didn't buy them illegally," he offers. "I bought them with cash at flea markets and gun shows, decades ago. Flea markets are the best places to find guns cheap. I never once thought about there being no way to trace them to bad actors who might use them in crimes." He looks at me.

Does he think I am a bad actor?

Homer takes three handguns from the vault and lays them out on the table, arranges them in a neat row as if offering the weapons up to a potential buyer.

I point at one. "Is that a good one?"

"For protection?" Homer says and picks up the handgun, ejects the empty clip from the magazine in the grip. He sets the clip on the table. "It wouldn't be my first choice. I wish I had a smaller caliber for you. A thirty-two or thirty-eight. This thing, the 1911, a.k.a. the forty-five ACP, or the 'GI forty-five,' as I knew it—it's a mule. Most people know it from movies and TV shows. Magnum used one on *Magnum, P.I.* It's the handgun in the game of Clue. It's the one millions of plastic army men carry. But we never think: Why did someone invent this damn thing to begin with? Not for some damn board game or TV show."

I see on Homer's troubled face that he has a need to tell a tale about this gun, so I oblige him with silence.

Homer picks up the .45's empty clip, turns it in his hand as if it is a relic that he's just unearthed from an archaeological dig, not quite understanding what he's found but knowing somehow it is of supreme historical significance in understanding a certain people.

"This handgun has killed more people than any other handgun ever made. I had one over there. This isn't the one. But I killed three men with mine. Boys, really. Like I was. Like we all were and always are."

He sets the .45 on the table as if setting down a piece of cake that's made him sick and he can't stand to even look at anymore. From a cardboard box of .45 cartridges, he digs out a single cartridge and holds it up to the light, its brass case gleaming, its blunt gray lead nose as dull as it is deadly.

"This gun, like *all* guns, was a solution to a problem, this particular problem being one the United States had with the Moro natives of the Philippines, who had the gall to stand up to Uncle Sam's colonization of their island. Defending their sovereignty was not seen as their defense of their culture and land but as a *rebellion* against old Sam. How dare a native people fight back against an imperialistic occupier. The Moro, they proved tough to kill in their jungle with just the thirty-eight revolver used by the US Army at that time, in 1911."

Homer weaves the cartridge between his fingers as a magician manipulates a coin. "The Moro fought with spears, knives, their bare hands. They charged through barbed wire the US strung in their jungle, torn flesh be damned. They threw themselves onto bayonets in suicide attacks. Men, boys, children, and women. They fought at night. In the day they disappeared back to their homes. Same old do-si-do we've seen since, we saw over there where I was. And it worked, as it does. Until the Colt M1911."

Homer seats the cartridge into the clip with a metallic snick and extracts another cartridge from the box.

"That old thirty-eight wasn't up to snuff. So Uncle Sam put a challenge out to gunmakers."

He works the cartridge into the clip.

Snick.

"Browning's answer won the day. A dream gun for CQK: close-quarters killing. It blasts vegetation and busts bones and smashes flesh and organs, obliterates spines on its way out."

Homer picks up three more rounds and thumbs each into the clip. Snick. Snick. Snick.

"This handgun, an icon for the past hundred and ten years, was made solely to kill a specific indigenous islander who refused to be colonized. Every single gun ever made, outside of a few sporting guns, was made to kill more humans faster. Even sporting guns are made to kill. There is no other intent or purpose for them. None. Forget about some Sunday fun at the range. Their purpose is to kill."

Homer takes me out to an old sandpit to shoot the 1911 and the LAR in its semiauto mode. The odds are slim, but I don't want to risk firing the LAR on full automatic and rousing the suspicion of anyone who might hear the rifle, even from miles away. Even if they are gun nuts themselves.

I take the LAR from Homer and brace myself, as instructed, in a wide stance, nestling the rifle butt into the soft pocket of my shoulder. Inhaling and then exhaling a slow leak of breath, my cheek flat to the stock, eyes focused down the barrel length, I squeeze the trigger.

I flinch against the expected mule kick and am astonished when it doesn't come. Just a polite nudge to my shoulder, like a friend trying to gently tap me awake from a catnap. The rifle gives a dry crack, like the snap of kindling.

I am impressed and appalled.

I put it to my shoulder again and squeeze another round, still half anticipating the LAR will buck and rage.

It doesn't. The second shot is just as kind to my shoulder and ears.

I fire another round, and another, and another, at the paper target Homer has set up in the pit. At times I see anguish etch Homer's face, the distress and doubt about what he is doing, what I am doing. What we are doing. Still, he is here for me.

I shoot another few clips of rounds until I can hit the target with consistency.

It doesn't matter. I won't ever be shooting it after today. This rifle is my Trojan horse.

I tuck the .45 under the back of my shirt and draw it and fire at targets five feet away. Close-quarters killing. The .45 bucks hard, and I have to work at keeping it steady, bracing my wrist by clutching it in my opposite hand.

Over and over again, Homer realigns my stance and positioning of my arms and hands, then steps back, coaching me on how to draw a weapon with one smooth movement and shoot literally from the hip with accuracy, as if for CQK.

After I've fired the weapon what seems a hundred times, I am confident I can hit a paper pie plate at five feet. A paper pie plate that approximates the size of a human heart.

"I'll need them back when you're done with them," Homer says. "I have one more use for the rifle."

I drive back toward home, the LAR hidden beneath a blanket in the bottom of the car trunk along with the loaded metal ammo box, the .45, and a crate crammed with Homer's books and magazines dedicated to gun collectors.

I plan to go straight home and hide the guns and ammo, but the closer I get to home, the more I panic that something dreadful has befallen Lydan and fear the hospital has tried to reach me without success. I remove my makeup and the blue contacts, then drive straight to the hospital, park in the lot, and dash inside. I take the elevator to the ICU, fidgeting and pacing as it rises. My stomach drops, and for that one weird moment I feel weightless.

When the elevator doors open, two women in scrubs are standing outside it, waiting to get on. I hustle past them and hurry down the hall to the nurses' station. Ella is there, head bent as she types on a computer keyboard. Clack clack clack. Sensing my presence, she looks up. Her face is slack and grave. The worst has happened, and I wasn't here for it. I am gutted by regret.

"I'm so sorry," I say. "My phone. I—"

"I hope you got some good shut-eye," Ella says, and her smile is warm and easy.

"Lydan's okay?" I say.

"Tremendous. He woke several times."

"Was he upset I wasn't here?"

"He never noticed, he was so foggy, and he fell back to sleep within minutes."

"I didn't mean to be gone so long."

"You did what you needed to do." She stares at me. She doesn't sound like she thinks I went home to shower and sleep. In fact, I am in the same clothes as I left in and am still clearly unbathed and more disheveled than ever.

"I slept," I say. "Almost the entire time. I never even showered or ate."

"You should eat, and you'll need all the sleep you can get in the coming days. Lydan, I believe"—she clicks keys and glances at her screen—"will be released to your care in roughly two weeks."

"Two weeks?" I say, stunned.

"If he improves as we believe he will."

I'm taken aback, terrified by the prospect. How can I care for him myself? "Home? In my care? How can that be? So soon?"

"He's been recovering and healing the entire time while in the coma. There will be visiting nurses and physical therapists and occupational therapists coming to see him regularly. But he won't need to be on his IV, and he won't need ICU care any longer. We can't keep patients admitted if they are conscious and their vitals are stable, and at least as we can judge, he will meet both criteria by then."

"But," I say, "I don't know what I'm doing. What if something happens? Some emergency and the nurses or whoever aren't there? I don't know how to take care of him the way he is."

"I know. It can feel overwhelming. But. You won't be alone. Dr. Downing will visit and be available. And Lydan won't be in this state at home. He will be conscious and, hopefully with the use of a wheelchair, then a walker or crutches, be partly mobile. And if he's not ready in two weeks, he'll take however long it takes. But I tell you, I think he'll be ready. Your son is a fighter."

"What if something happens that I can't—"

"We have protocols in place for such events. And Dr. Downing will be available at all times."

Protocols. Events.

Like hiding under a desk.

"And," Ella says, "we'll give you all the information and medications and instructions and support you need to make this transition as smooth as we can, for the both of you. You want your son to come home, right?"

Of course I want Lydan home. But I don't know how I will ever begin to care for him, to give him all he needs in his condition. And . . . and I don't know how I am going to do what I need to do if Lydan is home. It will be impossible to leave the house for the entire night I'll need, especially if nurses are in the house. And I can't leave him alone all night. Can I?

Perhaps this is a sign for me to not do what I am thinking of doing.

"God, yes, I want him home, more than anything. I'm overjoyed but overwhelmed," I say. "I just don't know how I'll—"

"We will be there for you both, every single step of the way. Once he's fully awake, you'll see a marked difference. His color will come back. His smile. You'll adapt. You're about to start a very new kind of life, and it's harrowing, but you can do this. For him. After what you did at that school . . ." She pauses, fixes her calming eyes on me, touches my shoulder with her hand. "You can do *anything* you put your mind to."

"Right," I say. Anything. "Can I see him?"

"He's asleep. Judging from his pattern the last thirty-six hours, I'd say if you want to catch him when he's awake, come back in two hours. But if you just want to sit and be with him, you can go see him."

I start down the hall to Lydan's room until Ella says, "Oh, someone came by to see you."

I look back at Ella. "Came by? Who?" I say. Fear radiates in me.

"She didn't leave a name."

She?

"Except for you," Ella says, "no one else is permitted up here to see Lydan. No friends, no family, as well intentioned as they are. But this lady, she got in here somehow. She seemed agitated. She said she'd been trying to get hold of you for days. I explained that you went home to rest. She said she'd been by your house and knocked and rang and you never answered. And your car wasn't there."

"Of course," I blurt, flustered. "I keep my car in the garage. And I was sleeping almost the entire time and ignored all texts and calls, since I gave you the landline number to call and that never rang."

"Makes sense. She said if I saw you for you to check your messages. It's urgent. I can't imagine what might be more urgent than you taking care of Lydan, but"—Ella shrugs—"I just wanted to pass it along."

"Did she leave a name?" I ask.

"She did, but I was consumed with other responsibilities, and really I just had to make sure she left the ICU as soon as possible. I never wrote it down. She said she'd keep trying to get in touch, but time is running out for you?"

"Time is running out for me?" I say.

"A figure of speech, I'm sure," Ella says. "You're just getting started."

I sit beside Lydan and, finally, check my texts.

There are hundreds, most from numbers I do not know. I cannot begin to navigate them. The countless numbers I don't recognize I delete.

The most recent texts, sent in the last few minutes, are from Juanita Ramirez, my teachers'-union rep.

Time is running out.

I'm relieved it is only her. I've no idea what is happening with the school. When and if it is opening again. If it's already opened, I cannot go back there. They ought to burn it to the ground. Juanita has sent dozens of texts, all variations on the same theme; the most recent is from minutes ago.

> Please contact me ASAP. We have to meet
> with superintendent and principal TODAY.
> It's imperative.

I need to contact her. I will. When I get home later.

For now, I sit with Lydan. The TV is off, the shades are open, and soft sunlight bathes the room in its warmth. A vase of fresh flowers, pink carnations, has been placed on the windowsill. Lydan looks the same, frail and vulnerable. *My boy. I will fight. For you. I will fight.*

I pull my car into the garage and sit at the wheel and sob until I can no longer sob. I am blind with exhaustion. I need to get the guns, gun magazines and books, and ammunition box out of the trunk, hide them in the basement. I get out of the car and pop the trunk and turn to shut the garage door behind me.

I'm startled to see a woman standing just outside the garage door. If she even glances into the trunk, she'll see inside it. I have no idea if the blanket covering the guns and ammo shifted during the ride, if the contents can be seen. I don't dare look and risk drawing her eyes to the trunk. I step toward her, force her to take a couple of steps back into the driveway.

"Sorry I startled you." The woman is Claire Kirk, the widowed neighbor from across the street. She clutches a cache of mail in her hands; a smear of melted chocolate stains her chin. She seems winded, as if she saw me and rushed out of the house to catch me but first grabbed her mail to make it seem that her timing was coincidental. Her big lemur eyes lend a sense of her being perpetually alarmed. She's a truly pleasant woman, kind and well meaning, judging from my interactions with her. Still, I can't risk her so much as getting a glimpse inside the car's trunk.

"I saw you pull in," Claire says, "and just—I had to say how sorry I am. How terribly, awfully, dreadfully sorry I am." Emotion strangles her voice. Her husband, Jerry, died less than three months ago of an aneurism in his sleep, leaving Claire alone with her two high school boys. Her raw grief has carved its name in her face; the weight of it squats on her slumped shoulders. She means what she says. She *is* terribly, awfully, dreadfully sorry, and I feel for her own grief. Still, she must go.

"Thank you," I say.

"I know there's nothing I can say," Claire says. "But. How is he?"

"It's . . ." I say. "Nothing will ever be the same."

"I know. I'm just so sorry."

Claire tilts her head, and I wonder if something in the trunk has caught her eye.

I turn, quickly, on instinct, not caring if my action seems odd, and slam the trunk, hard. Claire flinches. The blanket moved in transit, and the LAR's black case and the .45 atop it were both visible. My mouth is dry.

"I've kept an eye on your house," Claire says, staring at the trunk. "Since it happened. How can it have been so many weeks? Your house was mobbed by media for a long time, and locals and people from afar holding vigil. I saw you came home, but I didn't catch you in time before you left again." Her eyes meet mine.

"I came home for a shower and change of clothes." I regret my lie even before the last syllable fades. It is a needless lie. It's clear I haven't showered or changed clothes recently, and Claire of all people might understand this. "But," I say, "I never did. All I did was cry. And sleep."

"I understand that."

"I really have to go. I don't want to leave Lydan alone too long."

"Can I help you carry anything inside?" Claire nods at the trunk, raising an eyebrow.

"I'm fine."

My jaw aches with the effort to smile as Claire stands there unspeaking.

"I really do have to get going," I say.

"Let me know if you need anything. *Anything* at all."

Claire drifts down the driveway and stops at the curb and waves.

I wave back, resisting the urge to flick my wrist in a gesture to hasten her along.

With Claire finally back in her house, I lower the garage door and take the LAR case, the ammo, and the .45 from the trunk. In the basement, I set everything on a workbench near the washing machine.

I grab a hammer from a toolbox and crawl under the bench into the corner. Using the hammer's claw, I peel back a sheet of fake wood paneling. A tiny nail pops free, then another, and another, as the panel is jimmied away from the studs. When a span of four feet is pulled from the bottom, I work the LAR case into the recess behind the paneling, between the studs. I hide the ammo box and the .45 beside it and hunt around the floor for wayward nails, plucking up all but a couple of strays I cannot find.

I tap the nails back into the board. It's tricky. The nails are nearly impossible to pinch between my fingertips and tap gently with the hammer, which is too big for the delicate job. As I secure the paneling back in place as best I can, the doorbell upstairs rings.

I freeze with fear.

The doorbell rings again.

And again.

Is it Claire with a few more words of condolence?

I climb the stairs. The doorbell rings, insistent.

I pin myself to the entryway wall as a figure moves on the other side of the door's frosted window. I am jolted back in time to Lydan's classroom. I see the figure pacing on the other side of the classroom door. The pale face at the window.

I wait for whoever it is to go away, but the ringing continues, spelled by a rap of knuckles on the door.

I start for the cellar to get the .45, but a woman's voice speaks through the door.

"Elisabeth," the voice says. "It's Juanita Ramirez. I need to speak to you. Please. If you are in there. I must speak to you. We must speak. I know you—"

I unlock the door and throw it open.

Juanita straightens her posture and forces a smile. She wears adult braces, the kind that look like an athlete's plastic mouth guard.

"I'm so sorry," she says, "to intrude like this." She seems genuinely contrite as she fixes the lapel on her black pantsuit's jacket. "I wouldn't have come here if I did not absolutely have to, on your behalf. I tried calling and texting. Numerous times, and I got no reply or answer. I even went to the hospital."

"I know," I say.

"I would never have done so, but we cannot afford to miss your hearing."

My confusion must show on my face. A hearing is for individuals who are on trial, who are accused of doing something wrong.

"A hearing with the school superintendent and Principal Lamb. That's why I've been trying to get hold of you. It's scheduled in an hour at the superintendent's office, which is a half an hour away. I texted and left you so many messages about it and—I wanted to meet, to strategize with you. To help prepare your defense."

None of what she's saying makes sense.

"I've done nothing wrong," I say.

"I know. The union knows. That's why I'm here. To help."

I still don't understand. I am bewildered and vexed.

"So why a hearing?" I say.

"It's about your conduct . . . during the shooting."

"Conduct?" I say, angered now. "I saved those kids."

"Agreed. One thousand percent agreed. But that's not how the process works."

"The process. What 'process'?"

"They—"

"*They?*" I say, humming with anger.

"Superintendent Mitchel and Principal Lamb."

"Two *men* have decided they don't like *my* conduct?" I say.

"Unfortunately. And the only way to demonstrate your conduct wasn't wrong but absolutely valorous is to show up and defend yourself, on the record. I tried to put off the hearing. I tried to get them to dismiss their pursuit of this. We did. The union did. Frankly, it's vile. Outrageous. But they're pursuing it anyway. And we, you, need to show up or else—"

I am in utter shock. I feel ethereal, no longer a physical being. I am wholly detached from the galling reality of these *men*. "Give me five minutes," I say. "I need to shower, as you can see."

In the shower, my muscles are slack and weak, skin crusted and ripe with dried sweat. I am filthy and reeking.

I run the water as hot as I can bear it, scrub and lather, then run the water stunningly cold.

On the drive to the superintendent's office, Ramirez says: "In most cases, we would be aggressive in our defense. But this is a singular case. Personally, I wholeheartedly agree with what you did. I stand with it. With you. Professionally, too. But . . ."

"*But?*"

"*But* they have dug their heels in on this."

"Why would they do this to me?"

"I don't know. Remember, the union's advice, all my advice and counsel to you today, is entirely to make this easier on you, get you the best possible outcome. Preserve your livelihood."

"*Wait.* They can't remove me from my job. That can't be possible. Not that I'd ever even go back there. Still." It's as if I am in an alternate reality.

Ramirez's silence is disquieting.

"In our strategic meetings," she says, finally, "we decided the appropriate tack is contrition."

"I have nothing to be contrite about."

"True. But it's for the best, even if we know in our bones you shouldn't have to. We want you to keep your job and your medical insurance. If you take any other stance, you might be dismissed. Can you afford to face what's ahead for your son without medical insurance?"

We both know the answer.

Little pricks.

It's clear, sitting here at this faux-wood-laminated table in this generic conference room down the hall from Superintendent Mitchel's office, that this proceeding is the apex of hubris and folly. Yet its inanity does not make my job as a teacher any less imperiled. It makes it more so.

Mitchel and Lamb sit elbow to elbow across from me and Juanita, as close as two schoolboys at a cafeteria table sharing a dirty joke. The harsh sun illuminates the window behind Mitchel and Lamb and shines in my eyes. Its heat makes me feel drowsy and flushed and a tad nauseous. Its brightness makes me squint. A venetian blind hangs from the top of the window. One of the men could easily lower it with a tug of its string and relieve me of my discomfort. Yet neither man does so. Both wear what look like bargain-rack suits. They likely feel that they appear authoritative, representative of the system in which they are cogs, but instead they look cheap and pedestrian.

Mitchel's blue tie is knotted so tight that a ring of pink flesh bulges above his collar. His posture is poor, and the sunlight gleams on his scalp through thinned hair that he somehow has decided is made less conspicuous by his seventies comb-over. Before him on the table rests a Moleskine ledger and a manila envelope bursting with loose papers. He taps a ballpoint pen on the knee of his chinos.

Lamb is pale of face, and he looks undernourished, his suit too loose on his frame. His hands are bony and roped with blue veins. He glances at his smartphone placed face up on the table. The meeting is set to officially begin in five minutes, but there are no other attendees scheduled besides the four of us. The men could have started the meeting ten minutes ago, but Mitchel makes us wait, in silence, for no reason other than that he can.

Juanita fires up her tablet.

I hear a faint chiming sound.

Mitchel takes his phone out of his coat pocket, swipes a finger across its screen. The chiming stops. "Well," he says, cracking his knuckles, "shall we proceed with the matter at hand?"

By all means. Proceed.

Juanita nods.

"Okay then." Mitchel opens the Moleskine notepad. "First, let me say, Ms. Ross, I, we"—he nods at Lamb, and Lamb nods back, so somber, so serious—"sympathize with you, as parents, which is why we waited as long as we did for this to take place. We *know* this cannot be easy for you."

He knows nothing.

Nothing.

My eyes fix on him.

Mitchel glances at his notes. "You're here because of violations of the safety protocols put in place by the supervisory union. Measures we practice with methodic rigor every third Monday of the month to ensure the safety of our student body. Drills you have overseen the practice of dozens of times over your decade of teaching at Franklin."

"And a half," I say.

"Excuse me?" Mitchel says.

"I've been with Franklin Elementary for fifteen years. A decade and a half."

Mitchel glances at his notebook. "Mmm. Yes."

"You did practice the drills each month, did you not?" Lamb says and scratches at a patch of flaky skin on the side of his nose.

"Oh, yes," I say, "I practiced them."

"Yet when it came time to *enact* them, you did *not* follow them, what we worked so hard at, as a team, as a community," Mitchel says.

"I did not," I say. They know I didn't. That's why, inexplicably, I am here for this exercise of the absurd.

"You put your entire classroom and yourself at risk," Mitchel says.

Juanita glances at me. I know what I am supposed to do here. Apologize. Be contrite.

When it's clear I'm not going to reply, Mitchel says: "You would agree, would you not, that you put the students at risk, the students for whom you are responsible?"

Juanita nods at me, her eyes pleading: *Agree. Be contrite. Get it over with and keep your job. For your son.*

"I would not agree," I say.

"I'm sorry?" Lamb says.

"I'm sorry too," I say. "Sorry you brought me here for nothing."

Juanita rubs her hands together, nervous, and addresses Mitchel. "What Elisabeth means is—"

"What I mean," I say, "is that, by evidence of the irrefutable facts, I did not put those kids at risk. I saved them." My head vibrates with a sharp pain, and I am carrying Lydan, setting his limp and bloodied body down on a desk next to his murdered teacher.

"Elisabeth," a voice says. Juanita is nudging my elbow.

"This is bedrock fact," I say. "I got them out, and they *lived*. Other teachers followed your protocols, and their kids are dead, maimed, or traumatized. If my son had been in *my* class and not in the class of a teacher who followed your protocols, he'd be home playing with his Pokémon cards right now. You do see, do you not, how your sitting here and saying *I* put them at risk is literally beyond belief."

Mitchel stops tapping his pen on his knee. A bloom of blue ink stains his chinos. "You," Mitchel says, wagging the pen at me, freckling the table with ink, "elected to go rogue."

"Is he serious?" I snap, turning to Juanita, who stiffens, then clutches my wrist. I shake free of her grasp. "Are you serious?" I say to Mitchel. "*Rogue?* Is this the military?"

"Ms. Ross, *please*, I do have the floor," Mitchel says as he sits up straight, his chest and gut puffed up like he's some bird about to perform a mating ritual. "You did not follow the protocols put in place, protocols we worked like slaves for years to *perfect*, protocols you practiced, we all practiced, to ensure the safety of our students. You practiced them, but then you *ignored* them; you decided . . ."

I half expect Mitchel to leap up on the table and start strutting in circles as he squawks and preens. This is not about protocol, not about the students being jeopardized, not about rules. Not about the fact that I saved lives. This is about a *woman* disobeying *men*.

Mitchel is still blathering; he won't be denied his moment of pontification, his chance to lord it over *his* educator. Each word he speaks is a tiny blade nicking my flesh, meant to wound, meant to weaken my resolve. I wonder, if I continue to *resist*, how long it will take for his words to morph from tiny blades to swords and cleavers, bludgeons. For they always do with men of his make. For now, he speaks each word with a deliberate, controlled calm in an attempt to demonstrate that he is trying his utmost to be civil, democratic, fair, and he ought to be lauded for maintaining such constraint when he and the system he represents have been so egregiously insulted and challenged, *ignored*, by a woman. Yet his reasonable and constrained tone is also a warning: *Do not push me; you cannot expect me to remain this reasonable forever in the face of your gross disrespect and misconduct. Consider yourself lucky, very lucky, Ms. Ross, that I am a patient man.*

"So you see," Mitchel says, the red of his face fading to a deep pink, the skin slick with sweat, "we take exception to such affronts, to such *rogue* behavior."

"May I speak?" I say. "May I speak against this attack?"

"Attack?" Mitchel scoffs. "Now *she's* being attacked." Exasperated, he twirls a finger in the air for me to expound, as he leans back in his chair, his puffed chest deflating, his gut bulging over his belt. He seems not to notice that his face is freckled with blue ink, his fingers stained with it. "By all means, that's why we're here. We're here to understand. Are we not?" Mitchel says to Lamb. "Understand why she did such a thing, jeopardized an entire classroom of children. Please, proceed."

"Did they work?" I say, scratching a fingernail into the table's cheap, fake surface as I simmer with contempt.

"Careful," Juanita whispers.

"Did what work?" Mitchel says.

"These sacred protocols you worked 'like *slaves* over'—did they, *in reality*, ensure the safety of our kids?"

"What are you—"

"How many children were shot in the classroom just to the left down the hall from mine?" I say.

Mitchel glares at me, as if I've asked him how many feet are in a mile, a question to which one, it seems, should know the answer, but when asked the question, one realizes that they do not know the answer.

"*Five*," I say, recalling the faces and names from the newspaper I read in Lydan's ICU room, eons ago. "Five students were shot. Three died. Tim Jenkins, age seven. Jeremy Luciando, age seven. Malka Shapiro, age eight. One died a week later, Taylor Stewart. One girl, Penny Francis, remains in ICU. Just down the hall from my own son."

"A tragedy, no doubt," Lamb squeaks, "and we are not without—"

"*No*," I snap. "Not a *tragedy*. A tragedy is a shorted wire causing a house to burn down. This was not a tragedy. None of them are. They are willful acts of mass murder of our children."

Lamb opens his pale mouth to blat something, but I won't stand for it. I am in a lather. "And how many students were shot in the classroom to the right of mine?" I say.

Mitchel's face goes crimson as a boiled crab, then blanches, his flesh pale as Lamb's now, his jaw a slack sack of pudding. His fingers are polluted with dark-blue ink.

"You *both* ought to know this," I say. "You both ought to have these numbers, these names, these facts, seared into your brain. They ought to keep you up at night." I thrust a finger at Lamb. "Do they? Or is two months enough for you to rinse your mind of it? Let me ask again. *Do you know* how many students were shot in the room to the right of mine?"

I wait in the pounding silence.

Mitchel will not humiliate himself by referring to his Moleskine notepad, if he even has such notes with such numbers in it.

"Since you don't know what you should know," I say, "I'll just tell you. Seven. Seven children were shot." I give the names of the children and explain that two are dead, and the rest suffered injuries that will affect them forever and likely shorten their lives. "And one teacher. Mr. Taylor. He's dead. They died by observing your *protocol.*"

Mitchel's face darkens to the shade of pomegranate pulp. He clutches at his strangling tie. "How dare you," he croaks.

Juanita scratches a note on her pad and slides it to me: *You're right. But toe! The! Line!!!*

My blood spikes, evaporates in my white-hot veins. "They died hiding under their desks and chairs. Hunkered like frightened squirrels."

"I see where you are going with this," Mitchel says, "and while—"

"You *do know* how many kids were shot in my classroom?" I say, glaring at Mitchel. "*Do you not?*"

Mitchel's nostrils billow. He is apoplectic and aggressive when instead he should be mortified and apologetic. Such is the nature of such men. When trapped in a cage of facts that prove them wrong, they double down, triple down, quadruple down—instead of admitting fault, they lay siege to facts and the messenger, retreat to defensive spite and self-righteous outrage that spiral down a vortex of justifications and lies. All to protect their fantastical egos, as trembling and fragile as a soap bubble, from being pierced by reality.

I switch my focus to Lamb. "Neither of you know how many kids were shot in other classrooms, but you know how many were shot in mine. Because it's easy to remember."

"I caution you," Mitchel says. "Your behavior here—"

I bolt up from my chair. Mitchel and Lamb startle at my alacrity. "You listen to me," I say.

"Please," Juanita says.

Mitchel makes a furious note in his Moleskine, striking his pen with ferocious intent, blue ink freckling the paper and table. Lamb looks like a child who has just been slapped across the face.

"*Zero* kids were shot in my class. Zero had to even lay eyes on that man," I say.

"*This* time," Mitchel bleats.

"Excuse me?" I feel as if I've taken a blow to my skull. I take a step toward Mitchel.

Juanita clutches my forearm.

"This time," Mitchel says. "This time you saved them."

"Was there another, better time," I say, "some other universe that *matters more than the time it actually happened*? Some theoretical time where bullets are stopped by desks and sand tables?"

Juanita squeezes my forearm. I shake her free. "Is there some other alternate dimension that counts besides the one I acted in, the one that saved their lives?"

"There is no need to be combative," Juanita says.

"Let go of my arm," I say to her. "All I want is to know what world he's living in." I pivot to Mitchel. "What do you mean: *this* time?"

"I mean—" Mitchel stammers. His fingers work at his tie, as if he's trying to tighten its knot, as if this might stiffen his spine. All he succeeds in doing is marring it with blue pen ink. "I mean that it worked out this time but next time—"

"You plan on a next time? You'd prefer I obey your rules even if it gets kids killed than disobey your rules and save kids' lives."

"Don't put words in my mouth."

"I'm confused," I say. "Why am I here? How is my job possibly in jeopardy when I saved my students?"

"*Elisabeth*," Juanita says. "*This* is not helping you."

"Juanita," I snap. "*You* are not helping me."

I take another step toward Mitchel as Lamb looks on, his face now the sickly gray green of an overboiled egg yolk.

"*In what* magical dimension would you expect me to abide by rules that get my students killed just so long as I obey you?" I say, tapping my fingernail on the table. "In what world does that make any sense? Because I refuse to live in it."

Mitchel's face purples.

"A world," I continue, "where this sort of thing should *never ever* happen. Ever. Not once in a million years, let alone once every third day. I shouldn't have to be saving kids from being blasted into raw hamburger."

"That's a disturbing thing to say," Mitchel says.

"It's a disturbing thing to *see*," I say. "But neither of you would know, since one of you is never in the schools and the other was out that day with the sniffles."

"I know you're under some strain—" Lamb says.

I laugh. A loud bark. Mitchel and Lamb flinch. "*You* don't know shit," I say. "You know *nothing*." My spittle speckles his forehead.

Mitchel's face collapses like yeasty risen dough punched down with a fist.

"*We*," he rasps, "have rules. So we have order and not chaos. We cannot just make things up on the fly. We cannot just . . . flee."

There it is, the kernel. I fled. I retreated. As if I were a soldier and he the general with marching orders. I defied him. Embarrassed him by saving kids while breaking his protocols and thus showing that his protocols resulted in death and trauma.

Mitchel finally seems to notice his fingertips are stained with blue ink and gives a sour frown. "None of what you say excuses the fact that—"

A sharp keening deep inside my head, a whining peal, a long sharp needle of sound piercing my brain. It's all I can hear. My jaw aches and pulses with it; my skull reverberates. Mitchel's mouth moves, his tongue darting and poking, his coffee-yellowed teeth bared, and I know right now I want to shoot him. To shut him up. To stop him. I want to shoot him. I could do it. Right now. Easily. Just shoot him in the face. Without a single regret. He is the enemy.

Come back, that inner voice says. *Listen to what the enemy says.*

The ringing fades to a dull throb in my ear.

"You also went back inside the school," Lamb says. "Another breach that put others in danger."

"It put no one but me in danger," I say.

"You ignored the *FBI*."

"My son was in there," I say.

"You have a young daughter; you'd do the same," Juanita says to Lamb, without conviction.

"*My behavior* is not being questioned here," Lamb says. "I appreciate what she did, as a parent. But as a professional who develops policies and must make decisions to reprimand or suspend based on an educator's conduct, I cannot let my personal beliefs trump my professional responsibility. The matter of her misconduct is severe and demands action. I will recommend a semester suspension without pay to the board, not because I want to but because I must. And that is the best I can do, if she is contrite. Otherwise, I will recommend it be permanent." He gives me a thin, satisfied smile.

"You're both parents with daughters in grade school," I say. "Ironic your kids attend private schools, but let me ask: Which classroom would you have wanted your daughters in that day? Mine? Or any of the others?"

The men stare at me, unspeaking.

"Right," I say. "Mine. And I think every parent, when I tell them what you've put me through here today, how you've traumatized me, *again*, they will agree with you about which class they'd have wanted their kids in. And if you press forward, we'll see just who gets fired at the end of all this. So have fucking at it."

"Stag-15L Model 4L," I murmur in the dark of Lydan's room, the lexicon foreign on my tongue, defining a world cold and alien to me. "Made by Stag Arms in Wyoming. Chambers five point five six by forty-five millimeters NATO. Button-rifled bore. One-in-nine-inch six-groove. Right-hand twist. Barrel is *not* chrome lined like other Stags."

I sit alone this last week at Lydan's bedside and devote myself to memorizing flash cards cribbed from Homer's books and magazines, the makes and models of handguns and black rifles. I glue a photo of each weapon on the front of the card and write the name and description on the back. Deep into the many nights, I drill myself on DPMS M4s, AP4s, M16A2s, Stag-15L Model 4Ls, AR-15s. Make. Model. Caliber. Action. Use. Make. Model. Caliber. Action. Use. I must know what I am talking about. I must know this world.

When I learn a firearm cold, I put the flash card in a pile with others I've learned, and when I go home for a catnap, I burn the flash cards and all my notes in the charcoal grill on the back deck, until they are ash.

Tonight, I feel ready. I depart the hospital early, at 8:30 p.m., and drive south for four hours on a deserted stretch of M-42. I pull off on a random side road to a state park, turn onto a dirt lane that ends at a gravel parking area to a trailhead. The night is black.

I put the battery into the throwaway phone I bought on the way to Homer's and bring up Akers's website, the glow of the screen the only light in the dark. I am amped with adrenaline and have to concentrate to hold the phone tight enough to keep it steady. I study Akers's website, lurk in the chat rooms, and find mention of another infamous gun dealer, an apparent nemesis of Akers. Lance Bishop in Driggs, Idaho, a Second Amendment bedfellow but direct competition.

I find Akers's email address on GunsGunsGuns.com, and using a fake, encrypted email account—FreedomFighterSam—I write a subject line with no body copy in the email: Fusil Automatique Léger. Interested?

I consider hitting Delete. I wonder if this email account for Akers is monitored now that he's announced his candidacy. I doubt it. This is his private account, his private world. Guns are the obsession he cannot deny himself, just as another man cannot deny himself his gambling fixation or sexual pursuits. Still, I hesitate. I can hit Delete and go home. Or hit Send and not know where it will take me.

To a different life, for certain.

Yet still, my life.

I hit Send.

And.

Nothing.

For an hour. For two. Nothing.

I stare at my inbox. Empty. I reload it and reload it and watch it and wait and reload it. Nothing. I wonder if Akers reads mail sent to the address I used or if the address is even valid.

I turn off the phone, take out its battery and SIM card, and start the long drive back home.

I don't use the phone again until twenty-four hours later, when I drive back out to the same spot and turn on the phone and access the email.

The inbox is empty.

On the third night, I drive out again and check the email.

A reply from Akers: Who is this?

I respond: Interested?

A reply appears in seconds: Don't waste my time with bullshit. Who is this?

I reply: Don't waste my time with bullshit. I can get real interest in Idaho. You have a knockoff. It happens.

Ain't no knockoff.

The phone pings.

Send proof. Photo. Serial number.

ID it in person. You'll know it's the real deal at a glance. Thought you'd have interest. I'll see if our man in Idaho does.

Of course I can ID with a glance. Even if it's what you claim, I'm not interested in buying it.

Didn't say I was selling. Got 1500 rounds to burn through.

Five minutes pass. Perhaps he's worried I'm ATF, or a political rival, setting up a sting. Maybe he's considering the legal ramifications. But he wouldn't be in any legal jeopardy just from looking at the LAR or firing it in his range. Not if he isn't the owner. And, I hope, he can't help himself.

Interested or not?

Does the NRA protect your 2A rights? I doubt she's the real deal but if she is, I'll get her hot and bothered in my private range and I swear I'll tongue fuck her sweet black muzzle.

She's the real deal.

I send the date I'll be there. 11 pm. Sharp.

Why so late?

If that's past your bedtime, I'll keep going to Idaho.

Use the back entrance.

I get out of the car, and from the trunk I take a hammer and obliterate the phone.

I collect the shards and pieces in a bag and scatter them randomly along the highway fifty miles away.

I imagine Akers's face when he meets me and finds out "Sam" is a woman. It will make him skeptical, but it will disarm him and work to my advantage. I won't be glammed up like Suze. I'll be cold business. Scant makeup. A bulky sweatshirt to conceal the .45 in the back of my loose jeans' waistband. Sneakers. A ball cap. Short-cropped wig. Nothing to see here, except my fake blue contacts. But it won't matter that I'm dressed drab. Akers's ego will demand he impress me.

Taking the exit off M-42, I sing my favorite line from my favorite movie, *Mary Poppins*:

> *Though we adore men individually,*
> *we agree that as a group they're rather stupid!*

There are good men in this world.

But they remain too few.

And they are not the problem.

It is the other kind.

The fools. Fools for women. Money. Toys. Fools who cannot stand calm in their convictions and their vision of themselves, who get defensive when questioned, who vie for whatever drop of acclaim or stature or power they can squeeze out of life and everyone around them. Men who lie or cheat or steal to advance toward their arbitrary and mythical goal of "success." Boys in adult bodies without emotional or psychologi-cal maturity. They scarf junk food, play video games, read comic books, watch superhero movies; doesn't matter if they swill six-packs of cheap beer after a day on the jobsite or sip at three fingers of single malt scotch in hundred-dollar crystal snifters after a day manipulating hedge funds. They obsess over sports teams made up of men young enough to be their sons, worship the jocks who once likely ridiculed and bullied them in the locker room. They watch movies with infantile depictions of crime and violence and sex, quoting the same tired lines as they straddle spread legged and spray spittle everywhere, reenacting a celluloid myth that they seem to want to live in themselves. They mumble like slack-jawed Saint Bernards, lines like "I'm gonna make him an offer he can't refuse," believing these lines to be iconic, legendary in their appeal. Elevating the inanity of stuffing one's cheeks with cotton balls to genius instead of the schtick it is, even as confessed by the thespian himself, who did it for the paycheck that helped buy his island. Men whose entire pro-jection of themselves is a pathetic myth of smoke. Like Akers himself.

So I'll let Akers be the fool, bloviate about all he knows about the LAR. It will be his downfall, providing the distraction I need.

By the time he figures out why I'm there, it will be too late.

For him.

And for me.

BOOK II

At home this past week, I've been petrified as I watch Lydan, my eyes alert, my mind a seismograph sensitive to the slightest tremor that might forecast a violent seizure or fall. He is relegated to a walker, and a wheelchair when he is too fatigued to stand, which is often.

"Don't stare at me, Mama," he will say from his wheelchair or the hospital bed that was placed in his room, when I come in to check on him, to take the rail down or up for him. Adjust pillows.

"I'm just making sure you're okay," I say.

He is so broken, broken in ways invisible to the eye, to the physical world. He seems to have aged years, yet it is more than that, more than *years*, more than a human measurement of time or space. And not just bodily. He does look different. Somehow he looks younger and aged at once, and smaller than he was. Paler. Weaker. I've not yet seen the color return to his cheeks as Ella forecasted. The light he once radiated, the pure and magical light of youth and innocence, of wonder and curiosity, is vanquished. Yet this is not quite what I mean. He has not just aged; he's diminished in ways even I, who was there that day, cannot begin to understand. I cannot know what it was like to be there in his own classroom. To see what he saw. Hear what he heard. Feel what he felt. Fear what he feared. Know what he now knows about this world. In some ways he has regressed, and in others I see, at times, in his eyes a deep, ancient knowing, a sense he knows more than I will ever know, that I am the child and he . . . not the parent. Not the adult. But something else. It is as if his soul has aged. His therapist, who Zooms every other weekday, says it will take time for him to "find himself" again, that he will, in part, need to create a new self, piece himself back together and find out who he is now, in this aftermath. So much was taken from him; so much was stolen; so much of him, who he was, was left behind in that classroom. He must become someone new, someone else.

This, I understand.

Nightly, I sleep in fits, if the state I reach can be called sleep at all.

It is not a place of calm, that tranquil netherworld, that respite from the waking world. It is not a time of recharging, freshening, or rest.

Each night, I am forced once more, against my will, to revisit that day, the classrooms and hallways. All of it. And each time it unfolds as if for the first time, as if I have never experienced it before, in a dream or in the flesh. And I am plunged again into all of its horror. Every night. Every single night. I relive it again and again and again without reprieve.

When I finally awake before dawn, I am more depleted than when I first lay in bed, often not until 2:00 a.m.

Lydan, for his part, has his own strange dreams. He will awaken in the night muttering and weeping, sheathed in sweat. He does not share his dreams. And I do not dare ask too much; I do not want to pick at his psychic wounds. He does not tell his therapist about his dreams either. She says he appears to forget them entirely by the time they meet on Zoom in the afternoon. He either does not remember them at all or is very deft at deceiving her.

Daily, Lydan and I run our routine.

Physical and occupational therapists visit and depart on rotation in the mornings; his psychologist Zooms in and out.

When it's time for his Lovenox injection, a prescription to help prevent serious blood clots, I have Lydan lift his pajama top up to expose the soft pale flesh at his side. He's humiliated by the diaper he wears and the catheter tube and bag, so he doesn't pull the pj top up far enough. I ask him to hike it just a bit more. He does so, turning away from me.

I take the disposable syringe from its plastic box. The shot is easy to administer, but it still makes me nervous. I worry I'll do it wrong, hurt Lydan somehow, push the needle too deep and strike his hip bone or break the tip off inside him. But all of this anxiety is unwarranted; the injection could not be easier to give. The syringe is small, the needle capped. There is none of the dramatic pressing of the thumb to squeeze out a squirt of liquid medicine, no tapping the syringe to make certain no killer air bubbles remain. I just take the tiny cap off the needle, put the needle to flesh, and press my thumb to it. The needle jabs and retracts in an instant.

"Pinch your side," I say first.

Lydan grabs what little flesh there is and pinches it to gather it up.

"Ready?" I say.

"Mm-hmm," he says and squeezes his eyes tight. He's nervous too.

"It's not going to hurt," I say. "You've been through a lot worse. This is nothing. A beesting. Not even a beesting."

"Okay." His voice trembles. After all he's suffered, he is still just a young boy, afraid of the sting of a needle.

"Okay," I say, "on three. One. Two—"

I inject him on two, as Dr. Downing suggested.

"That's it, see? Easy peasy," I say. "Done."

Lydan lets go of his pinched flesh and looks at me as if I tricked him and I haven't really given him the shot yet.

"Nothing, right?" I say.

"Nothing." He lets his T-shirt fall.

"Tomorrow, we do the other side, so you don't get sore from me jabbing the same spot."

There is a week of tomorrows, until I pay my visit to Akers.

Lydan remains distant. There are times he seems to want to break out of it. Yet he doesn't dare.

Tonight, I sit on the couch and call for Lydan to come out from his room, where he chooses to spend most of his time, and join me.

I tell him I have a movie ready to go and doughnuts I had delivered along with the weekly groceries. He doesn't respond.

I check on him and find him sitting on the edge of his bed in his room, crying.

In another time, I'd simply ask, *What's wrong, sweetie?*

Not now.

I know what's wrong, and I know it can't be fixed or healed.

I sit beside him and put my arm around him. "Come on out and watch a movie with your mama," I say. "I have doughnuts."

He doesn't say anything. Doesn't so much as shrug.

"What can I do for you? Don't you want to watch a movie with me?"

"I guess."

"Then come out with me."

"I can't sit with you. I can't snuggle."

He's right. If he sits back on the couch, the angle of it will cause him great discomfort, and the catheter's tubing is likely to get tangled or pinched.

I never say the word *catheter*. The very word mortifies him.

Some of his friends have asked to come visit him, but he doesn't want them to see him like this. I told him no one will care, and if they do care, they aren't his friends. They'd be glad to see him. They've sent dozens of cards and texts to my phone from their parents' phones, a cascade of hilarious and heartfelt emoji.

I tried to get him to Zoom with friends. He tried once but didn't know what to say. "I'm not me," he said. He wants to be. But he isn't. He sobbed and I held him and kissed the top of his head. I told him to get it all out, and he said there is no getting it all out. "It's bigger than a million universes," he said.

"You can bring your wheelchair up close enough to the end of the couch to hold my hand while we watch the movie," I say now.

He looks at me.

"Would that work for you?" I say.

"I guess we can try," he says.

And we do try.

I sit on the end of the couch, and he wheels close to me, and we sit and watch one of his favorite movies and hold hands. He eats half a jelly doughnut but loses interest. He laughs at the movie, once, but mostly he just stares at the TV without any reaction to it at all.

Halfway through, he is asleep, making strange, strangled sounds.

He'll be fast asleep. He'll never know.

I stand at the stove and watch Lydan try to play solitaire at the kitchen table, flipping his cards with his left hand. The nerves of his right arm are too damaged for him to manipulate the playing cards.

We are just a tangled spiderweb of nerves. Pull one thread.

I open the cupboard and stare at one of Lydan's dozen bottles filled with prescription pills he takes daily. It's 5:00 p.m. I need to be out of the house in two hours if I am going to do what I need to do.

I pick up the amber bottle and read the label.

Take 1 to 2 pills for pain twice a day as needed.

In the time he's been home, I've never given Lydan two pills at once. One pill makes him listless and drowsy for a couple of hours. His doctor said two pills won't hurt him, but it will put him out, maybe for longer than I'd prefer. If he's having trouble sleeping, it might give him a night's rest, but I am not to do it regularly, and there is no prescription they can put him on for nightly use, even to combat his dreams.

I put the bottle back in the cupboard and check on the tuna casserole in the oven.

"Your favorite," I say.

"Why are you making that, Mama?" Lydan says and flips a card.

I set the casserole on a trivet. I'm caught off guard by his tepid response to my effort and by the suspicion in his voice. "It's your favorite," I say. "With extra-toasted, extra-buttery croutons on top."

Lydan eases himself out of his seat and adjusts the leg of his loose sweatpants where it has snagged on the catheter bag strapped to his thigh. He takes the crutches propped against the table edge and works his way over to the counter, dragging his left leg behind him, wincing. He takes a whiff of the casserole, then pinches a crouton between two fingertips and pops it into his mouth, crunching it. "How come tonight?" he says. "It's usually just for special things."

"You're special," I say as I spoon a scoop of casserole, blow on it, and offer it to Lydan. "See if it's up to snuff. Careful, it's hot."

Lydan takes a big bite, then huffs a breath. "Hot!" he says, waving a hand in front of his mouth.

"Told you. Good?"

Lydan offers a thumbs-up. Then he says, "I know what you're doin', Mama. You can't trick me."

His voice is flat, his look serious.

"You," he says, "put broccoli in it. Hid broccoli to trick me."

I gasp with relief. "Would your mama do that to you?"

"I want another bite. To check."

"Finish your card game and let dinner cool. I made peach cobbler too and got vanilla ice cream."

He frowns and glances down at his catheter bag, face flushed. "I'm gonna get into my pj's."

"Want help?" I say.

"I can *do* it," Lydan says.

He can, but it's a battle to get his sweatpants down and detach the bag and drain it into the toilet while maintaining his balance without his crutches.

"I know you can do it, sweetie," I say.

"I'm not a sweetie. I'm not a baby."

He crutches his way down the hall. When he is out of sight, I take out his Percocet prescription bottle. Listening to water running in the hallway bathroom, I tap two pills into my palm.

Between two spoons, I grind one pill to powder.

"Mama," Lydan shouts. I drop the spoon, the powder spilling.

"Mama!"

Lydan is standing in the center of the bathroom, his sweatpants sagged around his thighs, snagged on the catheter bag, his pajama top clutched in his left hand.

"I *am a baby*," he sobs.

"You aren't," I say. "Here."

I take the pajama top from him and set it on the back of the toilet. "Raise your arms," I say. "Let's get your shirt off. Go easy." The T-shirt is two sizes too large for him. It makes it easier for him to get it on and off. He starts to raise his right arm slowly but stops, going rigid with what I believe must be atomic-level pain, grinding his teeth with such fierceness I can hear it. "Easy," I say. "Try your good arm first." He raises his left arm, and I help him slip it down and out of the sleeve. He can't adjust his right arm enough to do the same. "We'll use the scissors." I take scissors from atop his bureau and carefully cut the shirt off him.

His meager torso is puckered and knotted with a constellation of raw scars, the flesh both pale and a livid purple, like lard marbling a raw steak. Among these wounds are a half dozen neat surgical scalpel slices, one a ten-inch curve along his abdomen and over his right hip bone. Tonight, the scars are particularly vicious. Crimson. If his pain is half as angry as his scars, his soul must be howling.

I hug him, breathe in his scent, feel the heat of him as he shivers.

"You are courageous," I say, holding him out from me, hands on his shoulders. "You are braver and stronger than you will ever know."

"It feels like lightning is inside me. Flashing everywhere. Like I'm full of lightning," he says. "I hate it. I hate me."

"Don't say that," I say. "Hate him. He's the one you should hate."

"What 'bout what he said?"

"He was crazy. I'd do anything to have listened to you that morning." I've avoided the subject for Lydan's sake, but I can't any longer. "How did you know it was going to happen? Why did you have that icky feeling?"

"How what was going to happen?"

"When you woke up after surgery, you said you didn't feel icky that morning but that you had an icky feeling, like something bad was going to happen."

"I don't remember that."

"You said it."

"I believe you, Mama. Maybe I just felt bad about going to school. Then maybe after what that man did, I imagined that's what I meant before school? Made it up when I woke up in the hospital. I don't remember."

"You were very clear," I say. "You said you felt it that morning, knew it, something bad was going to happen. I asked you several times if you were sure, and you said you were."

"I don't remember, Mama."

"I remember thinking maybe I should keep you home, but I didn't. I took my job more seriously than time with you."

"I don't want to talk about it anymore, Mama."

His chin quivers as he fights tears. If I could exorcise his anguish and make it my own, I would.

"Let's get your jammies on," I say. It's easier to get his arms into the loose sleeves of the open, button-down pajama top.

I help him step out of his sweatpants.

He stiffens as I unclip the catheter's tube from the bag and unstrap the bag from his thigh. The bag is swollen with a dark-amber urine stained pink from internal bleeding. This is an improvement. A week ago, the urine was still an alarming red with blood and had clots floating in it. I am relieved to see signs of his healing even if there is still so much healing left to do.

Lydan looks away as I drain the bag's contents into the toilet. I hope the bag won't fill up in the night and that the discomfort won't cut through the fog of his medication and awaken him. I hadn't thought of that. I worry about what else I haven't thought of.

Please, don't let him wake up in the night. Please, spare him. Spare us that.

I attach the emptied catheter bag back to Lydan's thigh.

"Need help with the bottoms?" I ask.

"This part is easy."

"It wasn't easy a week ago. Superstar progress, right?" I ruffle his hair. "Come out and eat your dinner and have some cobbler."

In the kitchen, he gobbles up his casserole while I scoop warm peach cobbler into a bowl and sprinkle the powder of the crushed pill into it. The oven clock says 6:00 p.m. I have one hour.

I scoop vanilla ice cream on top of the cobbler and hold the bowl out to Lydan. "Dessert," I exclaim.

I sit with my own cobbler and place Lydan's other pill next to him with a glass of water.

Lydan sips his water and swallows his pill.

He shoves the spoon deep into the cobbler and ice cream and takes a bite.

He commences to wolf the cobbler down and finishes with a smack of his lips.

"Look at you," I say.

I eat my cobbler. Lydan wants to play checkers. He used to excel at it with quick decisive moves and jumps. Time and again he beat me. Now he stares at the board, eyes dim with indecision, as if he's not quite sure what to do, or even what exactly the checkers *are*. He looks at me as if for approval, then makes a halting move. He yawns. "Tired," he says.

"Let's get you to bed," I say.

Lydan tries to push off the table with his palms but slumps back in the chair. "Tired," he says again.

I wrap my arms around his waist to help him stand. "Get your balance, sweetie," I say. "Lean on Mama." He is slack, as if drunk.

I manage to navigate the hallway with him and get him tucked into bed.

"Stay with me," he murmurs, "till I fall asleep?"

I have to leave in fifteen minutes or I will never make it. I cannot risk speeding on the way there, and I cannot be late.

I lie down and spoon him, mindful not to cuddle him too tight.

How I wish I could absorb his pain, let it seep deep into my own flesh and drain from his.

He's snoring. I worry now that the dose I gave him is too potent and will send him into a sleep that's too deep. Or that the dose is not potent enough and he will awaken alone in the night with me gone and no idea where I am. No way to reach me.

In a panic, I grab a pad of paper and write, Mama had to go out. But I'm close by. Don't you worry. Just go back to bed and sleep and Mama will be home when you wake up. I'll be home very very soon. So soon you won't even miss me. Promise. Mama loves you SOOOOO much. Don't worry just go back to sleep. XXXOOO

I read the note several times and scribble hearts next to the *XXXOOO*. Five minutes.

I prop the note up against Lydan's bedside lamp and watch him sleep.

I pull his Snoopy blanket up tighter to his chin and kiss his cheek and tiptoe out of the room.

I check the back door of the house. It is locked. I leave the bathroom light on.

It's time.

In a million years I'd never have believed I'd do this.

In a million years I'd never have believed I'd have reason.

The night is black and cold and silent.

My car sits in the driveway. I didn't want to chance the racket of the overhead door awakening Lydan or attracting the attention of a neighbor.

I start the engine and wait a moment. I can see Claire's picture window in my rearview. It's dark. I turn on the headlights and ease the car down the street.

I see the figure of a woman on the curb. Claire. She's out in her bathrobe smoking a cigarette while her cockapoo pees on her mailbox post. Claire lifts her hand to wave, the orange ember of her cigarette arcing through the dark of the night. I am unsure if Claire recognizes my car or me, or if she simply made the gesture out of habit without really looking.

Either way, it's too late.

Three and a half hours later, a half mile from my destination, across from an old train yard and a Little League ball field, I sit in my parked car and wait. There is one traffic light in this town. Through the trees it blinks yellow.

This, I hope, will be the only place a CCTV camera will be. There might be others at the doorways of the sleepy businesses, but I won't be walking by them. I've planned my route. And Akers's pride, if he's telling the truth in his interviews, keeps him from using any security other than iron bars on the windows and his guns.

If he's lying for the sake of theater, if he does have security cameras, I will be caught within days. Hours.

My armpits and crotch steam with sweat. I feel severed from reality, from myself. I ache for Lydan, to know he is okay. I imagine him awakening and wandering the house, pleading for me to answer his calls. If I come home and find that he woke with me gone, stumbled out of the house to ask a neighbor for help, or sat on his bed, enslaved by fear, I don't know how I'll begin to comfort him or explain my absence. How I will ever forgive myself.

I won't.

I can go back now. I have that power. To choose. I can return home and slip into bed with Lydan and wake up and face the world. I can choose to do as others have in the wake of these horrendous acts. I can speak out, speak up. I can run for office. Start a cause, a foundation. Try to hold leaders accountable in another way. All of these acts are both noble and honorable. They take strength, too. Mettle. Bravery. Perhaps what I am doing is weak. Is a surrender. I do not know if it takes more strength and courage to do what I am about to try to do, or less. Yet what have these other honorable and peaceful acts attained?

Nothing.

I put on the wig and tug the camouflage ball cap on, the words *Gun Control = A Steady Aim* reading backward in the rearview mirror. Concealed in the dot of the *i* is a minicam lens. In this light, I cannot make it out. The lens appears to be an embroidered dot. The hat was easy enough to buy at Walmart. But if Akers sees the lens somehow . . .

I take out the tiny remote for the minicamera from the glove box. I put the remote in my hip pocket. With my thumb, I can press buttons to stop or start the recording, with or without audio.

I step out of the car and tuck the .45 into my waistband at the back, underneath my sweatshirt.

I open the trunk.

Breathe.

I lift the case out of the trunk. It still astounds me how light it is. I grab the metal ammo box. It's twice as heavy as the LAR case.

A paper cup tumbleweeds on a breeze down this small town's grim and forgotten street, desolate and sleepy at this hour. The full moon hangs over the flat, endless horizon at the end of the long street.

A nothing town.

Akers is proud to call it home. He's proud to have established the world's most famous gun shop in this tired place. It informs his schtick.

Crossing the street, I crush the trundling paper cup beneath my sneaker.

At the front entrance of the shop, a sign in the window.

Intruders will be shot. Survivors will be shot again.

As instructed, I go around toward the back entrance.

At the side of the place, vehicles sit parked beneath a lone parking lot light, the first vehicle a spanking-new silver Mercedes SUV. Fixed on its rear bumper, a sticker: DON'T BLAME ME. I VOTED FOR THE AMERICAN.

A muddied Hummer from the 1990s, its paint job a flat matte army green. The Hummer's back window is festooned with faded stickers slapped on crooked, as if the person who'd stuck them there was too excited to get them straight. Among the stickers: STOP SCHOOL VIOLENCE! ARM TEACHERS.

At the rear of the shop, I set the ammo box down and knock on a solid metal door. No one answers.

I knock again. The sound of my knuckles striking the metal door is distant. Dead. The door itself feels distant. I feel distant from myself, outside myself. I am someone else. I am gone.

I knock on the door and wait.

I raise a fist to knock again. A metal latch works on the other side of the door, and the door swings open.

Akers steps back in the doorway. He looks behind me as if I have somehow chanced upon a gun shop by mistake at 11:00 p.m. on a Tuesday, or perhaps I am merely an assistant, knocking on the door for the man named Sam who must be arriving soon with the LAR. Still, instinctively, his eyes walk over me, head to toe despite my loose sweats. I can't be Sam. Sam is a man. Akers's confusion delights me. He glances at the LAR case, the box of ammo. His eyes creep back up my body and light on the ball cap. He stares at it. I don't know if he notices the camera's microlens or not.

"You going to let me in?" I say.

"You're Sam?" Akers says. "I didn't—"

"Mean to keep me waiting?" I say. The wig, the glasses, the clothes, the LAR, they are a costume. They cloak my real self, allow me to tap into a persona that emboldens me with a sense of command.

"You have," I say. "Kept me waiting. So. Strike one."

"You're a—"

"I'm aware," I say. I crawl my own eyes over his body with a look of disappointment I want him to absorb. He's barrel chested, his head big and round, face pink. His black mustache and hair are clearly dyed, badly, something not perceptible on TV. He is far shorter than expected. Maybe five feet six in cowboy boots that have a good two-inch heel. "You're not what I expected either," I say. "You're short, for one."

His pink face reddens. I can't tell if it's from shame or anger. I don't care. "Are you going to invite me in?" I say.

"I had an issue I was taking care of in my office upstairs," Akers says. He extends his hand. I shake it, look him in the eye, smile as I stifle my disgust.

"Come on in, then," Akers says and puts a hand on the small of my back as he ushers me inside and shuts the door behind us.

I walk inside. There's a door to my right, marked RESTROOM.

To the left a gargantuan flat-screen TV on a wall above a glass case of handguns plays a clip from a cable news show featuring Akers's announcement for candidacy in the presidential primary. The volume is loud. "Fight!"

The TV screen goes black. The interview commences all over again, on an endless loop.

I glance away and am struck to see four men now stand at the center of the shop, eyes on me. The room is charged. What is this? Who are they and why are they here? My heart pounds as I try to assess what to do now. Five men. Not one.

"Who are *they*?" I say.

"Interested parties. I'm nothing if not generous," Akers gloats.

One of the interested parties is a skinny old bald man who wears jeans and a black T-shirt. An AR-15 is slung over his shoulder by a strap, the muzzle pointed to the floor. His chest holster cradles what I know from my research is a Beretta 92G.

"Nice 92G," I say. The man grins. I can hear his thoughts: *Chick knows her shit.*

The second man, perhaps in his sixties, might have stepped out of the old frontier with his gold panner's denim overalls, round wire spectacles, and, bursting out from beneath a worn felt crusher hat, a frizz of wild white hair with a yellowish, antique tinge to it. His beard, which matches his hair in frizz and color, hangs halfway to his hip holsters, from which jut the handles of a pair of standard blued Ruger Black-hawks: .45 Colt revolvers, 7.5-inch barrel length.

The last two men wear matching navy-blue pin-striped sports jack-ets they might have purchased from a JCPenney's closeout sale. They're perhaps in their late thirties, but a middle-age pudge creeps over their belts. Their matching short haircuts are parted neatly to the side. One part to the left, another to the right. Brothers. Twins, perhaps. *Thing One and Thing Two*, I think.

The brothers and Gold Panner each cradle R4s in their arms.

I bolster myself. Empty my mind and smile at the men. This demon-stration demands veneration.

Against the long side wall of the shop are the M4s, AR-15s, A2s, and dozens more black rifles I studied.

I walk past the showcase of home-protection shotguns and the long glass case of handguns in matte black, silver plate, and nickel plate, with pearl, wood, and synthetic grips. Here are what I learned are the Rugers, Berettas, Smith & Wessons, Tauruses, SIG Sauers, Accu-Teks, Bersas, Brownings. An obscene march of weapons.

"Let's get this party started," Akers says.

With my thumb, I press the button on the remote in my pocket to record with audio.

The private firing range below the shop is state of the art, or so Akers claims publicly. It sports fourteen handgun stations and five long gun stations. The place is claimed to be twenty feet underground, sound-proof, climate and humidity controlled. At the far end of each firing lane hangs a target in the shape of a human silhouette.

Akers shows me to the first rifle station and gestures for me to open the rifle case.

The other men huddle close enough to see but not so close as to crowd, to betray fully how eager they are to set eyes on this weapon. This unicorn.

I produce a key from my pocket and unlock the two padlocks attached to the cleated latches at each end of the case. I slip the padlocks out, unsnap the latches. Slowly, teasing, one at a time.

Snick.

Snick.

Snick.

Snick.

I lift the lid.

I can hear the men swallowing, blinking. Salivating. Hear their hearts beat.

Akers licks his upper lip. "Mother of God. I joked in my email that

I'd tongue fuck her gorgeous muzzle," he says without compunction. "I may damn well do it. *Look* at that sexy thing."

The men laugh. They give off a ripe animal sweat. The air vibrates with toxicity. Akers's head is bowed, and he holds his hand out so it hovers over the LAR, as if he's the pope blessing a layperson more worthy of God's grace than himself.

"That right there," says Gold Panner, "will stop the fucking bad guy."

The men laugh. Their jowls ripple like rubber Nixon masks.

"Take her out of her case," Akers says to me. "Now is not the time to be shy." Akers's voice is loud yet remote, as if he is shouting at me from across a wide lake; his voice echoes yet is diminished by a vast space between us. His figure is smeared too, as if the lake between us is banked with fog. My head is empty.

Now is not the time to be shy.

Sweat trickles from beneath my wig down my cheek as I slide my hands under the rifle, cradle it, and lift it out.

I lever the rifle's folding stock out and lock it into place with a quick, efficient, practiced snap. I work its action open.

Akers ogles the weapon as if ogling a woman in a thong on a beach.

He is all but panting with anticipation.

I hand the black gun to him.

He accepts the weapon, licks his mustache as he scrutinizes the LAR from every angle with a salacious grin. With the men's eyes on the LAR, I reach behind my back and beneath my sweatshirt to feel the grip of the .45, adjust it.

"I gotta slip my finger in her and make her yelp," Akers says, winking at me, his voice wet with expectation. "How many rounds did you bring?"

I open the metal ammo box to reveal the stacked boxes of ammunition: 1,500 rounds in all.

Akers whistles. "Fuck me blind," he says, leering.

"We going to have us some fu-*un*," Thing One says.

Akers grabs the three loaded clips from the gun case. Each holds thirty live rounds. He picks up a pair of electronic earmuffs dangling on a peg, seats them over his ears.

The four other men and I follow suit. I dislike the muted dissonance of sound they create. It makes me feel even more detached, as if I am underwater, not fully here.

Akers turns his neck to one side, then the other, working out kinks, and seats a loaded clip in the LAR.

He positions himself at a rifle station, takes his stance, glances back over his shoulder with a grimy grin and another wink. He seats the LAR against his shoulder. His nostrils flare. He squeezes the trigger.

Just like that, thirty rounds spit downrange in fewer than three seconds.

I shut my eyes, but I can still see Lydan in that classroom closet.

I open my eyes. The target is shredded.

The acrid odor of gunpowder pollutes the air. I struggle not to vomit.

"Daaaamn," Akers says. "She's smooth as a twelve-year-old's . . ." He catches himself. "A twelve-year-old scotch." I know what he'd say if I weren't here: *Smooth as a twelve-year-old's pussy.* Or *snatch* or *twat.* Or *cunt.* And if any of his men objected, not that any would, Akers would lean back on the old reliable: *It's just a joke. Don't get your panties in a bunch. Lighten up.*

It strikes me, here and now, a cold hand slapping my face.

I am not here because of guns alone.

I am here because of men.

Men and their lust, their need, for violence.

For blood.

For killing.

For death.

That face in the school window.

It was a man's face.

It is always a man's face.

The shooter in Indiana.

A man.

Connecticut.

A man.

Florida.

A man.

Nevada.

A man.

Colorado.

A man.

Pennsylvania.

A man.

Texas.

A man.

Ohio.

Washington.

California.

Kentucky.

Vermont.

Louisiana.

Missouri.

Iowa.

Wisconsin.

Massachusetts.

Minnesota.

Oregon.

Utah.

Georgia.

North Carolina.

South Carolina.

South Dakota.

North Dakota.

Virginia.

Maine.

West Virginia.

A man

a man

a man

a man

a man

a man

a man

a man

a man

a man

a man

a man

a man

a man

a man

a man

a man

a man

a man

a man . . .

Every state.

A man.

Almost every single time.

A man.

Even the killer in China who stabbed his victims to death with a knife.

A man.

Akers and his ilk's fight, their *war*, is not about their right to bear arms. It's about their perceived right to violence. They do nothing about these killers, because they are them, in spirit; they just haven't pulled the trigger yet, or don't dare to themselves. They live vicariously. Let someone else pull it while they sit back and defend them, using their right as a straw man as they cash in. And we, we women, and our children, must sit by and be quiet, must stand back and suffer it, must *grin* and bear it, over and over and over again and again and again, down through the ages, while these same men do nothing, because they like how things are. They like this world they've created.

Men like Akers invented this *war*. As men have *invented* every war.

They shape the world through violence and conquest, pillaging and rape and genocide, oppression and control; they use their own language to mold a world that's male dominant, male centric, male first.

*Man*kind.

Hu*man*.

Wo*man*.

Without man there is no wo*man*.

Without the male there is no fe*male*.

Without he there is no s*he* or *he*r.

Reality is a story, an illusion spun with the spider's silk of the words of men (*his* story, *his*tory), man as the spider at the web's quivering center, the rest of the world—women and children—caught for millennia in their web.

In the beginning, there was man.

Just a man.

No woman.

Eve but an invention of man. Made from man. Nothing without man.

Eve, named by Adam. Her man.

Eve, the *helper* to Adam. Made from Adam's rib to keep Adam happy and less lonely in his little garden. The poor, lonesome little Adam needed a helper, a little woman.

Eve the villain.

Eve the ill.

Eve ill.

Evil.

Eve, nothing without Adam, the man, who said:

> *This is now bone of my bones*
> *and flesh of my flesh;*
> *she shall be called "woman,"*
> *for she was taken out of man.*

She is of me and from me and would not exist if not for me.
She is part of me.

She is mine.

Property.

Eve, the wo*man* punished and banished for seeking knowledge.

Eve, the *cause* of her man's banishment.

Eve, the guilty.

> *The woman you put here with me—*
> *she gave me some fruit from the tree, and I ate it,*

said Adam.

Blame *her.*

The woman.

Not me.

The man.

The man absolved of accountability, a victim tricked by his wo*man.*

The wo*man* blamed by man's god, *him*self.

God said to the woman,

> *What is this you have done? . . .*
> *I will make your pains in childbearing very severe;*
> *with painful labor you will give birth to children.*
> *Your desire will be for your husband,*
> *and he will rule over you.*

Rule over you.

What is this, the word of God?

It is story. Myth. Each and every single word written by and for men.

Not a word written by or for a woman.

The words of men who seek to *rule* over you. Lord over you. Over women.

God is but men's words on a page.

Because of sinful Eve, who sought knowledge, poor Adam had to actually *work*, to labor with the thorns and the thistles. All of it Eve's fault. If she had only adhered to her role as her man's little helper, paradise would have forever reigned.

Eve, who failed to know her place.

Eve, a fictional character in a book written by men.

No woman allowed to write her own story, or if she did, those pages were burned. Or *she* was burned.

Ask Lilith, the real first woman of the world, who came before Eve, but who was not made of man, not created of Adam's rib, who was her own separate being, so whose story had to be ground into the mud by the heels of man. Lilith, who would not do. No. Even if she too was conjured by the words of a man.

If man is made in God's image, then God is a man and man is God.

I am here to rewrite the myth.

I will no longer live in the myth of man, the myth of servility and pain and guilt and death, and be told this is a war but I cannot fight back with equal force and violence against the men who feel it is their God-given right to deal it out.

I will write a new myth.

Her story.

Herstory.

My story.

And I will write it in men's blood.

BOOK III

Gunfire.

Where am I?

Here.

With these men.

"I can knock out rounds quicker in just semiauto with this sweet thing than I can in full auto with my AK," Akers boasts.

I eye the men. Their handguns tucked in their holsters. Rifles slung across their chests. Armed to the teeth for a gunfight.

"Let me at her," Gold Panner says.

He sets his R4 down on the adjacent station's table.

"Not yet." Akers extracts the spent clip and seats a loaded one in the rifle. He steadies the LAR and fires, lights up the tattered target, muzzle ablaze. Ecstatic, his eyes shine. "No way I'm going to let any of you clowns buy this out from under me," he says.

"We'll see about that," says Thing Two.

Gold Panner takes the LAR from Akers as a fresh target is sent down the range.

He takes position and fires the black gun.

Finished, he holds it out in disbelief. "Not bad."

"*Not bad,*" Akers says. "Fucking liar. *Not bad.*"

The other men take turns with the LAR, each setting their rifle aside to lean against the wall.

I touch my fingertips to the butt of the Colt.

The men fire the LAR in turns, whoop and snort, slap each other's backs and punch each other's arms as they shoot more than a thousand rounds in five minutes. A haze of gun smoke floats above their heads as they grin like high school boys who've sneaked their first bottle of liquor from their old man's cabinet.

"This here will wipe some liberal assholes clean," Skinny Old Man says.

"This here is the new AR," Gold Panner says. "The Asshole Remover."

The men roar, the mood fraternal. Tribal.

Akers is drunk with gratification, taking in the camaraderie with a proprietary pride. He handpicked these men to join him for this august occasion. Good men. American men. His men. "Why'd the gunman kill all the kids in the classroom?" Akers quips, in his element, his domain. His eyes on me.

For a moment I believe he knows who I am. The hero from Franklin. And he is testing me.

He repeats the joke, except now it is not a joke awaiting a punchline; it is a question of initiation in search of the right answer. I am being hazed.

I know the answer. I've seen it posted on his site. I steel myself to deliver the answer and prove I am one of them.

I press the remote's button to record without audio.

"Because," I say, "he supports No Child Left Behind."

The men roar.

I record with audio again.

"Yes!" Akers exults, laughing so hard he has to wipe his tears with his beefy thumb. "Yes!"

The men repeat the punchline in unison: "He supports No Child Left Behind!"

I nod at the LAR in Thing Two's possession, its clip empty. There is no more ammo left. I take the LAR from him.

"I know you said it wasn't for sale," Akers says. "But maybe we can work it out. I'll buy the fucking thing in cash right here, right now. I got it upstairs in a safe. I'll get it and I'll pay whatever it is you want."

I nest the rifle back in the case and shut the lid.

I stare at Akers. I turn off the audio. "I have a joke for you," I say.

The men's eyes lock on me.

"Want to hear it?" I say.

"I want to buy that goddamn gun is what I want, and you know it and knew it all along. What are you playing at here?"

"What," I say, "do you call five gun nuts who come face-to-face with their wet dream?"

Akers scowls, but the other men smile: *The woman can joke too. Now. Now.*

I draw the .45, train the muzzle on Akers's gut.

The men's smiles die. Their eyes lose focus for a half heartbeat.

A half heartbeat too long.

"Dead," I say.

I shoot Akers in the gut.

Blood blasts the wall behind him as he sags to the floor, baying like a hound.

For another heartbeat the four men stare at this woman they allowed to enter their circle out of greed.

Another half heartbeat too long.

"Jesus," Thing One says.

I shoot him.

He collapses, the wall behind him painted with his blood.

Time dissolves.

The sight of Akers and Thing One writhing sedates me.

My mind is a gentle breeze.

My vision telescopes to focus on the next man in front of me.

These men have not prepared. They believe they have, but they have not. They can shoot their paper silhouettes of "bad guys" until they're blind, play at cowboy and mercenary every Sunday with the boys, brag and pound their chests, dream their myths of heroism, but what did they think was going to happen when they were caught off guard by a shooter in a mall or a school or a place of business? Or here. Right here. Right now. Playing pretend has not prepared any man for this reality, for sudden, unexpected violence that takes one off guard. Simulations do not account for the adrenaline now detonating in the men's veins, nor for the fear abuzz in their brains that short-circuits their gross motor skills.

Thing Two glances down at Thing One on the floor.

I shoot Thing Two in the stomach. He howls, blinks at me, still standing. I shoot him again and pivot to Skinny Old Man. He seems to awaken now from a trance. He grabs his R4 from the station nearby, raises it, fumbles for the trigger, seemingly forgetting in his escalating dread where it is located.

I shoot him in the knee.

His kneecap evaporates in a mist of blood and bone, and he crumples to the floor, screeching, his good leg kicking him around on the floor in circles.

Gold Panner raises his R4. He fires a few shots, wide even at this perversely close range, he's so shaken.

I shoot him in the groin, blood misting as he joins the fraternal knot of groaning men. This is no movie. None of these men will overcome their pain and shock to gather themselves and seize a weapon and shoot me. None of them will save the day. None will be the hero. None of them will be the good guy with the gun.

Their agony and terror will entomb them.

I step over to Thing One, press the muzzle of the Colt to his forehead.

I pull the trigger, and my face is freckled with hot blood.

I step to Thing Two and shoot him between the eyes.

I straddle the skinny old man: "Please," he whines. "Don't."

I shoot him in the chest.

Gold Panner lies face down, his body slack and still in a lake of blood.

I shoot him in the back of the head.

I stand over the men now, wiping at the blood on my face with the back of my hand. Endorphins sing in my veins and my mind is afire with dopamine. Blood storms my heart.

A mewling behind me grabs my attention. Akers. He is curled on his side, clutching his gut. Blood pumps and froths from his abdomen, polluted with viscera. He weeps.

There will be no gritting of the teeth here, no brave last words, no last-gasp valiancy as he shoots his assailant, this nasty woman.

I kneel at Akers's side. "Go ahead. Tongue fuck it."

"Please," he says. "My daughter."

I shove the barrel of the Colt deep into Akers's mouth and pull the trigger.

Upstairs, I set down the ammo box and LAR case. I am ragged of breath. My skin is cold yet steeped in a tropical sweat.

I take medical gloves from my pocket and enter the restroom. I scrub my face and hands of the blood speckling them. Rinse the sink. None of the blood is mine. It cannot be traced to me.

As I am working the back door's lock to exit the shop, I hear a voice behind me.

I wheel around, snatch the .45 from my waistband, and press its muzzle to the forehead of a young girl.

My heart stops.

The girl stares past the muzzle straight into my eyes, as if the gun does not exist.

I take my finger off the trigger, trying to calm my mind, calculating the girl's age. She's maybe four years old. To her I am not me. I am not a woman with long frizzy brown hair and brown eyes. I am a woman with bobbed black hair, a ball cap, and blue eyes, in a nondescript gray sweatshirt.

"Where's Daddy?" the girl says. "I was in his office sleeping and woke up, and he never come back up."

I had an issue I was taking care of in my office upstairs.

"Daddy," I say and lower the .45 to my side, "is busy. Downstairs.

Don't bother him. Go back up and wait. Don't leave until someone gets you."

"Okay," the girl says and trudges sleepily back up the stairs.

Outside, the night is cold in the silver glow of the moon.

I am alive.

And I need to hurry home to my child.

I am panting in the car, seized by panic and nausea.

My scalp itches and sweats.

I rip the ball cap off and tear off the wig, clawing at my scalp.

I take out the eye contacts.

I don't know what to do with the .45.

I don't know what to do.

I planned to toss it out of the car somewhere along a deserted stretch of road in the middle of nowhere. But I don't know now. I don't know if I can risk doing it in the dark. How will I really know if I am in the middle of nowhere, or if it just seems that I am because it is dark? What if there is a house or many houses tucked away nearby unseen, maybe with curious kids who live in them and walk along the road? What if there is an early-morning road crew who does tree work, or bottle collectors, or I don't know what else. If I drop it off a bridge into a river, is the river deep? Do kids jump from the bridge into it? Do families swim there? Do people fish there? Camp and picnic along it? What if I miss the river and it lands on the bank, right on a sandy little beach for all to see? I can't get out of the car on a bridge. I don't dare.

Keep it. I need to keep it, for now. I cannot risk anyone finding it by chance. The only way the gun can jeopardize me is if I'm connected to what happened at the gun shop in another way. And if I am, I might need it.

I put the .45 in the glove box and slam it shut.

The LAR is in its case in the trunk.

I know what I want to do with that. What I need to do. For now.

I hook the cap's minicam up to a new burner phone and upload the footage and set it to go live to Akers's chat rooms in a few hours.

I use the name Lilith.

I can't breathe.

Halfway home, the dead air inside the car is suffocating.

The image of Akers's daughter plagues me.

I can't breathe.

I power down the windows, and a rush of cold night air pours into my car, but it doesn't cool me. The stale heat of the car is not to blame for my sweating and my shortness of breath. Fear is. My chest is crushed by it. I turn off onto an old forest road. As soon as I'm out of sight of the two-lane, I stop the car and stagger out onto my hands and knees and vomit.

"He was her father," I murmur, wiping at my face with my sleeve.

The world is better without him.

Is it?

They wanted a war. I brought it. They created their myth. I broke it.

The thunderous *thwump* of a helicopter's blade breaks the calm night silence. Law enforcement. They've tracked me from above. No. Not a helicopter. My blood clobbering my head.

I must get rid of the wig and the glasses and bloody clothes and contacts. All of it. The phone. All of it. I take a duffel with fresh clothes and a can of lighter fluid and a box of wooden matches from the trunk. I bring them and the belongings into the woods.

I strip and throw my clothes in a pile with the wig and phone and the rest. From the duffel I take a flannel shirt and jeans and sneakers and dress in them. I douse the heap, saturate each item. I light it on fire and watch the flames glow in the dark night, feel the orange heat on my face.

When the fire ebbs, I stir it with a stick to breathe oxygen into it and make sure everything is afire. It's 2:30 a.m. I am off the main road a half mile, yet fear creeps into my bones. What if I *am* seen? What if the fire is seen? But by whom? Who would be out here now?

I shine a flashlight on the ashes, poking the stick around in them. The phone is a melted glob of charred plastic in a bed of ashes. I collect bark and branches and ferns and cover the spot. No one will ever find the remnants buried beneath forest debris, fifty feet off a random spot along a road that's seldom used. If anyone ever does find the spot, they'll think it's an old campfire site and never give it a second thought. There is nothing to see, and no one will be looking anyway. Not here. Not 110 miles northeast of Maximillian Akers's gun shop.

I park the car in the driveway and open the garage door.

Birds perched unseen in the trees announce the dawn.

I pull the car into the garage and lower the door behind me. I grab the .45 and tuck it in the back of my waistband. From the trunk, I haul out the LAR case and ammo box and enter the house by the door from the garage to the kitchen.

Inside, I set down the case and ammo box.

The house is quiet.

I hope Lydan is sleeping. I hope he never woke in the night.

My phone chimes on the counter where it sits charging.

I glance at its screen. A weather update. I pocket it.

I need to see my baby.

I sneak down the hall toward his bedroom, my mind wild with unholy scenarios.

With a fingertip, I ease open Lydan's door and see in the shadows the hump of his blanket and pillow, but I don't see Lydan. He must be here; he must be under his sheets. But even as I pull the sheets back, I know he is not here.

The bed is empty.

I flip the light switch on and scream.

Lydan is behind me in the hallway, leaning on his crutches. He yawns, grinds a balled fist against his sleep-puffed eyes.

"You scared me half to death," I say, relief washing through me. I bend to hug Lydan and stop when the .45 jabs against my tailbone.

"Where were you?" I say, taking a step back.

"Where did you go, Mama?"

"Nowhere." I can barely speak.

"You did." He has the same look of certainty on his face that he had in the hospital when he told me he was dead. "You were gone," he says. "That's what your friend said."

Lydan continues speaking, but I can't hear his voice. His lips move in slow motion. His tongue and teeth shape soundless words.

"Friend?" I manage to say.

"The lady in my doorway last night."

He's been dreaming. No one was here. That's not possible. "There was no lady here last night," I say.

"Mmmm-hmm," Lydan says.

"You dreamed her," I say.

"She was in the hall at my door. I asked where you was, and she said you went out and she was a friend and she was here to look after me. She told me to go back to sleep."

I hear my voice but seem to have no control of it. "That was me in the doorway. You were so groggy from your medicine. Confused."

Lydan's face is a mask of suspicion.

"It wasn't your voice."

"My throat was dry and scratchy," I say. "You woke me up from a dead sleep with your screaming about a lady in your dreams."

"It *wasn't you*, Mama." He doesn't seem himself. He doesn't seem like my little boy, or any little boy. He seems knowing. Old. Older than me. Older than time. It feels as if he's interrogating me, giving me a chance to confess the sin he *knows* I committed.

"It *was* me," I press. "You know how I know?"

Lydan doesn't answer. He doesn't even look at me.

"Because I was here," I say. "I have nowhere to be except here, do I?"

The note, I suddenly think. Did he see it? Read it?

"I don't know," Lydan says.

"You *do* know, sweetie," I say. "You know I'd never leave you without telling you. And where would I even go at night? And if I was going to get a babysitter, I'd get Wendy like I always did before—wouldn't I? I don't even know any other babysitters."

"But—"

"Okay," I say and kneel before him, taking his small shoulders in my hands. "Let's say there was a lady. There wasn't, but let's say there was. What did she look like?" If there was someone here, just by chance, I need to know what she looks like, who she is.

Lydan shrugs. "A woman."

"Did you see her face?"

"She was in the doorway, and the light was behind her."

"You didn't see her face?"

"I was sleepy too."

It was a dream. It had to be.

"I *didn't* go out," I say. "That lady was me."

"You said I dreamed her. So how could it be you?"

"You sort of dreamed it in your sleepy head. I stayed in the hall because I wanted you to get back to sleep."

Lydan stares at me.

"Okay?" I say.

Lydan digs his fingernails into the foam padding on his crutch's grip. "I hope you're not lying to me," he says. His voice is so cold it chills me. "I hope not."

"What do you mean by that?" I say.

He doesn't answer me. "What's in the case and box on the kitchen floor?" he says.

I try to swallow but can't.

"Did you open them?" I manage to ask, even though this isn't possible either. The rifle case and ammo box are both locked tight.

"I know what's in them," Lydan says.

His assuredness unnerves me.

"Art supplies," he says. "Paints and stuff for school. When you go back."

I'm never going back. That life is gone.

"Right," I say.

"I knew it. Because of the red paint on your neck."

"Paint?" I say, as if I don't know what the word means.

"On your neck."

Blood. He means blood. Terrified, I wipe a hand at my neck.

"Other side," Lydan says, pointing.

I wipe at it. Caked dried blood flakes off my skin. I examine it on my fingernails, scales of rust.

"Let me tuck you back into bed," I say. "It's still really early."

Lydan scrutinizes my neck where I scraped away blood.

"I can go back to bed on my own," he says. His voice is cold again. "But where did you get the art supplies?"

"They were out in the trunk of my car," I say. "I bought them a long time ago and forgot I even had them until this morning. I remembered. So I got them out of the car."

"Are there extras enough for me?"

"Maybe," I say. "Let's get you back to bed."

I step past him and enter the room to grab the note from the bedside table.

It's not there.

I look on the floor, peek under his bed.

From behind me, Lydan says, "What you looking for?"

I straighten up.

He's staring right at me.

"Nothing," I say.

My eyes glance around the floor by the bedside table, behind it.

I can't see it, but I know it must be here.

With Lydan asleep, I look around again for the note, carefully, using my phone's light.

But I don't find the note.

It's not here.

It's gone.

In the bathroom I shut the door and sag against it.

When I can breathe again, I strip and examine my neck and body in the mirror.

I don't see any more blood. It seems it was just that one flake. But just because I don't see it doesn't mean it's not there.

Or in the car.

On the seat or the steering wheel. Blood I cannot even see. Invisible blood.

I scrub my neck with a soaped washcloth. Scrub and scrub.

I thought Lydan must have imagined the woman. That no one was here. No one could get in. No one knew I was gone. And the place was locked.

But the note is gone.

Someone was here because someone took it.

In the shower, I scrub harder. *Stupid*.

Stupid.

I scrub and scour my flesh beneath a hard stream of scalding water.

What other nooses have I knotted for myself without my knowing?

What did I think? I could get away with it?

I have jeopardized everything. Jeopardized my son.

I examine my hands, scrub them. I work a soaped fingernail brush under and around my nails and between my fingers until my fingers are pink and raw.

I wash my entire body over and over again, shampoo my hair three times, until I can't stand it any longer.

I must destroy my clothes. Burn them or get rid of them somehow.

Dressed, I sneak the gun case and ammo box down to the cellar and crawl under the workbench and pull away the paneling.

A floorboard squeaks above me.

Lydan.

The thump of his crutches in the hallway.

"Mama?" he cries out. "Someone's here!"

I shove the case and box behind the wall. I feel for the .45 behind my back. I keep it there.

I push the paneling in place, tap it back in as best I can with a hammer, and dash up the stairs.

Lydan is in the entryway, staring at the door.

"She's out on the lawn," he says. "I got up to pee and saw her."

"Go to your room," I say to him.

"Why were you downstairs?" he says.

The drubbing continues.

"Doing laundry. Go to your room."

"Why are you holding a hammer?"

I'm not just holding the hammer; I am clutching it so hard my fingers ache. "I was going to hang a picture up," I say. "Now. Go to your room." I nudge Lydan along and watch him hobble down the hall, glancing back over his shoulder at me and at the hammer, before he shuts his bedroom door behind him.

I go into the kitchen and peek out the window. A dark-blue van is parked out on the street, askew against the curb. I can only make out the rear quarter of it from my angle.

I set the hammer on the counter and go to the door, my hand on the cold .45 at my back.

I peel back the curtain at the door's window.

A woman and a man stand outside my door, their expectant faces inches away, only the thin pane of glass separating them from me. I know the woman. It's the reporter from outside the hospital. She's latched onto my survivor story, staked her budding career on it.

I release my grip on the .45 and open the door.

The reporter advances.

I want to shout at her. I want to yell that this is private property, that she should get out of here and leave me alone, but I know the man's camera is recording. I have to behave, accommodate, not come off as hysterical. I know the drill.

I am balanced on a high wire.

Composure is my net.

"What do you think of this shooter, this Lilith?" the reporter asks, microphone held aloft as if it's a torch to fend off night's darkness.

The video.

The cameraman levels the camera at my face. I want to swat it away.

"What's happened?" I say.

The reporter wields a smartphone to show me the video from the firing range. "It's *everywhere*," she says.

"I don't want to see it," I say.

"She shot these men last night," the reporter says. "She shot the most prominent gun dealer in the *world*, a candidate for president. Maximillian Akers. She killed him and four other men. They were all armed and trained to kill, and she shot them dead. You haven't seen it?"

She seems keyed up, nearly elated to share this with me.

"I just woke up," I say.

"This Maximillian Akers," the reporter says, "he was going to buy a *highly illegal fully automatic* weapon. He was making graphic sexual jokes, joking *about kids being shot in schools*. Awful things. And—"

"Do you think I want to hear or see that?" I say, biting the words in half. I catch myself. I must keep composed. "After what happened to me and my son, do you really think I want to see or even hear about *that*? I don't." It's true. I don't. "Why are you here, at my house? Preying on me."

"For a comment," the reporter says.

For your career, I think. *You vampire.*

"I thought you'd care," the reporter says. "After what happened to you. After what you did. This Lilith did this because no one in power cares. No one *does* anything to stop shootings. She sought to prove that having a gun doesn't keep anyone safe. If it couldn't keep Akers safe, five armed men safe, then how is anyone safe just because they have a gun? And that men like Akers aren't the good men, the good Americans. Good patriots. Aren't patriots at all. As someone who's been a recent victim, has a child that was a victim, you must have an opinion."

"I think," I say, biting the inside of my cheek so hard I taste blood, "it was inevitable."

"So. You support her?" the reporter says, edging closer.

I am distracted by movement on the street. Claire is walking across to my side of the street to stand at the end of my driveway. She folds her arms across her chest, watching. Two other neighbors stand out on their lawns, one with his bathrobe clutched at his throat as he sips from a coffee mug, and another in gray sweats and bare feet, her orange tabby cat threading figure eights between her legs.

"You support her?" the reporter says again.

"I said it was inevitable." The .45 digs into my tailbone.

"What does that mean?"

"It doesn't matter. I'm no one."

"You're not 'no one.' You're idolized for saving those children in your classroom. Rescuing your son. Maybe not as many people idolize you as they do this Lilith, but—"

"People idolize her?"

"The video's trending number one on every social media platform. It's on so many places it can't be taken down, even though the social media companies and government are trying to get it down. It's been shared millions of times already. People are praising her. Celebrating her. Women especially. Online *and* in the streets. Not everyone, of course. Some despise her, vow to find her and hang her in the streets for doing this to 'good men.'"

Claire has made her way to the top of my driveway, openly

eavesdropping now. It's as if she's playing a children's game, sneaking closer each time I take my eyes off her and stopping when I look up. I wonder if Claire saw me leave last night. If Claire knows I was gone, left Lydan home on his own. Was she in my house?

"What do you mean, 'inevitable'?" the reporter presses.

"Inevitable that a woman finally said, 'Enough.'"

"Enough of what?"

"The vigilante lynch mobs tell us everything."

"How?"

"Who do you think these people are that want to hang m—" I stop. I almost said *me*. Hang *me*. I gather myself. "Hang this Lilith? Who are they?"

The reporter glances at the cameraman as if he might have the answer.

"Men," I say. "Now. I have to make breakfast for my son."

I back my way inside, keeping the .45 from sight, and shut the door.

I check on Lydan. He's sound asleep.

Out in the garage, I check the seat of my car, the steering wheel, the console and gearshift. I don't see any blood. But I know this means nothing. The eye does not see everything. Many invisible worlds exist. I take some bleach cleaning wipes and wipe down the steering wheel, the gearshift, and the console. Then I rub my hands all over them. Start the car and work the wheel, grab and shift the knob. I can't leave them looking wiped clean.

The seat has a vinyl cover on it, to guard it from crumbs from all the snacks I eat and spills from the coffee I drink. I take the cover out and put it in the trash can. The trash removal comes later today. It will be long gone soon.

I collapse on the couch and click on the TV, the .45 in my lap.

A cable news network is airing a digital composite drawing of Lilith based on Akers's daughter's description.

The rendition bears no resemblance to me. It is not me. The face is not my face. I wouldn't be able to identify myself from the image.

This doesn't give me relief.

I need to be vigilant.

I fear what I missed.

One day that knock will come.

One day my door will be broken down.

One day the car following behind mine will flash its lights.

I think about the blood specks on my neck.

I think about not being able to turn time back.

I think about my boy all alone.

I think about what I've done.

I think about the day that I and my boy and all of us will be gone.

Gone gone gone.

I wonder what I've overlooked.

I awake with a start.

The light is different, the sunlight violent at the window.

The TV cuts to scenes in various cities and towns, showing women and girls out on the streets hoisting handmade signs:

WE ARE LILITH!

IT'S ABOUT TIME!

A BADASS WOMAN WITH A GUN STOPPED BAD MEN WITH GUNS

I go down the hall and check on Lydan.

He's snoring in bed.

On the TV, graphics show tweets and Instagram posts:

WE RISE WITH LILITH!

WAKE UP, MEN!

ENOUGH!

More bumper sticker slogans.

More trite inaction.

More of the same.

Words words words words words.

The news story shows an image of an LAR, and for a second, I am dumbstruck and think I left the LAR there and did not bring it home. But no. I did. An expert is talking all about the LAR, how coveted it is. How impossible it is to come by. So impossible he doesn't have one to show the talking head but must rely on the images shown in the video.

"For someone to get their hands on this rifle, especially in the United States, she'd have to be very connected. And wealthy. So that narrows it down some, her profile."

More images of an LAR show on the screen in close-up.

"Oddly, this 'Lilith' did not kill the men with it. She killed them with a handgun. She lured them with the LAR. A unicorn. A Trojan unicorn, if you will."

I stare at the image. The weapon is frightening.

I am startled by a noise behind me.

Lydan peers from the living room entrance, eyes fixated on the TV screen, the LAR. "What's that?" he says.

"The news," I say and take the .45 from my lap and hide it on the other side of me, between two cushions.

I switch to another channel, only to bring up the artist's rendition of me, of Lilith.

Lydan looks at me. Looks back at the TV. Looks at me again. Does he see me in the sketch, see the sketch in me? I shut off the TV.

"Who's that?" he says.

"I don't know," I say.

Lydan winces as he lowers himself slowly and sits next to me. He leans his head on my shoulder, and it is all I can do to not break down.

"I'm sorry you had such a tough night," I say. I mean it. I am sorry.

"It's okay, Mama," Lydan says.

I jump as my phone rings on the coffee table.

I know the number.

I answer it. "Hi," I say.

"How are you?" Homer says.

"As good as can be expected," I say. I am not good. I stand at the precipice of a bottomless pit.

I cup a hand around Lydan and draw him closer to me.

"It's remarkable," Homer says, "what happened."

I don't know exactly what he means, yet I know he can only mean one thing. Akers. Perhaps his friend has apprised him already. Perhaps there is no earthly way to keep the arrow of such news from piercing even the bubble of his hermetic life. I note he doesn't say it's terrible or awful. Just . . . remarkable.

"It is," I say.

"These are troubled times. We all need to be so careful."

I don't answer.

My mind is a ghost town.

Homer never believed my lie about the journalist. He's known all along. Going back to that day we picked blueberries. The day he said he had a special weapon waiting for a special use. He knew even then I, my mama's special child, was destined for this.

He speaks now, but I can't eke out meaning from it, his consonants and vowels sputtering like a damp string of firecrackers.

"You should visit," he says, his voice finally coming in clear.

Lydan clutches at me, wrapping his arms around my neck.

"Mama."

I hold up a palm for him to wait.

"Mama."

"What, sweetie?" I say.

"Who is it? You look scared." He glances at my hand clenching the phone tightly, my knuckles pale. "Am I gonna have to go back to the hospital?"

"No, sweetie." I hug him, feeling the heat of his life; it burns hotter than mine. "It's nothing to do with you."

"I'm here for you," Homer says, "for anything at all. I'll wait."

Just as the LAR was waiting for me all these years.

In the days that follow, I attempt to fall into a rhythm of normalcy. I do not just want to attend to Lydan; I want to dote on him. I let him sleep late and prepare a banquet brunch of French toast and bacon, pancakes and cinnamon rolls. Grapefruit too. He loves grapefruit. He loves to slurp the juice from the bowl when he's done spooning out the wedges.

Yet I do not fall into a rhythm. There is no normalcy. It is not possible. Each simple action is an act. Each ring of my phone, chime of a text, or knock at the door makes my heart jump as I steel myself. Any moment might bring my end.

"Want to come with me to the store for a bit?" I say to Lydan some days later, after breakfast.

He's not been out anywhere in public. Neither have I. I want something normal. Crave it. And I feel, after the reporter's visit, I need to behave normal. Appear normal. Innocent.

"It'd be fun," I say, "to do something normal. Just grab some groceries, maybe a treat at the coffee shop. An éclair or something?"

"Can I stay home while you go? Please. I used to do that. That's normal."

I hesitate. I cannot leave him here to run chores, even if that is what I did before.

"You used to leave me when you were gone for less than an hour," Lydan says. "As long as I kept the door locked and I don't answer the door or phone."

"I don't know."

"I want normal. Please."

"If you promise. *Promise.* Keep the door locked. Don't answer the phone. And don't use anything in the kitchen."

"Promise."

I push a shopping cart with a wonky wheel down an aisle beneath the glare of fluorescent lights. I go down my list and pick out various cheeses, butter, and breadcrumbs for mac and cheese. I grab cereal—Special K for myself, Apple Jacks for Lydan—plus his favorite junk snacks, cinnamon-brown-sugar Pop-Tarts and Snickers and Pringles. I select some apples and pears and tomatoes and turn them in my hand to inspect them for bruises and those first indications of rot. I sniff cantaloupes and rap a knuckle against watermelons. I can't recall the last time I've done this. As I pass the meat and butcher section, I gag on the tang of bovine blood so metallic and potent in my nose that it makes me weak from the memory of all that blood from children.

Children.

I lean against a cooler and close my eyes and try to breathe to keep from passing out, from being sick.

Having regained my equilibrium, I buy a magazine with the story of the shooting of Max Akers splashed on its cover.

I perform these simple tasks with a sense of ephemeral respite.

Still, I cannot forget.

Still, my very blood is contaminated with violence.

After the grocery store, I sit in the window of a café across the street. I want another few minutes to myself in a normal setting. I sip a double espresso, a sour tang on my tongue, molasses in my throat as the coffee slides down, hot, warming me. The café is an old favorite spot I have not been to in many months.

For an instant, I almost feel like myself.

I open the magazine. I can read it without worry. There's no tracking of what I read here. The magazine has profiles on all the men I killed. There is a photo of Gold Panner sitting on a couch near a Christmas tree with, according to the caption, his three grandsons. He was recently retired from his veterinary practice, which also served as a rescue shelter for dogs and cats. He was a "community man" held in high regard by folks of all walks of life, according to some of the quotes. He was also a fine watercolor artist, his scenes depicting his favorite rivers in Colorado and Montana and Wyoming. He was a regional chairperson for the Make-A-Wish Foundation and St. Jude Children's Hospital.

He was also a cancer survivor. He'd recently undergone radiation and chemotherapy treatments that had put his cancer into remission.

His widow said, "We'd finally got to where we didn't have to worry constantly anymore and could simply enjoy our new retired lives, concentrate on the animal-shelter part of things. It's not work when you enjoy it. We just started to relish free time with our children and grandchildren."

The skinny old man I killed was the owner of a hardware store and lumberyard. His name was Edwin Mack. His wife of twenty years, Dawn Mack, was a dental hygienist. The two had three grandchildren, four, nine, and twelve years old.

"I don't know what to tell the kids," Dawn Mack said. "Except that there is evil in this world. I used to think there was more good than evil. Now, I don't know. Some people are evil. Sick. They have no respect for human lives. My husband could crack some crass jokes. But he didn't deserve to die because of that. I didn't abide his crassness at home. He was forbidden to make such slights to any of God's people in my home. We are all God's people. It was beneath him. Beneath our family. But for anyone to think that tasteless jokes should be met with violence, death, they are ill. Sick."

I stop reading.

I glance at the door, watch the sidewalk through the steamed window. Outside, snow falls, big fat flakes fuzzing the gray day.

I dip a cake doughnut into the espresso and take a bite.

A bearded man to the side of me swipes at his phone's screen as he drinks a latte. Two young women wearing coats with the nearby college's women's basketball logo on them huddle at the laptop screen on the table, exchanging conspiratorial looks. No one pays me any mind.

One of the girls takes off her winter coat and hangs it on the back of her stool. I am dumbstruck by what I see. An image of my face is emblazoned on the front of her T-shirt. Not my face, not really, but the rendition of Lilith's face, in the color scheme of the famous "Hope" shirt of 2008. Beneath it are the words *I AM LILITH*.

"You like?" the girl wearing the shirt asks me.

I lift my eyes to meet hers.

The other girl, who has a tattoo of Tinker Bell on her neck that looks raw and sore, elbows the girl with the shirt and says, "She makes them herself. She's got them in all sorts of color combos and, like, Warhol- and 'Hope'-type prints. I'll text you the link to her Etsy I created for her. She's sold like a thousand already."

"At least," the girl in the T-shirt says. "You like it? You want to buy one?"

"It's not for me," I say.

"It's *so* for you," Tinker Bell says, twirling a finger at me. "It'd look straight fire on you. And these are the best ones out there. Made by a real woman who gives a real shit about this cause. Not like those hundreds of corporate-paid 'influencer' shills cranking out T-shirts for QAnon. We make them because we *believe*, and ten percent goes to a fund for Lilith's bail, if they catch her, which we hope the hell not. I'll text you the link," she adds.

"I'm not giving you my phone number," I say, my voice sharp. I want nothing to do with these girls. The more they speak, the more incensed I grow. They don't know anything. The sacrifice.

"Smart," Tattoo Girl says. "I wouldn't give a stranger my digits either. I'll scribble the Etsy account name down for you." The girl digs through a canvas backpack and grabs a pen, starts to write on a napkin.

"I don't want one of your damn T-shirts," I say.

The two girls look as if I've just slapped their faces.

"You," I say, standing, pushing my stool back, "are *not* Lilith. You are the opposite of Lilith."

The girls, aghast, trade looks, their fresh faces collapsing with devastation. What I've said goes against their script, goes against the response they've likely garnered—*What a great cause! You go, girl!*—and sought out for their triumphant efforts at social justice.

"We stand with Lilith," Tinker Bell says.

"We do," the other says. "We truly, truly do."

"We get her. You know? We *get* it. We understand. We *are* her."

The girls have their dander up now, prattling on about varying degrees of victimhood, about social justice and activism, about *aggressions* they've *endured*, and about how everyone has to play their part.

"You make a mockery of Lilith with your T-shirts," I say. "You give ten percent? How about you give one hundred percent? That would be the *very* least you could do. Instead, you profiteer. You want to be like her, *be* like her. Act. Words are meaningless. Profiting off a goddamn T-shirt is meaningless. Everything but action is meaningless. Act."

I zip my coat to leave.

Everyone is watching me.

Tinker Bell has her phone trained on me. I don't know how long she's been taking a video.

"Thanks for coming last minute," I say, swiping a sponge over the countertop even though it's already clean.

"No problem," Wendy says. She is sprightly. Effervescent. Brainy and bursting with goodwill and promise. An AP senior who volunteers at the homeless shelter and food bank and old folks' home and has since she was twelve, all her good deeds undertaken of her own volition, because that is the soul she had when she was born.

May we all have her soul.

"My cell phone is kaput," I say, though my phone is dry and turned off in my bedside drawer. "I dropped it in the sink doing dishes. I'll grab a throwaway and text you using the number."

"Put your phone in a bag of rice," Wendy says. "That usually does the trick." She sheds her army cap and shakes out her hair. Her bangs are cotton-candy pink, the rest of her hair onyx. A new stud, a tiny shimmering sphere of silver, graces the wing of her nose.

"I did," I say.

Wendy unslings her backpack, which I know is crammed with puzzles and games for Lydan, as well as a book for her to read if Lydan decides he wants to do his own thing. Lydan likes her. He looks forward to her visits. Or he used to look forward to them. I don't know how he'll respond now. Wendy and Lydan haven't seen each other since that day.

I lecture Wendy at length about Lydan's new needs and leave two pages of printed notes on the counter. The medications he must take and the times he must take them. The times during the day when a visiting nurse will stop in and what that nurse does in her hour here. The catheter, which Wendy is not to so much as glance at. His mood swings. I caution that Lydan might not interact with her.

"And your parents," I ask again, "they don't mind you staying overnight?"

"They love Lydan and you. They feel awful. We all do. What's happening in this world, it's just so sad. It makes me feel so helpless. They say hello." She sniffs. "You've earned time for you, and I'm so ready to be with Lydan, even if he ignores me."

Wendy doesn't ask where I'm going, and I don't volunteer a fake excuse, though I am prepared to tell her that I'm going to visit family.

"You're a savior," I say.

"You're the savior," Wendy says. "You and Lilith."

I drive down the block, past Claire's house.

I see Claire at her kitchen window, the drape pulled back as she watches me leave the neighborhood.

Hours later, I park near the Fayville Corner Market on a side street in Fayville, Michigan. A backwater town. A store I know from when Lydan and I drove back from Toronto, several lives ago. Lydan was carsick, so I pulled off at the first exit and found my way here to buy Dramamine.

I apply my makeup in the rearview, heavy blue eye shadow to accent my eyes. I adjust a blond wig taken from the Halloween trunk and get out of the car.

In the window of an old-time dress shop, I catch my image.

I'm not there.

That's someone else.

My shoes squeak on the linoleum floor of the quiet store. I feel conspicuous. I hoped to be invisible.

The cashier is an old woman whose cat-eye glasses lean crooked on her face as she tips her head down, focused on an object that I can't see.

I don't want to appear like I'm on a mission for a phone, so I grab a shopping cart.

The narrow aisles are a schizophrenic selection of goods. Green plastic bottles of vitamins and pink boxes of tampons alongside mass-market paperbacks and Wonder Bread. I stroll past a rack of sunglasses and pick up a pack of English muffins, a plastic key ring, and a paperback by some guy named John Sheldon.

At the counter, the old woman reads a *National Enquirer*, transfixed by two grainy video stills of a dead Akers, the headline: WHO IS LILITH??!!

I unload my items from the cart and say, "I'd like to pick out a phone, for my niece." I don't know why I say *niece*; it was unnecessary.

The woman gives a last gander at the *Enquirer* and gestures for me to follow.

"That one," I say, pointing.

The woman unlocks the phone and hands it to me.

"And a forty-dollar card," I say.

Back at the counter, the woman asks, "Are you a member of our Fayville Market Shoppers' Club?"

I tell her I'm not.

"Would you like to be? It takes only a minute. Probably thirty seconds; all I need is—"

"Not today."

"Just passing through?" the woman says.

I don't want to engage her, give her any reason at all to remember me.

"Just not interested. Thanks, though."

"But you aren't from here. I've never seen you before."

The silence stretches taut and thin, and I fear that if I say so much as a word, I will pierce its membrane and encourage questions. Perhaps a chain store would have been the right choice; a pharmacy in a hectic suburban wasteland might have left me entirely anonymous. Here, I am a notable stranger, off the beaten path, for what reason?

The woman glances at her *Enquirer*.

I hand her eighty dollars in cash, bills I've picked up as change along the way and kept in the kitchen drawer, bills handled by many hands, not new bills easily tracked back to an ATM.

I glance at the article as the woman counts back my change.

"What do you think of all this?" she asks and holds up her tabloid.

"I don't know," I say.

The cashier waves the paper at me. "Everyone knows. Right or wrong. We know. What do you mean, you *don't know*?"

I'm thrown by her aggression. "What do you think?" I say, deflecting.

The woman smooths her palms over the belly of her smock, straightens her posture, as if all along she sought to be asked her opinion, as most people do. "I think if I ever saw this Lilith, if she walked in here, I'd give her a tongue-lashing she wouldn't forget. She shoulda never done what she done."

I didn't expect this. "You think she's a villain?"

"No. The poor thing," the woman says, "but she should've known that if a woman rises up against men, it only ever ends one way. Old as time, that story. She's brave as they come, but there ain't but one way it's gonna end for her."

Homer stands outside on the camper stoop, hunched beneath its battered tin roof, as rain pours down. A mug steams in his cupped hands. I pull up behind an old ATV. It's the three-wheeled kind, discontinued forty years ago. They tipped too easily and killed some kids. Its tires are flat.

I get out, and the sodden loam soil yields beneath my feet.

The temperature has dropped and the sky darkened. Up here, two feet of snow could fall any day.

"Come," Homer says and elbows open the door for me to enter.

His face is unsmiling and inscrutable as he shuts the door behind us and sets his mug down beside a pencil and a spiral notebook resting on the table.

I am about to speak when he suddenly draws me to him and holds me as closely as I do Lydan. His affection seems real, but there is theater in his behavior, an underlying intent I cannot understand. "Shhh," he whispers into my ear.

He pulls away from me.

"Sit," he says and sits at the table. "How are you? How is Lydan?"

"It's—" I say, baffled.

"He's a warrior," Homer says. "Like his mother."

He jots a note on a page of the spiral notebook, tears out the page, and with a fingertip slides the piece of paper across the table to me.

He's written: I know.

Homer squeezes my hand. "It's all going to be all right," he says.

He lights a wooden match and burns the page to ash in his fingertips.

"How about we go visit the blueberry patch?" he says.

Homer's old Jeep starts with a rattle. He drives it in silence, taking a rugged spur road into the forest. He keeps peering up through the windshield at the sky, as if he's keeping an eye out for a UFO or a drone.

"I don't remember driving to the blueberries that day," I say. I do not know what else to say.

"We didn't. We hiked." He rubs a knee. "My knees can't hack that hiking no more."

The Jeep chugs through deep puddles, climbs up a degraded logging road, deeper into the tall pines.

"Here we are," Homer says.

The woods open up onto a field of wild blueberry bushes.

The blueberry field is real and surreal. I am struck with déjà vu. It is both the field as I remember it and a fogged, distorted dream. The lushness of summer's greenery on that day long ago is gone, and in the lavender mist early winter has turned the landscape brittle and brown. Snow is in the air. I can feel it.

The bushes shiver in a stiff wind blowing off Superior Bay so many miles away.

"Pretty," Homer says and exits the Jeep to wander among the blueberry bushes.

As I walk beside him, I miss my mama. I long to be the little girl I was, picking blueberries in the sunshine with her and Homer.

I am staggered by the loss of those days.

By the loss of my innocence.

I want those days back.

I would do anything to have them back, to start over again.

I do not want to be here.

I want to be home.

In the gray sky above, a hawk arcs and screeches as crows harass it toward a stand of pines.

"Why are we here?" I say.

My voice is not my own.

I put my fingers to my face.

My face is not my own.

Where have I gone?

What has become of me?

You are dead.

Elisabeth is dead.

"You have no idea what they can do," Homer says in a whisper as he stands close to me. He picks a dead leaf from a blueberry bush and inspects it. No longer does he seem like the affable uncle; he is a wary and somber mentor with momentous knowledge to impart. "They have so many ways of listening, of watching." He looks around at the pine forest and the silver sky. "Parabolic microphones," he says, his voice quiet. "They can hear people from miles away. Drones and satellites to track you most anywhere. I doubt they can out here. I hope not."

"I don't have a phone on me that can be tracked," I say, whispering back, confirming why I am here without confirming it. "I paid cash for gas in my own neighborhood. And will pay cash on the way back. There's no way to track me." I say all this without thought, without concern that it will leave him confused. He knows. He's known all the time, somehow, all these years, this would come.

"There are always ways. More ways than ever. You've put your boy in grave danger," he says. "And you lied to me."

His words cut me. If I am caught, I know Lydan will be taken from me, and I from Lydan. My son will live with the legacy of a mother who, famous or infamous, hero or villain, chose violence.

I can live with what I did, free or jailed.

But I will have left Lydan a legacy hard to bear.

"I did what I needed to do," I say.

Homer's silence feels like judgment.

"Someone needed to act," I say. "I couldn't stand back and let it all be. Like the ones who whine and piss all over themselves on social media, all their words and characters and memes and *emoji*. A 'protest' online. Virtue signaling how sick they are of thoughts and prayers, but they do nothing except profit off of T-shirts. They're no better than the ones who give empty thoughts and prayers. None of them ever act. *Do* anything. They sit back and they *wait*. Wait like kids hiding beneath desks. Wait, like I did, once. I was tired of waiting. Tired of doing nothing. Tired of talk. Of words. Of expecting someone else to do something for me. The only way for those so in love with their guns to ever get it is to *feel* it, feel what I feel, know what I know, suffer what Lydan and I and too many others suffered. Because until they do, it just doesn't matter to them. It just isn't real."

Homer stares.

"You think I'm crazy," I say.

Homer pinches the blueberry leaf between his fingers and thumb as if to extract its oils. Instead, the dry leaf crumbles to dust. "I think you did what you needed to do and have to live with it. I've lived with the ugliness of this world. I've contributed to it. As you now have."

"Don't judge me," I say.

"I don't judge you. I respect you. Your bravery, if not your methods. I've done far worse to far, far less deserving people. The things they had us do. The atrocities we boys have been brainwashed into committing across eons to appease powerful, narcissistic, greedy men. Boys young enough to still believe we're immortal, believe our violent acts are valorous and for the betterment of country or of mankind, when this is only true in a few rare worthwhile wars. And over the last generation they've done it to girls. Made it even worse. Made us all killers. At least I could seek help after what I did, even if it didn't work. Only isolation worked. What you did, you can't seek help. Can't admit what you've done to anyone. Except me, I suppose. Not that you have, exactly, and I don't want you to. And not that it leaves here if you did. It won't. Ever. You know that. But I'm sorry for the consequences it might cause you. Sorry you did not tell me up front what you planned to do."

"You knew. You sent me away with an illegal military firearm. You knew I wasn't going to meet a journalist friend."

"I never imagined you would do what you did."

"*But* it didn't surprise you."

"I suppose not. No. The specifics, maybe. But not in general. Not in hindsight."

"That day we picked blueberries, you said you had a special gun and one day a special use would come for it," I say. "Mama always called me chosen. Special. Said that I should use my gifts. And the day I left here with the LAR, you said it's always been mine."

"You have it wrong, Lizzy."

"*That* day you taught me how to shoot and told me about a special gun led me to this very day. To this very moment. Right now. That day forged this day. The LAR was the special gun. And I was the special use. It was my destiny."

"If you believe that, then you believe what happened to Lydan was his destiny, that he was meant to suffer as he has just so you could do what you did."

I'd not thought of that. Again, his words wound me. But perhaps he is right. What else might have spurred me to such an act other than Lydan's suffering? Did I have to feel the pain too before I would rise up and act? Forge my words into action through the revelation of pain? In this way, yes, Lydan was destined too.

"Maybe," I say. "I don't know. But I needed the only gun in the world that could be my Trojan horse and gain me access to Akers. And you are the one person who owned it, the very weapon I needed. *The very gun*. A gun you said was rare and special and meant for a special purpose one day."

"What I meant was that I would sell it when the time came. For a lot of money. On the underground market it's worth *a lot* of money. I know that market. That gun is the only thing I own worth anything, and I was going to leave the money to you. Every cent. That's what I meant by its special purpose."

"No," I say.

Homer seems suddenly very old and tired.

"How did you find out about it?" I say. "The shooting?"

"My friend. She knew you weren't going to use the LAR for an article."

"You *told* her you gave it to me?"

"She's the only person in the world I trust. The friend I was with in Asia in seventy-five when I bought the LAR. In nearly fifty years, she's never told a soul. And she's not about to start."

"Who is she?"

"A nurse I befriended over there, my last tour. The things she saw. We GIs, we see our own horrors. *Commit* our own horrors. That's what we are for, after all. I saw savagery maybe every two months. Between the savagery was monotony. No one knows monotony like a GI at war. But the medics. Nurses. In surgical triage. They saw the worst of the worst of the worst, every day, all day, for *years*. Bodies profanely destroyed by AK-47s and M-16s and forty-fives."

I hold up my hand for Homer to stop, but he doesn't stop.

"She's never forgotten the waste," he says. "And for decades she's seen the same damage done to our children in schools and everywhere else we should enjoy ourselves. Pursue our happiness. Slaughters using weapons designed for soldiers at war being bought like candy by clowns. It was hard enough when everyone could agree on the awfulness of it all. Her anger has deepened, *calcified*."

The hawk perches in the top branches of a rotted pine, bullied by the violent crows that dive and peck at it without cease. The hawk takes flight, and the crows give chase.

"When I told her I gave you the LAR, she was distraught. She was very, very angry with me," Homer says.

"And when she figured out I was the one at the gun shop, she told *you* instead of the *police*? Why would she ever do that?"

"She was distraught I'd put *you* at such risk. Distraught I'd jeopardized your safety. Perhaps your very life. And Lydan's. She is not distraught by what you did or who you did it to. She lauds you for it. There are thousands of people who do, apparently. She showed me newspapers about it all. The last thing she'd do is turn you in. She'd die first. When I told her about you leaving here with the Colt and LAR, she asked where you lived, and she went there and watched you and your house, to keep an eye on you."

"She was at my house," I say. It was she in Lydan's doorway. In our house. She who took the note.

I am left cold at how easily things can unravel.

"When you left that evening, she became troubled by your absence and found her way into the house to find Lydan dead asleep. She sat all night on the couch in the dark until in the early-morning hours she heard him stir and went to him and convinced him to go back to sleep. That was the same night Akers was killed. And the LAR and a forty-five soon made it into the news. She came over with the newspapers shortly after."

My recklessness renders me speechless.

"I should have never come here," I say. "Not that first time and not today. I should never have taken that rifle. I should have figured out another way. Never involved you and put you at risk. But after everything that happened and getting your letter, I remembered what you told me about the LAR and its purpose. I believed it was fate."

"Who am I to say it wasn't. Perhaps it was." Homer sits on a tree stump with a groan of pain, stretches his legs out, rubbing his thighs. "Some say destiny can only be seen when we look back upon our life; it cannot be seen beforehand. I should have known your intent. I probably did know it and left it unquestioned so as not to deter you. In that way I suppose I felt whatever you did with it was fate, as you say. I trusted that whatever you did with it, after what you went through, you had your reasons, and it would be just. As I said, I have *done* far worse for far less a cause. I did and I *do* want to help you any way I can, no matter the risk to me."

"Why?"

"Because I understand. Sometimes, when we suffer sudden traumatic violence, another part of us emerges. It was always there, dormant, until excruciatingly violent circumstances awaken it. We experience a dissociation. We break apart. We become many. We do things we would never normally do. Or perhaps in your case, do things we were always meant to do. This is what war does to the human mind and spirit. I know this myself."

I feel wrung out.

He pushes off the stump to try to stand, unsteady on his feet.

I take his elbow. He inhales the damp air deeply and exhales a cloud of breath.

"I put Lydan in danger," I say. "And I put you in danger. If they ever suspect me, they'll check with relatives to find out more about me and look for places I might hide or try to get help."

"It's a good thing I'm not family," Homer says.

"A great-uncle counts, if they dig deep," I say.

"I'm not your great-uncle."

"*Second* uncle."

"I'm not any sort of uncle. I'm not family. Not by blood anyway."

I feel as if I've stepped into a hall of mirrors, where nothing is any longer what it appears to be, and perhaps never was.

"I thought you knew. It wasn't a secret. Your mother called me 'uncle' since she was a little girl," Homer says. "And I felt like her uncle. I was her father's, your grandfather's, closest friend. Two naive boys called up, rightly or wrongly, by their country." Homer looks at me. "Blood doesn't always matter."

The rawness of the day insinuates itself into my bones. I want to drive home to Lydan and forget all this, go on with my life. My real life.

But I can't.

This is my life. I created it.

"If they get onto you and they look for family, they'll never find me," Homer says. "You didn't put me in danger, but I put you in it. I want to help. That's why I called you. To help you."

"How?"

"The guns. If you still have them, you need to get rid of them. As soon as you can. Forever."

The thought of them in the basement now terrifies me.

"I know a place no one will ever find them," Homer says. "But we need to plan it. When you're ready, call me and tell me you'd like a break from it all and want me to take Lydan fishing."

Halfway down my street, my house coming into sight through my car windshield, I know something is wrong.

Neighbors mill about in the street in front of the house, talking, shaking their heads, and moving their hands and arms in an animated fashion as they glance at my house. Claire is among them, central as she holds court with a clutch of neighbors. Wendy stands beside her Toyota in the driveway. As I pull in, all eyes train on me.

Wendy rushes to me as I get out of the car. Her face is pale, mouth slack with fear.

"Elisabeth!" she shouts, her breath short, as if she's been underwater for several minutes and just surfaced. "There's something wrong with Lydan."

I grab her shoulders, my fingers digging in. "What's wrong? Where is he?" I look around. I don't see Lydan.

"We were playing hide-and-seek and having fun, and he was normal. But when he came out from his hiding place, he was acting funny. Weird. Not doing anything, just sitting there not moving, like he was asleep, or like in a coma, sort of, but his eyes were wide open. Like, not seeing anything. He wouldn't respond to my voice. To my touch. Even when I shook him. I wanted to call, but you never sent the number for the phone you were going to pick up."

"Where is he?" I demand.

"I called an ambulance," Wendy says with a sob. "I didn't know what else to do."

"You did the right thing."

"They left a while ago. I was going to the hospital now after talking to the police."

The police.

"Where are they now, the police?"

"They just left."

"Go home," I say. "I'll call you. He'll be okay. I know he will."

He has to be.

I roar out of the driveway in my car, its tires chirping.

In my rearview mirror, I see Claire standing in the middle of the street, watching me.

The bright lobby is all glass and white tile with a strange metal object suspended from the ceiling, artwork that reminds me of Kittyhawk. I find a woman at the desk and inform her of who I am and why I am here.

She pushes her wire-rimmed eyeglasses higher up on her nose and types on her keypad. She gnaws her bottom lip, which looks dry and raw.

"He's in ICU."

Again.

I arrive at the ICU and am told by a young man at the desk that Lydan is in room 312 and I can go in.

"I need to speak to his doctor in charge, to his nurse, someone who can tell me what's going on," I say.

"Dr. Lehman is with him now."

I enter, cautious, quiet, and solemn, anguished to see Lydan here again, in this state.

"Ms. Ross?" a voice says. I am fixated on Lydan in the bed and don't respond right away.

"Ms. Ross?" the voice says again. "Elisabeth?"

I blink and see the doctor, for it must be the doctor; after all, it is a man in a tie and white coat standing in a hospital room. His short black hair matches his black glasses. His posture is erect, his skin pale, and his fingers long and slender. He introduces himself.

"What's going on with Lydan?" I say.

"He had an episode of sorts, as the EMT report shows, and judging by what the babysitter said. We wish she had followed your son in as she said she would, but she seems to have disappeared. Her information, as the only person who witnessed what happened, would have been invaluable."

"Can't Lydan tell you what happened?"

"His state is quite precarious, and he wasn't quite present."

"Did he do something to himself?" I say.

"No," the doctor says. "I don't doubt your concern is real. He likely suffers PTSD, as you do, I am sure. It takes its toll. Depression isn't the only manifestation. It can create a sense of separation from oneself, from others, from the world, a sense of being out of body, disconnected. As if the world is no longer real." He clears his throat. "But he is not here at his own hand. We did some imaging."

His voice is calm, flat. I do not like it.

"What did it show?" I say.

"Your son experienced a seizure brought on by microscopic particles of lead in his blood that amount to an unnatural blood clot. One of them freed itself in his bloodstream and found its way to his brain."

"A stroke," I say. When does this end? And I realize: It doesn't end. There is no recovery, no way to forget, no way to put it behind us. It lives inside Lydan, inside me. A toxin. Even if he were to recover absolutely from his physical injuries, my boy is poisoned and broken.

"It was not a stroke, technically. In layman's terms, yes, he had a foreign obstruction in his bloodstream that resulted in blockage that led to his seizure."

I sit down on the arm of the chair and put my face in my hands.

"We located the clot and were able to go into the vein, insert a catheter, inflate the vein, and remove the clot."

"This is from his injuries?"

"This clot was, and he was at risk from the surgery itself, which is why he was on the Lovenox."

"Is he okay now?"

"We don't believe he's suffered lasting damage. Time will tell."

"Is he okay or not?" I say.

"It's not possible to know if he has a clot elsewhere or if any more will develop. There is shrapnel in him that the surgeons did not dare try to remove at the time. He does not appear, through imaging at this time, to have any other major blockages, but the obstructions do not have to be major to instigate major damage. That said, I want to get him back on the Lovenox so that if he does have any troubling natural clots that we cannot detect, they will be diminished and absorbed by his body and not lead to threatening emergencies such as these. You two have already been through enough. I would plan to stay close to home the next few weeks so you can be near him, closer by than you were today, to be sure."

"Where were you?" Lydan says as he awakens.

A nurse and another doctor are in the room, going over his charts.

Lydan is dumb with medication. He is unable to lift his head from the pillow. "Where were you?" he says again.

I sit beside him and touch his face. His skin is cold.

"I got here as fast as I could," I say.

"I was worried."

"*You.* Worried about *me?*"

"Worried something bad happened."

"Nothing is going to happen to me. I'll always be here for you."

"Nuh-uh," he says. "One day you will be gone."

Yes, one day I will be gone from this world of the living and be one of the dead. I will no longer be here. But where will I be? My remains interred in the ground, sealed away in a dark box, body reposed on a quilted bed of pillowed satin, lips waxen and eyes glued tight, mouth stuffed with cotton, veins emptied of blood and infused with formaldehyde and methanol, all so my corpse can decompose over decades, instead of naturally, within months. Or my remains incinerated, reduced to a coffee can of ashes and bone chips and teeth. All for what? For whom? Who will visit me at my grave? Lydan, perhaps, for a spell. But even I, who love my mama, have not visited her grave in a few years, and I live a mere fifty-two miles from where she rests. Will my ashes be kept by Lydan, or will he spread them in a place I once liked while I was here? Perhaps among the wild blueberry bushes.

I will not be here to help him. Death is final. There are no ghosts. Or spirits. There is no afterlife. There is no heaven. Or hell.

Mama used to say that when she was gone, I shouldn't worry, as she would be looking down on me from heavenly bliss.

I told her that wasn't true.

"I believe it is," she said.

"Believing it doesn't make it true," I said.

"Doesn't it?" Mama said.

"If it is, then heaven sounds like hell for the dead," I said.

I was disappointed that she believed in such magic in order to comfort herself that we, the living, are not all alone in our living, that the dead are with us too and can see us, watch over us. She'd never considered her belief from the perspective of the dead who had to watch their loved ones, unable to touch them or speak to them or in any way communicate with them. How awful. How perverse and excruciating to watch your beloved in their worst moments of grief and pain and not be able to touch them, speak to them, comfort and aid them, or embrace them in their most celebratory moments, to be mute and invisible. Not there at all, really. What torture to be on the other side of the glass.

How long can the dead look down on us? I wanted to ask. *Forever? What happens when we are dead, too, and everyone we ever knew in life is dead along with us? Who do we watch then? Do we watch generations of descendants we never knew in life, for eternity? When do we ever get to truly, simply rest in peace?*

And if Mama would be looking down on me, would she be omnipresent, able to see me anywhere, when I used the bathroom or shower, or during my most intimate and private moments, when I would want to be alone? What if I did not want her to watch over me? I left these questions unasked. They were moot. The dead watch over no one. The dead are dead, and the idea of them watching over loved ones is meant to comfort the living in their grief and to give them hope about their own demise, that they will continue on and still be here in some way after death.

I find no comfort in it, eternity, everlasting life. When I am dead, I will be gone, and I will never know I existed. I will not know I ever was. Just as when I am asleep, I do not know I exist or ever existed.

I am not saddened or frightened. It is this that brings me comfort. Confidence. Confidence to do something now, in this life, with my life. This one and only life of mine. I have done what I've done, and I am glad I did it. Despite what Homer said, this is my destiny. But I worry about Lydan's destiny. I do not want him destined to live a life without his mother.

"Mama," Lydan is saying.

"Hmm," I say.

"You look far away."

"I'm here," I say. "Rest. So we can get you home."

"I need to be normal again," Lydan says. "I need to be me. And you to be you."

"I am me."

"You're not, Mama. You're not."

"I am the me I am now. And you will always be you, and you were never normal, my silly little man; you have always been exceptional. Extraordinary. Special." I hold his hand. "What happened changed our lives. But they are still our lives to live and to create. No one else's. We can still do whatever we want, be whoever we want. Maybe you'll be someone even more exceptional than you were, though that seems impossible. Maybe more exceptional in a different way."

"I don't want to be exceptional. I just want to ride my bike."

I am at the kitchen sink scrubbing a pot when the car pulls up to the curb out front. It's a four-door sedan. Silver. American. Nondescript yet with an official air to it. I set the pot and sponge down in the sink.

"What's wrong, Mama?" Lydan says from the kitchen table, where he works a spoon through his bowl of oatmeal for a lump of undissolved brown sugar. It is nice to have Lydan in here with me while I do simple chores. After a few days, the scare of the blood clot has subsided. I want him to stay here in the kitchen, but watching the car out front, I know he can't.

"Nothing," I say as I watch two women get out of the sedan. "Why don't you finish your oatmeal in your room. You can have extra screen time."

"For how long?" Lydan says, excited, getting up from the table with his crutches.

"As long as the visitors are here."

"Even if it's all day?"

"Even if it's *forever*."

The sedan's doors snick shut, and the two women stand beside the car and stare at the house. The taller and clearly elder woman of the two, perhaps fifty, dark haired and complected, speaks to the younger, who nods her head of short-cropped red hair in agreement or at least understanding. Each woman wears dark slacks and a white shirt and a neat, fitted dark blazer.

The women stride toward the house, eyes forward, shoulders square, officious, neither speaking nor acknowledging each other. Grim and sober.

I open the door a moment after a single knock. The two women's faces are open, and the taller of the two offers a smile that I have seen, one that says, *I am sorry for your pain. I know you are in pain, and I know I can never know that pain; I am humbled by it. Still, I am sorry for it.*

"Ms. Ross," she says. "I am FBI Special Agent Alicia Saavedra, and this is Special Agent Folsom. We'd like to speak with you, if you have the time."

What am I supposed to say? That I don't have the time to speak to the FBI; I'm too busy scrubbing a pot?

"Who is it, Mama?" Lydan says behind me, giving me a start.

"I thought you were in your room," I say.

I must play this right, smart. Calm and casual. I must see the FBI as an ally, as helpful to me. I do not know if I should ask why they are here. I should assume they are here about the Franklin shooting, even though it's been months, and I recall telling someone from there, in the fugue of the first weeks following the shooting, what I could bear to tell them.

"Lydan, go to your room, sweetums," I say.

"Who are they?"

The agent who calls herself Saavedra smiles.

"They're the FBI," I say. There is no reason to lie about who they are. It might be good to have him here.

"What's an FBI?" Lydan says.

Saavedra steps into the entryway and crouches so she's eye to eye with Lydan. "We're like the police," she says. "But for the whole country. Not just for a town or city."

"Come on in," I say and yield the kitchen entrance to the agents with a sweep of my hand.

Their eyes catalog the living room as they pass by it into the kitchen, continue to peruse the kitchen in a practiced, efficient, and only mildly discreet manner, absorbing and recording details and wanting me to know they are doing it, looking for anything out of place or odd, as if I might have the LAR propped in the corner like a broom.

I nod toward the kitchen table. "Can I get you a coffee or water?"

I expect them both to decline, to get to business, but Saavedra says, "I'd love a coffee. It was a bit of a slog here. Black is fine."

"I'll take an ice water," Folsom says.

"Mama," Lydan says at my hip.

"One sec," I tell him and drop a K-Cup into the machine and fire it up.

"You must be Lydan," Saavedra says, planting her hands on her knees.

Lydan gives her a curious look.

"I'm sorry for what happened to you," Saavedra says. "There is too much of what happened to you in this world. One time is too much."

I hand Saavedra the mug of coffee and get Folsom's glass of ice water.

"Mama," Lydan says. "Your tablet is dead. I can't find the charger."

"Grab my phone, on the counter there."

He wraps his arms around my hips and presses his face into my flesh, and I want to burst into tears but don't. He says, "Thanks, Mama," and glances at the agents. He hugs me again, and when I bend for a kiss on the cheek, he whispers in my ear, "I don't like them."

He breaks away from me, and Saavedra says to him, "I bet you're glad to be home. Just you and your mom. It must be nice, just you and your mom."

I don't like this. I don't want them speaking to him.

"Before you go," Saavedra says, "I have a few questions for you, Lydan. If it's okay with your mother, that is."

"It's not," I say.

Lydan looks at me.

"What's this about?" I say.

"It's about what happened at your school. What else would it be?" Saavedra says, as if there could be no other reason.

I recover my wits. "I assumed it was about what happened at

Franklin, but that you had questions for me, not him."

"We have questions for both of you," Folsom says.

"We spoke to the police or agents or someone, months ago. It's all a blur. I don't want you speaking to him now. No good can come of making him relive it," I say. "The shooter is dead. I have only Lydan on my mind. Only him. We don't talk about it."

"Except for when that reporter cornered you outside the hospital," Saavedra says.

"And again on your doorstep," Folsom adds.

They've seen the interviews. Of course. They've probably studied every word, every tic and mannerism and gesture and pause. What have they learned from them? Why mention them now?

"I wanna go play on your phone, Mama," Lydan says.

"Yes. Go play," I say.

With Lydan in his room, I turn on Saavedra. "He doesn't need to relive that nightmare. It's a day we want to forget and can't. We don't need anyone else picking at our wounds, parasites picking at us. You should see how many texts and calls I still get. Some offering obscene money for our 'story.' It's not a story. It's our lives. It never resonates with anyone just how awful it is. People say they can't imagine what it's like. They're right. They can't. Because it's not *like* anything, to go to school as a teacher or a child and have that happen. I've avoided questions as much as I can at every turn. I didn't leave the hospital for weeks and never leave home unless I absolutely have to."

"Mama." Lydan is back in the kitchen doorway. I look at him, winded. I didn't mean to say all that. I shouldn't have said all that.

Saavedra folds her hands on the knee of the leg that's cast over the other leg. Folsom's hands rest on the table before her, fingers laced together.

"Mama," Lydan says. "Are you all right?"

My left eyelid twitches.

"I'm fine, sweetie," I say.

"You were shouting. I thought something bad happened."

"I'm sorry," I say. "I won't raise my voice anymore."

He turns away for his room.

To steady myself, recalibrate, I make myself a mug of coffee and sit with it, keeping my hands cupped around it, an act to perform to keep my hands steady and nerves calm. I sip my coffee, blow on it.

"So," I say, "I don't mean to be rude, but Lydan needs my attention. What about Franklin do you need to know at this point?"

"We had new information come to light. We want to know more about the shooter's behavior. To help profile for future incidents."

"He was an unhinged lunatic," I say. "What else is there to know? You have to be unhinged to do that."

"You'd be surprised how normal some are. Or seem, anyway. You could share a coffee with them, like we are now, and never know that he or she was a shooter. But inside, they're cold, no sympathy or empathy for the deaths or for the pain they've caused. Others, of course, enjoy the pain they've caused, get off on it. The whole point is to create pain and suffering and grieving. Sadists."

Neither of the shooters she describes is me. I know what I've done. I know the pain I've caused. It inhabits each cell of my body. I did it to awaken others who are asleep.

"It seems impossible," I say. "That they could appear so normal."

"People ask how murderers sleep at night or live with themselves," Saavedra says. "Most sleep like babes. The bad sleep well. Because they feel justified. Superior in their thoughts and acts. They convince themselves that what they are doing is a moral act in ways known only to them. So what is there to lose sleep over? Some have compunction, commit their violent act out of duress or pain or anger, of feeling helpless. They believe that there just isn't any other way to achieve what they need to achieve.

"There is a difference between someone malicious and someone who has made a monumental mistake but who is remorseful and accountable."

She's speaking of me, I know it. She's trying to tell me she knows I did it, but I am one of the good ones, an otherwise good person.

"And the Franklin shooter," I say, because I need to say something.

I cannot just sit and stew in the silence she leaves to swell between us. "Which is he?"

"The former. He planned it. Plotted it. For months. Cold. Calculating. Rational and deliberate."

"So you think he was sane."

"You tell me. We found his journal in which he wrote about how certain children are evil, seeds planted by demons, working in league with the devil himself to corrupt the world. He knew what he was doing was *legally* wrong, would be seen by society as wrong, evil, but in his view, it was a noble service to humankind."

Saavedra runs a finger around the rim of her coffee mug but has yet to take a sip. She stares into her coffee as if into a cup of tea leaves, divining the future.

"We'll never know. He might have written all of that as a smoke screen, to come off as if he were ill. Many have done the same. Written journals or diaries far ahead of time to show themselves as ill, that they are victims of a compulsion and paranoid schizophrenia and the like. They are slaves to mental disorders beyond their control."

"Something beyond their control," I repeat.

"Many shooters, by the time they get to the point where they are going to act out a violent fantasy, they can come across as unstable, obsessed with grievances with a boss or coworkers, colleagues or an institution. 'The system' or 'the man.' They often post about it online. Others keep all of that to themselves. Bottled up. They simmer rather than boil over. For some, the secret is part of the attraction. They feel it gives them power, to dupe those close to them, dupe the police or even us, the FBI, into thinking they could never even think of doing such a thing, let alone actually do it. 'I wouldn't hurt a fly.' They like to think they are smarter than us and that we are fools.

"Take Lilith, for example," Saavedra says. Her finger stops tracking circles on the mug's rim, and she looks up at me. At the mention of Lilith, I feel myself flinch and let out the tiniest gasp I try to cover by coughing.

This is why they are here. Lilith. It is clear now.

"Makes you wonder what kind of woman would do that. What drove her to it," Folsom says.

"Who cares," I say.

"You don't care?" Saavedra says.

"I don't care why she did it. Why any of them do it. I can't afford to invest my emotions and thoughts into these strangers' motives. I hardly have any emotions left except those for my son. You two, as agents, have to obsess over it. It's your job. For me, forward. That's the only way for me. I must have blinders on to care for my son."

"You needed them that day. Blinders. To go back in there that day and save him as you did."

Saavedra taps a ring on the handle of her mug.

Clink. Clink.

She still hasn't taken a sip of her coffee. Folsom hasn't taken a sip of her water. "I'd bet," Saavedra says, "Lilith comes across just as normal as can be. Just as normal as you."

"That's crazy in itself." I laugh. It is a genuine laugh. It is crazy to me. Crazy I can sit here and appear calm, even while my heart feels as if it might explode in my chest. "To do that and act normal. She has to be a sociopath."

"She might have learned how to compartmentalize. Or she keeps a ledger. Her good deeds on one side—community service, volunteer work, being a good parishioner and the like—balance out her *bad deeds* on the other side."

"Sounds batshit to me," I say.

"We all do it," Folsom says. "To some extent. Keep that ledger. I do. I'm sure you do too."

"For normal bad stuff," I say, "like yelling at Lydan when I'm tired and making up for it by baking cookies. Not killing people."

I glance at the clock on the stove.

"Lydan's physical therapist will be here soon. I doubt you came all this way to try to convince me how normal this crazy Lilith is."

"Maybe she's not crazy, just angry," Saavedra says.

"That's a lot of anger," I say.

"You must have been pretty angry after what you went through," Folsom says. "It's normal to have thoughts of revenge, vengeance. Some people act on them. Like those local girls."

I don't know what girls she is referencing, and it must show on my face.

"The girls who were arrested last night," Saavedra says.

I shrug.

Saavedra leans in, tapping her ring on the coffee mug again. Louder. Click click clack.

"There were two girls who grew up here in Franklin County, were first-year students at a college in Detroit," she says. "They were back for break and took two shotguns from one of their fathers' gun cabinets, sawed off the guns' barrels, and went to a football field where several boys they graduated high school with last year were tossing around a ball. The girls opened fire and killed two of the boys at point-blank range. These two boys were allegedly responsible for the sexual assault of both girls during a camping trip they all took last June. The girls had gone to the police. Charges were brought, but the judge dismissed the case because one of the girls and one of the boys had been an item at the time, and all involved had been drinking. The judge said something along the lines of, the alleged victims and perpetrators were drunk at the time, *illegally* inebriated, so it was impossible to untangle in a legal manner what happened between these drunk teens and if a crime had even occurred. Said it should be a lesson to all teens about underage drinking and the dangers of it."

Saavedra brings up a YouTube video on her tablet and slides the tablet across the table to me.

"I don't want to see it," I say.

A recording plays of the girls being taken into the courthouse for arraignment. As they walk, one of the girls turns and shouts at the camera, "They got what was coming!"

I suck in a breath. The girl speaking is one of the girls from the café, the girl who was selling the Lilith T-shirts. The other girl is her friend. The girl with the tattoo.

Except now she is in handcuffs, being led by officers up court steps.

"The boys laughed after that judge dismissed the case," she shouts at the camera. "Asked *what got our panties in a bunch*. If the law isn't going to do anything for women, we need to *act* on our own behalf!"

A reporter follows her, the reporter who has followed me. "You advocate for vigilante justice?"

"Justice for women," the girl shouts, hurried along. "If we can't get it in court, we'll get it on our own. We swallowed the judge's injustice for too long! We're not victims anymore. We *acted*."

"So you condone killing in cold blood without there being a conviction?"

"We were raped. You're a woman. Do you need a judge or jury telling you whether you were raped or not, or because you shared a hard seltzer with a girlfriend, you don't know you are being raped, or because your rapists drank a few beers, they didn't know they were raping you? We killed them for justice. So other young women won't be raped by them in the future. You know they'd do it again. Imagine them in college. We spared other young women what we suffered. That's worth it. I'll gladly go to jail for that for a few years. I am Lilith!"

She is at the top of the stairs, being led in. She seems to think she'll be released from jail when she turns twenty-one; she won't. She'll serve a long time in a rough prison instead of a small jail like the county lockup she's probably being held in now.

"Lilith inspired this?" the reporter says.

"You bet! And a lady in a coffee shop too. Me and Holly were selling Lilith T-shirts I made, I was wearing one, and this woman said selling T-shirts was an insult to Lilith. T-shirts don't help. Only action does. We need to act. All of us women. Act. Fight. I was mad at first, but then I saw the light."

The video ends.

I'm astounded and unnerved, yet a part of me is pleased. They were let down and deserve more than a judge dismissing the case. Deserved at least a trial.

"That was you," Saavedra says, "in the coffee shop."

"Holly took a video of you in the café, and you say you expect girls to act like Lilith," Folsom says.

The video. I forgot.

"I didn't mean for them to shoot people," I say. "It angered me they were making money off crummy T-shirts. That doesn't mean I suggested them using a gun. There are a lot of ways to act. Run for a state legislature. Work to change gun laws."

"That's what you meant?" Saavedra says. "Running for state legislature?"

"That's one idea," I say.

"And what have you done, to act?" Folsom says.

"I saved my classroom students, and I saved my son," I snap.

"What have you done in the aftermath?" Saavedra says.

"Taken care of my son. There's no time for anything else. What have *you* ever done? As people? Not as agents. As human beings. As *women*. What have you done to *stop* shootings? You go in and shoot the shooter. Or arrest him. I applaud you for that. I do. But what do you do besides clean up after the mess? Anything? Do you do anything to stop it? Help put an end to it?"

Folsom starts to say something, but Saavedra shakes her head for her to stop.

"I'm curious why you engaged those girls at all in the café," Saavedra says.

"*They* engaged *me*. Tried to sell me a T-shirt. I never said for them to take up a gun. I never knew what they'd been through either. I was out of the house for the first time in months, trying to treat myself to something normal, a quiet cup of coffee, and I get solicited to buy a damn shirt, after what happened to me and Lydan. Like a shirt helps anything. I took offense."

"You left Lydan home alone?"

I pause. They keep trying to corner me, take me off guard with new information.

I sip my coffee. "For less than an hour," I say. "More like a half hour. I used to leave him longer when I ran errands. He's old enough as long as he doesn't answer the door and keeps it locked. He wanted to feel like a normal kid again. It was the first time I left to get groceries. I had them delivered till then. And people still drop off food on our step."

"Do you have a babysitter?"

"If I need one."

"Have you? Needed one? At night, say?"

"Where am I going at night with Lydan the way he is? I'm not going on a date. Or out with the girls."

"What's the sitter's name?"

"I can't see how that matters."

"Can't you?"

"I can't," I say. "We have help from a slew of professionals. And a few neighbors and friends. They were all affected too, the neighbors. Touched, that is, by the shooting in one way or another. Their own way. The entire town is. Region. You don't have to be shot to be a victim."

"Like the girl in the Iowa gun shop," Saavedra says. "Akers's daughter."

"I don't know anything about her or it," I say.

"Except what the reporter told you on your doorstep," Folsom says.

I wonder again what they've learned from the video of that interview, how many times they watched and rewatched it, paused it to take notes about my words and manner and facial expressions. "That's a blur," I say. "I was ambushed and delirious with exhaustion. But that gun shop thing and those girls from the café are the last thing I want to think about."

"Akers's daughter was a victim of the sort you're talking about," Saavedra says. "She wasn't shot, but she was left all alone to find her father and his friends lying dead in their blood. Imagine the damage."

"I don't want to talk about shootings. You're as bad as the reporter."

"Maybe she is a good person, at heart, this Lilith," Saavedra presses. "Sometimes a good person commits a bad act they regret. Whatever justification they created in their mind is shattered upon executing the act itself. The act brings the shooter back to a cold reality. They despise what they've done, can't live with it, and want to confess. Need to confess. But the fear of incarceration prevents them from coming forward. So they live in a self-made prison of fear that any second they will be found out, that the knock on the door will come one morning. Any morning. A morning like this one."

Saavedra pushes her coffee mug away from her, turns it in a circle. They know. They both know.

"I've seen it," Saavedra says. "Otherwise good people, very good people, respected in their communities, from all walks of life—a pastor, a local insurance agent, a teacher, like yourself—have committed murder in moments of delirium driven by rage or jealousy or fear or greed, blinded by one or the other or several, and afterward they could not live with what they'd done. Because they were good people. At the core. Decent. They confessed, and every single one, without exception, who actually felt remorse, told me they felt freed by their confession and were more imprisoned by their fear and guilt than they were now even behind bars. Their soul is freed, their conscience cleared, and because they confessed and pleaded guilty in a deal, they served less time in less harsh environs."

Saavedra hooks a finger into the mug's handle and drags the mug back to her. Folsom stares at me. Unspeaking. Inscrutable.

The kitchen is dead silent.

For a heartbeat, I believe Saavedra. But I know what she says is a lie. For what I did, I will spend my life in prison, if I am spared my life.

I need to get the guns out of this house, but I don't know how to do it. Homer does. But the FBI will be watching me now. Listening. Recording my calls. Monitoring my texts on the phone they know I own. If they haven't been doing it already. They'd need a warrant for such surveillance. And if they can get a warrant for phone taps and for following me, they can get one to search the house, it would seem. I don't know. But they're not searching the house. They would be if they had enough evidence for a warrant. I think. I don't know. Maybe different types of warrants require different levels of cause. They don't have enough to arrest me. If they did, I'd be in cuffs.

I know this: I am a good person.

That is why I feel no guilt or shame or remorse for what I did.

Because I am a good person.

Because what I did was the right thing, the moral thing.

"I really need to attend to my son," I say. "Unless there is anything else."

"Not at the moment," Saavedra says.

With the agents gone, I want to go straight to the cellar and retrieve the guns. I should have ditched them along the way. It was a monumental mistake to keep them. I do not know what I was thinking. I wasn't. Yet I don't dare even enter the basement now. The agents might be watching or listening from a van down the street. There is no way for me to know.

I step outside to see if they are parked down the block or if some other car or van might have agents inside watching, listening.

Saavedra's car is still at my curb, without the agents in it.

I see the agents standing at the end of Claire's driveway, speaking to Claire.

Claire is nodding with enthusiasm, as if she wants to impress Saavedra with how much she is in full agreement with whatever Saavedra is saying. Yet Claire is hugging herself too, arms wrapped around her belly as if she is cold or uncomfortable with what is being said. Folsom nods back toward my house. If she sees me, she makes no indication. She looks back to Claire, who is speaking now. Folsom is writing something in a notepad.

The agents end the conversation, and Saavedra hands something to Claire, which Claire glances at, then tucks into her hip pocket.

I duck back inside, and from the kitchen window I watch as the agents return to their car and get in and drive away without a glance at my house.

I go back outside and look to make sure they are really gone. All the cars in the driveways are familiar to me. The right cars. There are no cars parked on the street. Down toward the cul-de-sac, a backhoe drops a load of rocks into the back of a dump truck with a loud boom.

Claire looks toward the sound and sees me on the lawn.

She is hoofing it to me, carrying an object with both hands.

"I saw the ambulance the other day, and my heart just sank," she barks as she gains on me, out of breath. She's holding out a casserole dish in offering. "What on earth happened?"

She makes no mention of the agents.

I want to ask her why the agents wanted to talk to her, what they asked or told her, but I don't want it to appear as if I was watching, as if I am prying.

"You two have been through enough," she says, presenting the casserole to me. The plastic wrap stretched across the top of it is opaque with steam. "Why is it some of us get far more than our fair share? It just isn't right, is it? Makes it hard to have faith, but then my mother always said God never gives you more than you can handle. When I saw you come back home from the hospital and you had Lydan with you, I just . . . I sobbed." She thrusts the casserole at me, forces me to take it. "My son Trevor," she says. "When he was Lydan's age, he just loved my mac and cheese. It was the only thing he ate for months. I sneaked in frozen peas to try to give him some actual nutrients, vitamins and minerals, but I skipped that with this one for Lydan and added extra buttered croutons on top. He deserves it. How is he?"

Claire glances behind me as if to get a glimpse of Lydan, to decide on her own how he is faring.

"Managing," I say.

"He's lucky to have you. What happened? With the ambulance?"

"A setback. What did those—" I begin to ask about the agents, but Claire cuts me off, as if she knows what I am going to ask and wants to deflect it.

"I saw you were gone the other day and pulled in just after the ambulance pulled away," she says.

She's a grain of sand in my eye; the more I try to get rid of her, the more lodged and irritating she becomes.

"You know," she says, "I'm happy to watch Lydan anytime. I'm right across the road, after all. I'm here. I hope you know that. I raised two boys, and I just love them. Boys."

"I appreciate that," I say. "But I have plenty of help."

"No such thing," she says. "Even the smallest gesture can make a monumental difference during times of trauma. Take the casserole you left on my doorstep after Jerry's death. Very thoughtful, even if the boys didn't care for it. You know how finicky boys can be with what they eat. I for one loved it."

I've never seen a teenage boy finicky about food. They are vacuums.

"We were all grieving, too, of course," she says. "Their appetite was poor. They didn't hardly eat anything. It certainly wasn't your casserole's fault. I just wanted to come over and tell you I want to return the gesture in any way I can. I am here, for anything. I've seen you've needed to be away, which I'm sure is trying for you. Was it for work or—?"

"There is a lot going on," I say.

"Of course. I read what they're trying to do, that awful superintendent and principal. Simply vile. They should erect a statue of you, a plaque at least. Just the opposite of what they want to do. They should be sacked."

"What was it that those agents wanted?"

"It must have been important," she says, ignoring me, "whatever it was. For you to have to leave Lydan. I imagine you wouldn't leave unless you absolutely had to."

"I wouldn't," I say. "And doubt I will again for some time."

"That's good. Stay close to home when the world is going insane. It seems every time you leave the house, something just dreadful happens."

"Every time I leave the house?" I say and wish I hadn't.

"Not *you* you. But any one of us. In general. Like every time we turn around, I mean, there is something terrible happening in this world.

More bloodshed. Death. People shooting each other. Sometimes I think my poor Jerry, rest his soul, is better off not being here, and I wonder what kind of world we brought our kids into. Murder as spectacle. Since that Lilith, things have gone even more to pot." She pauses, waits for me to respond. To react.

I don't. I must get away.

"I saw you on the TV," she says.

My mouth is dry and it's hard to swallow.

"Saying you thought it was about time someone did something," she says.

"I said I wasn't surprised," I say. "That's not the same thing."

"I think she's despicable. That Lilith. No better than the rest of them. I don't care if she's a woman or not. She's worse than a lot of the men. She's what, in my day, we called an instigator. Likes to stir the pot. Calling on others to take up arms and murder folks in cold blood."

"I'm not really following it, but I don't think that's what she said."

"You hardly have to follow it. It's practically in the air we breathe; a new shooting every hour, it seems. Multiple shootings. And she doesn't have to say it explicitly," Claire says. "She's clever, that one. Trying to make it all about men. All about the, what do they call it? 'Patriarchy'? Pff. Men have their role in life and women have their role. It's when you start to blur the roles, the lines, wanting more than you need, more than what God has prescribed, when you get greedy, that you muck everything up and cause it to go haywire. Me? I hate having to work. I liked it when Jerry went off to the real estate office and showed houses and kept us afloat and secure and I took care of the house and the kids and him, ran errands, made dinner for him and the boys. It was nice. Things went smooth as silk. There was a measure to it. There were no surprises, no upheaval. I liked taking care of my family in my way, and Jerry respected what I did as much as I respected what he did. Our roles were different but equal. I didn't submit; I wasn't oppressed. I was liberated. And I dare say it was a privilege, as the youngsters like to say, to have that option, not have to work, as I understand other women, like you, must. And you know, Jerry, the traditional men, they do a lot; they miss a lot; they sacrifice a lot. Jerry missed more than his share of Little League games and other events. Was late for dinners or birthday parties on occasion. And it stung him. He knew as well as anyone that each moment is its own, no getting it back. That's sacrifice. But this patriarchy business. *Really?* If a woman wants or has to work, she can. She can do anything she likes. No one is stopping her. But do women really want to work like men or be in power? Want that responsibility? You think for a second the world would be safer, less violent, more peaceful, if women ran the show? Please. No. Oh my God, no. I know women well enough, we women know women well enough, and girls well enough, to know how vicious some of us can be, all of us can be, at times, how manipulative and petty. I'm just being honest. Power and greed would go to the heads of women just as they do to men. Men don't have a monopoly on that, believe you me. You see it every day even now, with women in positions of power. Power knows no sex or gender when it comes to corrupting most people, bringing out their most cruel and selfish instincts. Women wanted to be equals and be soldiers. Great. Now they can kill just like men kill. Now we just have more people willing to kill more people. Isn't that just dandy. Look at what those young girls across the country have done. Killing those boys. That judge. Acting like animals. Monsters. It's sick. Shooting a judge in cold blood."

"What judge? I thought they shot the boys who raped them, not the judge?"

"There are judges being shot now. All kinds of people. By women now. Fabulous! And women willing to kill just as much as men. Is it surprising? Not to me. Like you said, I guess, it doesn't surprise me. If given license, a reason, if instigated, women are as violent as men. Do you see any difference in the women who are in power now from the men? As CEOs or senators, do women in general have a kinder way of going about things, or are they as beholden to the almighty dollar as any man? If you believe men and women are equal, wouldn't it be fair to say that they can be equally greedy and corrupt and violent? That Lilith. Look at what she did. I tell you this, I wouldn't mind gathering that reward for information that leads to her arrest. What I could do with that money. One hundred thousand dollars! Jerry, bless his soul, didn't leave me a pot to tinkle in, beyond the house and our spare savings. We didn't have life insurance, because who thinks they'll just . . . go like that? At fifty-two years old. A jogger, no less! I could use money like that reward for Lilith. One hundred thousand dollars. That kind of money changes a life like mine."

Claire finishes her treatise with a hard blink.

I shouldn't respond. I know better. Yet I am curious about this judge.

"What about this judge?" I say.

"They killed him. These girls who were victims of sexual assault. Allegedly. And that judge gave that boy who did it a legal sentencing that he judged fit the crime and circumstances. He was within the bounds of the law. And they did those awful things to him. Do you think it's okay? To kill a judge just because you disagree with his sentencing. That's lawlessness. Chaos."

"What did those two agents want with you?" I say.

"Who?"

"The FBI agents you were talking to," I say. "Just five minutes ago."

"Oh, them," Claire says, as if two FBI agents speaking to her isn't the biggest event of her life. "Nothing much. I saw them coming out of your house, and I called them over. I thought maybe they were media or insurance people or some other people bothering you, and I wanted to tell them off, not that you can't handle such things for yourself, but these types, these bottom-feeders. I was shocked to hear they were from the FBI. Then I was miffed."

"How so?"

"They said they were here for follow-up, about what happened at Franklin."

I tell Claire it's true, even if I don't believe it.

"I find that strange. Don't you? This long after," Claire says.

"They were tying up loose ends," I say.

"They are derelict in their duties if they were just following up now."

"What did they ask you or tell you?" I say.

"They were so tight lipped. Snobby. Acted like I was bothering them.

Like we don't pay their salary, you and I. All of us. They can give me the time of day; I'm a citizen. They said you mentioned me."

"Did they?"

"Well, that you mentioned neighbors anyway, helping you out. And I said the least I could do was bring you and Lydan some food and offer to help in any way I can. To help with babysitting or whatever, give your babysitter a break, though she seems like a responsible girl when I've seen her over here—never seen a boyfriend over or anything like that. Wendy, isn't it?"

Lydan long asleep, I surf cable news stations on my bedroom TV.

I do not want to search online or on my phone apps. I do not want to leave a trace.

TV is still safe.

I believe.

I don't know.

I am in disbelief of the stories of shootings I watch.

In Columbus, Ohio, the state's governor staged an outdoor event on the capitol steps, where he planned to sign a bill into law that would allow individuals to carry concealed weapons without a permit, anywhere at all. He is picking up where Akers left off. The snake has a new head. Already.

In attendance in Ohio were dozens of armed supporters dressed in military fatigues and black riot gear. They were armed with AR-15s and R4s and other various black rifles. They hoisted flags and signs that read, *My Gun Is My Business.*

The governor made a speech. "This is the dawn of a new day. From here out, the state of Ohio will keep its grubby hands off your guns and your rights. As our motto states, 'With God, all things are possible,' and so this is. If you legally own a handgun or any other firearm, you ought to be able to carry it anytime, anywhere. Even in federal and state buildings. These places should not be sacrosanct. They of all places should be where citizens are most allowed to exercise their constitutional rights. Today is an example of how those who carry firearms, concealed or open, can come together at a peaceful event and celebrate liberty and justice for all. Ohioans are finally free from the tyranny of government overreach, free to bear arms, as we bear witness to this historic bill, aptly named, in the spirit of Max Akers, the Keep Your Hands off Our Handguns Bill, being signed into law."

As the governor raised his pen into the air, a young woman, Joyce Mallory, a first-term legislator who opposed the bill, drew a handgun from behind her back and shot the governor in the side of the head, shouting, "Justice!"

Meanwhile, from the crowd below, four young women shed their winter jackets to reveal T-shirts emblazoned with the words WE ARE LILITH! They drew handguns and opened fire on those who sat at either side of the governor. Among those slain were the lieutenant governor and the House Speaker.

During the frenzied melee of gunfire, many militiamen in attendance opened fire on the young women. As many as nine other militiamen were killed; it is unclear how many by "friendly fire" and how many at the hands of the women who initially fired. The one of the four women not killed escaped on foot. Her whereabouts are not known.

Joyce Mallory and two armed women who supported the new law were also shot and killed.

In sixteen other shootings across the country in the past two days, a total of one hundred and thirteen people were shot and killed, and another thirty-two were shot and hospitalized.

Portland, Maine, saw a group of nine young women break into the home of district judge Lawrence Sheffield, who, in a highly publicized trial, had shown leniency to a member of a fraternity house accused of rape that occurred on a college campus. While the young man was found guilty of sexual assault, the judge sentenced him to the minimum of eighteen months allowed by law, with all but six months served.

This must be the judge Claire spoke to me about. It has to be.

At the sentencing, the judge said, "We don't have to compound this tragic situation further by destroying the promising life of this young man, who by all other accounts is an upstanding member of society and whose family has been esteemed for generations. He has demonstrated remorse, and I do believe the fear of God has been instilled in this young man, who made an awful mistake when he succumbed to the temptations every young man must learn to resist."

The young women entered the judge's home dressed in ski masks and filmed their invasion and what can only be described as an execution. They tied the judge to a chair, and each girl asked him a question. "How long do you think Carrie Bishop's trauma will last?"

The judge could only stammer.

"Forever," one girl said. "Is this just?"

"I—"

"Do you think she'll be over it in six months?"

"I can't sentence based on—"

"Based on what? Decency? The life ruined? The actual crime and not the criminal's 'good standing'? Despite his being a rapist."

"Based," the judge said, gasping, "on emotion. I must weigh—"

"By all accounts," one girl said, "not by 'all *other* accounts' but by *all* accounts, Carrie Bishop is a good person. A loving and caring and generous person. You could have sentenced her rapist to twenty years. Instead, you slapped his wrist because other than the inconvenience of being a rapist, he's a good boy. He's not the first you've done this with. The list is long of poor, good young men who've made the 'mistake' of rape. Except . . . they aren't poor. They are rich. Very rich. Their families, anyway."

"That has nothing to do with my sentencing."

"The records show otherwise. The records show your leniency to the wealthy. The severity and leniency of sentences you've handed out are in direct proportion to the wealth of the defendant."

"My sentences all fall within the legal parameters and guidelines. If I have shown what you call leniency, it is based on previous criminal offenses, likelihood of repeat offenses, and my discretion, which is what it means to judge."

"Do you think the victim will be recovered by the time her rapist is released in six months?"

"It's not that simple."

"Yes or no?"

The judge hung his head. "No," he said. "No. She won't. But—"

"There are no 'buts.' Not anymore."

The young women shot him.

Another report covers wives across the country who've been telling their husbands if they do not abandon their guns, the wives will leave their men and take the children with them. The movement is named Your Guns or Your Wife.

Thousands of men have brought their firearms to communal burn pits set up on town greens across the land, where in ceremonial acts, they dump their firearms into the trenches, spray them down with kerosene, and light them afire, then pour cement over them and bury them for good. At one recent event in Indiana, a group of armed men charged from the nearby woods and fired upon the men who were burning their guns, screaming, "Traitors! Traitors!"

While many men have disobeyed their wives and kept their guns, and the wives have resumed lives that are less than domestic bliss and now perhaps more perilous, many wives have lived up to their promise and walked out on their husbands, taken the kids, the dog, the cat, and left their men alone with their guns.

The names, faces, and addresses of Second Amendment activists have been posted on social media. Scores of individuals have been targeted and attacked, many shot and killed or wounded. Some attackers eschewed firearms and used primitive weapons: axes, shovels, and knives. In one instance, a sword was wielded, slicing a man nearly in half at the torso.

Big-box stores and small gun shops alike are experiencing a run on any and all guns and ammunition, their racks and shelves wiped clean of both. Certain gun shops refuse to sell to customers they do not personally know or to customers who they believe support Lilith. "We don't sell to murderous traitors and scumbag commies," Henry Grant of Toledo Guns and Ammo remarked.

Plenty of shops continue to sell guns and ammunition to whoever strides in with the means of legal purchase. "It's still a free country, for now," said Martha Sheridan of Sheridan's Guns in Waloop, Montana.

The outsides of other gun shops and manufacturers now look like fortresses, with armed sentinels around their perimeters and shooting towers erected at corners of their properties.

In a twist, ammunition stocks in many regions have been all but wiped out, so those who have bought firearms in the recent weeks cannot even use the weapons if they did not already have ammunition for them.

I am stunned by these stories and sit here in disbelief.

I could never have foreseen this.

Part of me wishes to stop it. Yet I know I can't stop it.

I might as well try to stop water from running between my fingers.

This is war, and as with any, some factions and some people are drawn into it who ought not be a part of it, who are bystanders. Yet part of me, too, I must confess, is pleased.

What was it I did envision? If not this, what? What is war if not chaos and mass death? One side left standing, the other on its knees. Even if I end it now, it's back to square one. Nothing has changed. Is that what I want, to surrender?

I watch Lydan from the kitchen window. He is outside for the first time since the shooting. The sun shines bright, big, and yellow on this unseasonably warm day. He holds his face up to the sun. It must feel soft and warm to him, like a dream. The window is open, and I can hear birds in the trees twitter and chirp. A breeze stirs the net of his basketball hoop at the edge of the driveway. He can't shoot a basketball. He can't move certain ways, extend or exert himself, without pain. Many days, in the afternoons and evenings when he is tired, I can tell it hurts him just to breathe. But he says he feels better lately. He says he feels good. He claims he doesn't feel the pain. He feels strong. I find it hard to believe.

The garage door is open, and I can see he keeps looking into the garage. His bicycle is in there, leaning against the back wall. It would be a nice day to ride it down the block to the cul-de-sac. He can't do that either. I wouldn't want him down there, not with the construction going on, the trucks and earthmovers coming and going to the jobsite.

He looks toward the street. A cat is sitting at the end of the driveway by our mailbox. The cat is orange and white and fluffy. It licks a front paw and looks at him.

"Kitty," he says. "Come here, kitty."

The cat does not come.

Its ears twitch. It lies down in the dirt by the mailbox and rolls on its back and squirms.

"Here, kitty," Lydan says. He stands and sways. I want to call out to him to be careful, but he tucks his crutches beneath his arms and works his way down the drive to the cat. I've never seen the cat before. It doesn't have a collar.

The cat minces up the driveway toward Lydan as Lydan crutches his way toward it.

"Kitty." Lydan bends to pet it. The cat swishes its tail, lengthens itself, and arches its back.

Lydan looks up. I do too. Claire is crossing the street to Lydan.

"Found a friend," I hear Claire blurt.

Lydan doesn't say anything.

"Looks like a stray," she says.

Lydan scratches behind the cat's ears.

"Nice to see you outside," Claire says. "That cat likes you. You've got the magic touch. Cats don't like most people. They don't like me, that's for sure."

Lydan scoops up the cat and tries to walk back without his crutches.

"No babysitter today?" Claire says.

I march out of the house.

As I head out the door, I hear Claire say, "I told your mama I'd watch you anytime. Where'd she go, overnight like that?"

"Lydan," I say. "Use your crutches."

"He's found a friend," Claire says.

I don't say anything to her. Don't even look at her.

I take the cat from Lydan. It struggles as I set it down.

I hand Lydan his crutches.

"I want to bring the kitty inside," he says.

"No," I say.

"Why?"

"It's someone else's."

"He doesn't have a collar."

"That doesn't mean it's not someone else's. Give it one last scratch. It's lunchtime."

"Early for lunch," Claire says.

"He gets hungry early," I snap.

"I'm not hungry," Lydan says. "I want to stay with the cat if I can't bring it in."

"Come inside. You've got medications to take too."

"I took it already, Mama."

"Not this medication. It's new."

"Must be hard, keeping track of everything," Claire says. "But we do what we need to do for those we love. Is there anything we wouldn't do?"

In the kitchen, Lydan says, "What new medicine, Mama?"

"I made that up," I say. "To get you inside. That lady is a nosy Nellie. Bothering you."

"I don't like her. She's always looking at the house."

I look out the window. The cat is gone. Claire is still there.

A week later, I sit at the kitchen table. It's long after midnight. I can't sleep. I still rarely sleep, and always the dreams, the nightmares, still come. My body has forgotten how to really sleep, and I wonder why we need sleep at all. Why are we made so our energy depletes after only hours of being awake and we need to shut down to recharge? For one-third of our lives, we are unconscious, unaware of the world, of our very existence. In our sleep we do not know we exist. We forget ourselves. Our lives. If we don't dream, we are literally dead to the world. This is what we will find when we die. Nothing. Less than nothing. Beyond nothing. Absence. If I shut my eyes and doze for a second, I am *gone* for that second. I do not exist to myself.

I am sleepless yet I am not tired.

I hear a sound. In the hall. I look up.

Lydan is there.

Walking.

Without his crutches.

Walking as well as he's ever walked.

No limp.

No hitch.

No pain carving a grimace in his face.

He steps into the bathroom.

I blink. Astonished.

I fell asleep. I am asleep.

Dreaming.

I must be.

Or Lydan is asleep. Sleepwalking and unaware of his pain, of what he can't do.

I wait for the bathroom door to open, for Lydan to appear.

I wait for an age.

The bathroom doorknob turns. Snick. I keep my eyes on it. Try not to blink. It feels as if a single blink will take a thousand years.

Lydan steps into the hall and pauses. I want to go to him. Catch him before he falls. But I can't move.

Lydan does not fall. He walks into the kitchen and startles when he sees me. "Oh," he says, "you're here. You're up."

I tell him I can't sleep.

I am vapor, barely here. I wonder if he is here. If we both died in the shootings or I did or he did, and I am a ghost or he is a ghost, or maybe we never existed at all. Maybe I or he or we are someone else's dream. An alien's dream. Or nightmare. I must be drowsing. These are dream thoughts, the thoughts of the drowsed.

Lydan looks out the kitchen window at the darkness, then opens the refrigerator door and ducks behind it, out of sight. There is the rattle of glass bottles and jars as he takes something from the refrigerator. He comes back up into sight and closes the door. His mouth and fingers are red with blood.

"Lydan," I say. I mean to scream it: Lydan! But it comes out as a whisper, as if I don't want to frighten him. He's been frightened enough.

He lifts his eyes to mine, too much of their whites showing. He grins as if his mouth is being slit at the corners. His teeth are bloody. His lips. Blood dribbles down his chin. He raises a bloody finger to his lips as if just realizing his lips are bleeding, and I see he is not bleeding. In his fingers he holds a fresh strawberry with a bite taken out of it, its livid juice trickling down his wrist.

"Mama," he says.

"What are you doing?" I say.

"I had to pee. Then I was hungry, so I got strawberries."

"What are you *doing*?" I say.

He doesn't understand. Maybe he is asleep. I've heard of people who can converse in their sleep. I am confused. And tired. My body feels hollow. My mind an empty room with the windows and doors open.

"You don't have your crutches," I say.

He looks at me as if I'm speaking a language unknown to him.

"Your crutches," I say.

He looks at his hands. "I don't need them anymore."

I am so cold my bones crack.

I should be ecstatic.

Instead, I am terrified.

"What's wrong, Mama?" he says.

For one miraculous moment, I know the shooting never happened. It was all a nightmare, and I have awoken from it at the kitchen table. I can shake it all from me with a shudder.

Lydan keeps standing there, sucking the bitten strawberry. He makes a sound like he used to when sucking on a pacifier. He drops the strawberry stem to the floor, smiles at me.

I don't smile back.

"You do need your crutches. I don't want you to fall and get hurt or overdo it and relapse."

"'Relats'?"

"*Relapse.* It's when you go back to how you were."

"I want to go back to how I was."

"I don't mean back to how, who, you were before. I mean back to being in pain. You can't rush recovery. Like when you have a stomach bug and you start to feel better again, start to feel hungry. And you eat something you shouldn't too soon. And you throw up again because you trick yourself into thinking you're better than you are."

"I'm not tricking me. I am better."

"I don't want you without your crutches. I don't want you to fall."

"I won't. Look." He bends and touches his toes, teetering.

"Please," I say. "Don't."

"Don't you want me to be better?"

"More than anything in the world."

"Good!" He bends and twists.

"Don't!" I shout. "Don't do that!"

He continues bending and twisting.

"Stop it. Lydan, stop it now!"

Lydan stops. "I'm all better."

"You're not."

"I am. I am me again."

"It's not possible."

"You used to say anything is possible."

"You might feel good, but you need to be careful not to hurt your-self again. There are internal injuries still healing."

"Aren't you happy for me?"

"I am happy."

"You don't look it. You look scared."

"It's normal for a mama to be scared."

"Of what?"

"I don't want to worry you with my mama problems."

"I won't worry. Tell me, Mama. I'll listen."

I can't tell him, though. I can't tell him the simple truths. They are too painful.

I can't tell him that when people get older, we get scared of more and more things. Scared of ourselves. Scared for our children. Scared of what the future holds for them.

There will be a time when I will not be here to guide or protect you. Hug and kiss you. Take care of you. Love you. I'll be gone. We are here and then we are gone. I see you, right now, right here. And I want to hug you. Forever. Have time stop. But that's not possible. That's not life. I am here now. But I already miss you with every heartbeat. I ache for missing you. There is so much of your life I will not be here to live with you. And you will go on without me. As we all must. Still, it breaks my heart. Breaks my heart that you don't understand it yet. You do not know how much of your life you will live without me, that I will never see. Perhaps I should have let my saving you be enough. I don't know. I've done a horrible thing. Horrible. Yet what is most horrible, and what I know you cannot understand, is that I do not regret it. I do not. Despite my immense love for you, despite the fear of losing you, I believe I would do it again.

"Don't cry." Lydan hugs me, and I sob.

I'm tired. So tired.

I cannot bear lying to Lydan, living a lie, yet I cannot bear having him know the truth either. I am his loving mother, and I am Lilith too. I own them both, with pride.

"Go to bed, Mama. Sleep," he says and takes my hand. "Come, Mama," he insists. "I'll put you to bed like you put me to bed."

I let him guide me down the hall. I am so tired.

He lays me in my bed and snuggles beside me, but I can't sleep. I know he will stay here until I do, so I pretend to sleep. He waits. I can sense him watching me. Finally, he leaves my room and shuts the door behind him.

I open my eyes and lie in bed on my back, staring at the ceiling.

I can't tell anymore if I am asleep or not, awake or dead. In the moonlight coming into my room through the window, I study the topography of the wrinkled skin at my knuckles. The pale dead skin at my cuticles. No blood there, that I can see.

I stare at my right hand. Its index finger. I curl the finger and uncurl it. A simple motion.

I don't know how I do it.

I don't know how I do anything.

How any of us do anything.

How does my finger know what to do?

How does my brain know what to do?

How does it know to tell my finger to scratch the itch at my elbow?

How does it know to point to a hummingbird on the feeder outside the window for Lydan to see?

How does it know to dip into a bowl of frosting and come back up for my tongue to lick?

How does my tongue know how to lick my finger?

How does it taste the frosting?

How?

How. How. How. How. How. How. How. How. How. How. How.

How does my finger know to squeeze the trigger?

It did as my brain commanded.

Every action, voluntary or involuntary, is at the will of my brain.

Not my *mind*.

My mind is not my brain.

My brain is not my mind.

I have killed five men.

Not murdered them.

Killed them.

As a child, I asked my mother how come we allow wars, fight wars, when the first commandment is *Thou shall not kill*?

She said that the translation is not exact. The original commandment was *Thou shall not murder*. What Cain did to Abel, that was murder. A sin. The gravest of sins.

But there are times when war, violence, is necessary, for an individual. For a society.

Such killings are not murder.

They are justified.

"How?" I asked.

"I don't know," she said.

They said to fight.

I fought.

I hear a snick.

I jolt up against the headboard, listening.

A door shutting.

The kitchen door.

"Lydan?" I say, but he does not answer. "Lydan."

Silence.

Someone is here, in the house.

I need the .45, but it's in the cellar.

I grab Lydan's baseball bat from the corner where I keep it and sneak my bedroom door open, tiptoe toward the kitchen.

I hear a strange noise coming from the short hall that leads to the deck door.

My muscles tense.

I peek around the corner to see . . .

Lydan. His back to me as he looks out the window of the door.

I exhale with relief. "What are you doing?" I say.

Lydan startles at my voice and turns to face me.

He's holding the cat in his arms.

He looks at me with the fear of someone who has been caught in the act of a crime.

This is why he wanted to put me to bed, so he could sneak outside and get the cat.

I can't help but smile.

"You can't be going outside in the middle of the night," I say and notice he's not wearing shoes. His bare feet and hands are dirty. "Especially in your bare feet," I say. "You're filthy."

"I . . . heard the cat outside my window," he says. "He crawled under the deck, and I had to get him."

"Put him outside."

"I just want to snuggle it. Please."

"For tonight. In the morning, we need to let it out again, to see if it goes back home or its owner finds it."

"I'm his owner now. He's my buddy now."

"He seems to be doing very well," I tell Dr. Downing when I speak to her on the phone, explaining to her about the other night in the kitchen. "Extremely well. I don't want this to come out wrong, be taken the wrong way, because I am astoundingly grateful for it—but this sudden fast improvement toward recovery is alarming. Scary."

"Scary in what way?"

"'Scary' might not be the right word. Unexpected. So fast. I wonder if it's real."

"I don't follow."

"'Real' isn't the right word either. I don't trust it. I'm scared he'll have a setback and be devastated."

"I don't see him having any major setbacks. He will experience plateaus. And they might last months and months, and those can and will be a cause of frustration and perhaps even anger. Resentment."

I am not speaking the truth. My truth. I cannot speak it. I will sound unwell. But the truth is that I am scared he is recovering so fast because there is something wrong.

He is not the son I've always had.

He's changed.

"This is good," she says. "I understand the trauma has left you untrusting of practically everything. And everyone. Of reality itself. Extreme violence, I'm sure you've heard and are aware, alters our brain chemistry, our emotions. The PTSD can bring seismic damage, fissures in one's psyche. Are you eating?"

"When I remember," I quip.

"And your sleep?"

"What's that?" I laugh a pealing laugh.

"Are you still not sleeping? You need to."

"Not much, if at all. Fits and starts. An hour here or there."

"I wish you would permit me to prescribe some hydroxyzine. To help you sleep. You can't go without sleep this long. It's essential to your well-being."

"I don't like to be on drugs."

"It's no stronger than Benadryl and won't leave you as groggy. Likely you won't be groggy at all."

"I don't know."

"Do you have racing thoughts at night from anxiety? I can prescribe something for that."

"You make it sound as if I don't have them during the day too," I say and laugh again. A big loud laugh. A genuine laugh at the absurdity of it all. Sleep? Eating? Racing thoughts only at night?

"The medication will help calm your thoughts."

"It won't calm these thoughts. I don't know if I want them quieted anyway. Some are beneficial. They help me solve problems. I don't want to be drugged."

"Have you ever taken antianxiety medication or sleeping aids?"

"I never needed or wanted them."

"So you don't *know* how they will affect you?"

"I don't like the idea of it."

"Of sleeping, of having a mind more settled?"

"Of drugs swimming in my veins and altering me. Am I not supposed to feel what it is natural to feel? Am I not allowed to go through the natural process of grief and anger and trauma and pain and fear and all of it without having to mask it, dull it, erase it with drugs? Make it go away because it's . . . unsettling. Not *nice*."

"It is natural but can be debilitating."

"That's natural too. Debilitation."

"The drugs I'd prescribe are not opioids. Lexapro helps anxiety. All it does is balance serotonin in the brain so you're not overwhelmed. Neither it nor hydroxyzine are addictive. They're both mild, and the doses are flexible. If you do not like how they make you feel, or if you experience any side effects, like headaches or mild dizziness or stomach issues, you can stop taking them. We can—"

"Tweak the dose? Try another? Give me something else? Give me something for the side effects?"

"The level of anxiety you have is extremely high, understandably. Your anxiety and racing thoughts can be reduced so that you are not unnecessarily worried about things you should not be worried about, things that in fact you should be pleased about. Your son's remarkable recovery is something to celebrate."

"You agree it's remarkable?"

"It is remarkable, for certain. It is at the extreme end, in the most encouraging way, but it is not outside the spectrum of possibility, obviously. It is what every parent would wish and pray for."

"I don't pray."

"Each person's body recovers in its own way. We help with surgery and medications and numerous physical therapies; still each body responds differently. This is the best possible outcome. Celebrate and enjoy it. You ought not be plagued with worry about something so positive."

"Have you ever seen a boy recover from such injuries so fast?"

"I've never seen a boy who has suffered half the injuries he has, let alone survived them. That he lived is against all probability. But I know of instances where individuals have healed and recovered far faster and more fully than anyone could have predicted or hoped for in their wildest dreams. I've seen people walk again who we thought were paralyzed for life. That you are so worried worries me. I don't know how else to say it except 'Just be grateful.'"

"I am," I say. "Or I want to be. One day he is in pain and can barely hobble down the hall with his crutches without pausing every few steps because of the pain or to gain his breath. The next day he's walking into the kitchen, not just without crutches but without any pain, without so much as the slightest limp or hitch."

"You don't literally mean the next day, but I can assure you—"

"I do. Because it was."

"Perhaps it seems like that. But it must have been a bit more progressive than overnight."

"It wasn't."

"This is where the need for sleep enters," she says. "Getting any sound sleep at all will help you exponentially. Bring more clarity. Sleep deprivation makes our senses muddy, the passage of time gauzy."

"You think I don't *know* one day from the next, a day from a week, just because I haven't slept well?"

"For months. That's far, far too long without good sleep. You can't be faulted. It is natural. You are right. But you don't have to suffer just because it's 'natural.' Childbirth is natural too, but we'd never expect you to go through it without an epidural or some sort of pain relief."

"I gave birth to Lydan at home with a doula, in a tub."

"Yes, well, if you'd let me prescribe—"

"I don't *want* it."

"You need it, I believe. For your sake and Lydan's. When an individual is sleep deprived for as long as you've been and doesn't eat well, time does get warped; reality can become warped. This is not professional 'opinion.' It's fact. Biological fact. Psychological fact. The individual is the last one to recognize it because the change is slow. A day bleeds into a night into a week until we lose all sense of time and perspective. If you change your mind, call, and I'll have you come in straightaway so I can see you in person and write you a prescription. You're an extreme case, and I will treat it as an emergency."

"I *saw* it," I say. "I saw *him*. The night before he was using crutches, and then . . . he wasn't, and he said, 'I'm all better, Mama,' and that—"

Terrifies me.

I am watching the news at 7:00 a.m. when the story breaks. A reporter is standing in front of a garish McMansion saying, "Lola Akers, the five-year-old daughter of Maximillian Akers, has reportedly died by a self-inflicted gunshot wound to the head."

A man at a podium wipes the lenses of his horn-rimmed glasses on the hem of his pink polo shirt before replacing the glasses on his nose. He plants his palms on either side of the podium. His flowing mane of white hair is tucked behind his ears.

"I am Noel Bravden, Mrs. Greta Akers's attorney," he says in a grave voice. "Mrs. Akers is in no condition to speak now and has permitted me to speak in order to try to answer your questions. After this, however, she wishes for privacy. She wants you to know that yesterday, her daughter, Lola, did indeed end her own life with a handgun. Since her father's murder, Lola has been in great emotional and psychological distress and grief. In the end, she wanted to be with her daddy, to join him in heaven. Mrs. Akers wishes you to know her daughter did this out of love for her daddy. She missed him that much. She loved him that much. And while this of course upsets Mrs. Akers, and she is grieving her daughter, she at least takes comfort that her daughter is with her daddy now, for eternity."

"How did a five-year-old get hold of a handgun?" a reporter asks.

"It was one of Mrs. Akers's handguns."

"It wasn't kept in a safe? There was no trigger lock on it?"

"That's an appalling and, really, a shockingly insensitive question."

"Was it in a safe or was there a trigger lock?"

"Mrs. Akers kept it at the ready in her bedside table drawer, for home protection. Against intruders. As you might imagine, the savage murder of her husband has brought out gangs of disturbed people, women in general, who view her as a villain in this simply because she was married to Mr. Akers."

"And the gun was loaded."

"If one keeps a handgun in one's bedside table for protection, one keeps it loaded."

"The child knew how to use the handgun?"

"Mr. and Mrs. Akers trained their daughter on operating a hand-gun, and other weapons for that matter."

"A five-year-old?"

"They wanted to keep her safe. Mrs. Akers also wants all her sup-porters to know that this death, her daughter's blood, is on Lilith's hands. Her daughter might as well have been killed at the hands of that evil woman. That's all I have for now. Thank you."

He takes off his glasses and again wipes them on his shirttail as he departs the podium and walks back toward the McMansion.

The reporter adds that the incident will be investigated, that Greta Akers might be brought up on criminal charges of manslaughter related to the ready access to the handgun that killed her daughter, and that the death might have been not the girl's intent but an accident that should never have happened.

A montage of photos of the daughter is shown on the TV. She's smiling as she swings on a swing set, her red hair trailing. She's blowing out five birthday candles atop a three-tiered pink cake. She is squeezing a Pikachu stuffed animal as she holds it aloft in triumph, knee deep in the litter of Christmas wrapping paper.

She is a cute girl. A joyous, gleeful girl. Or was.

She is gone because of me. On this count, Greta Akers is right: I am to blame. The girl should never have had the means to do it, never have had access to the handgun. But there is no ducking it. If I'd not done what I did, Lola Akers would be alive. I am as at fault as the handgun. She is dead as surely as if I'd pulled the trigger.

I cannot think of this. I cannot.

I will not.

I ponder what Saavedra said about confession bringing a sense of peace, of dignity. I know she is lying. Yet as with the best of lies, there is a grain of truth to it.

I shut off the TV and walk down the hall. I peek into Lydan's bedroom. He is asleep, splayed on his back, mouth agape and drooling as he snores. My boy. My lovely boy.

What have I done to you?

Whatever Akers's wife believes, whatever her own responsibility, whatever her husband did or might have done, I have taken her child's life as surely as if I struck the child down with the jawbone of an ass, and how can I ask others to own their parts in the play that is this terrible world if I do not lay claim to my part in it?

What example do I set for you, my boy, if I try to duck my accounting?

Still, son, I cannot leave you to the wolves.

I cannot.

Whatever trial confronts us, I must assess it and use it to our advantage.

"Adapt," Ella said in the hospital. "You'll adapt. You're about to start a very new kind of life, and it's harrowing, but you can do this. For him. After what you did at that school, you can do *anything* you put your mind to."

I am considering all this when a single rap sounds at the door.

I know that rap.

I stand to answer it.

Saavedra is there, with Folsom. Neither is smiling this time.

I want to tell them to leave, but what excuse do I have?

Saavedra denies my invitation to sit at the kitchen table.

"I'll stand," she says.

Folsom accepts my invitation and sits, staring at me.

"More follow-up," I say.

"Something like that," says Saavedra.

I pour myself a tumbler of water and drink from it, lean back against the sink.

I do not offer them drinks this time.

Saavedra looks around the kitchen. "Where's Lydan?"

"Sleeping," I say. "I'm not waking him."

"That's probably for the best," Saavedra says.

Folsom is still as can be, except for her eyes, which work over me and the room with deliberate calculation.

Silence thickens.

I sip my water. It's lukewarm and does not refresh me.

"You know what I don't get?" Saavedra says.

I shrug.

"We have footage of you buying gas at the Mobil station on Green Street. You must have topped your car off, because you got eleven point four two gallons."

Saavedra locks her eyes on mine, but I do not blink. I hold her gaze fast.

"Must have," I say.

"What's even funnier, though, is you seem to have filled it up again about two weeks later."

"Doesn't sound funny to me," I say.

Folsom picks up a saltshaker and sets it back down with a clack.

"It does to me," Saavedra says, "for someone who said she hadn't been out of the house hardly at all to run errands and the like, who never needs a sitter and has groceries delivered. That's a lot of driving."

"You know what's funnier?" I say. "The FBI spying on a single mom while she pumps gas."

"You paid in cash both times too. Do you normally do that?"

"If I have cash on me. Why would you be watching me pump gas? Don't you have better things to do? Criminals to catch?"

"Where did you go?"

"Not to run errands 'and the like,' as I said before."

"So. Where were you when your son had to be taken away by ambulance?"

"Nowhere."

"That covers a lot of area, nowhere does."

Folsom glances down the hallway.

"I drove around, for miles, for hours," I say. "No place."

"Odd behavior," Saavedra says.

"You know what's odd?" I say. "Having your child shot five times. Finding him bleeding out in a closet when all he should have been doing was his addition and subtraction tables. What's odd is a protocol where we have our kids wait in a room for a killer to come slaughter them rather than have us flee out the door and run away from him. It's odd being shot as I escape out a window with my dying boy in my arms." I pull up my shirt at my side and show my ugly scars. "When all I was doing was teaching kindergarten. That's odd. So pardon me if I needed some hours to myself to just drive around and do nothing, try not to think, to just be alone for the first time in weeks and weeks, drive with the radio on. Maybe you wouldn't think it so odd if you were in my shoes. Maybe you'd know just how normal it felt to drive around aimlessly for hours."

Saavedra scratches the side of her cheek with her pinkie.

"I know you're a good person. A good mom," Saavedra says. "I can tell."

I sip my water.

"There is a certain way to do this so it's as gentle on him as possible."

"On who?"

"Your son."

"Leave," I say.

"I feel for you, I truly do. For all you've been through," Saavedra says. If she's lying, she's practiced. "You seem like a decent person and definitely a good mother who had something awful happen."

"Get out," I say and look from Saavedra to Folsom. "Both of you. Leave."

"I wish I could do that."

"If I tell you to leave, you have to leave. You're trespassing."

"I want to make this as easy as possible on you and your son. Believe it or not. None of this is easy. I wanted to try to talk with you before—"

"Get a warrant if you think I've done something."

"I know you've done something."

"I haven't done anything, except what I've needed to do. Care for my boy. Now, I want you to leave or get a warrant."

"I have a warrant."

I'm taken off guard by this. I don't know if she is bluffing or not. I don't know if she's allowed, legally, to bluff about such a thing.

"You have to announce that," I say, but I have no idea if that's true.

"That's only on TV. You allowed me in. I've taken extraordinary steps to do it this way, discreetly, to try to convince you to do what's best for you and your son, to not have us have to tear your house apart to find what we need, and we will find it, if it's here. We will find it today."

She reaches into the inside pocket of her sports coat and extracts a cache of papers.

I look down at them.

It is a warrant, as far as I can tell with a glance. My focus is blurred, but I make out *Search and Seizure Warrant* and *United States District Court.*

"The press doesn't know. I want to do this discreetly for as long as possible, for your son, if for nothing else."

I've slipped up. They know. They suspect, at least. Perhaps I am one of dozens of female suspects, mothers with motive, and they need simply to try to eliminate me from their long list. Except they won't eliminate me. They will search the house and will arrest me when they find the guns in the cellar.

I think of Lydan in bed, asleep, unaware of what is about to transpire, unaware of what his mother has done, who she is.

Who I am.

"We are going to search your house," Saavedra says without any other acknowledgment of Folsom's presence. "Two experts are down the street, awaiting my orders. We are going to check your computer and your phone. Scour them. And turn your house inside out. It is going to be a mess, if you force us to have to look. We're going to start searching at my command, but before we do, you can tell me anything you'd like to get off your chest."

I want a lawyer. I need a lawyer. But if they find what is in the cellar, no lawyer will be able to help me. I know enough to not say anything. I am not under arrest, yet.

"Is there anything you'd like to say before we start?"

"Am I under arrest?" I say.

"Not at the moment. But know that any cooperation now will be seen in a positive light by a judge, when the time comes."

"What time is that?" I say.

"I think you know."

Folsom glances down the hall again.

I hear a sniffling sound, and I see Lydan in the hallway just outside the kitchen, rubbing his nose with the heel of his palm. He has his crutches tucked under his arms. I don't know why he's using them now when he doesn't need them, but I am glad he is.

"Mama," he says.

"Baby," I say, and he comes to me and sits in my lap.

"What's 'under arrest'?"

"Nothing," I say.

"Why are the ladies here again?" Lydan says and looks at me, then at them. Then at me again.

This is it. The time has come.

There is no way out.

They will tear this place apart and find the LAR and .45 in no time.

I've no idea now why I kept the guns. It's destiny, I suppose. I should have contacted Homer, told him I wanted him to "take Lydan fishing." But I feared they were watching. Listening.

I pull Lydan close.

If only I had stayed home with him that morning.

It is too late for such thoughts.

There is only forward.

It is time for my son to learn who his mother is.

"I need to talk to them," I say to Lydan.

"It's going to be okay, Mama."

When he hugs me tight, I feel I might burst with anguish, yet also with joy. Because he is here, with me now. Because I saved him. I close my eyes and breathe him in. I kiss his forehead and hold his face in my hands and tell him he is a good boy, a sweet, fine, funny, smart boy, all the boy I could ever hope and dream to have. The best boy. "Mama needs to talk to this lady now," I say. "You can have my phone or tablet to play with in your room."

"I don't want either of them," he says. "I'll just go wait."

He kisses my forehead and leaves, and I try to keep from weeping.

"I'm her," I say.

Folsom sits up straight in her chair as Saavedra takes a phone from her pocket. "I'll turn my phone's audio recorder on, if that's okay," Saavedra says, as if she's asking me if it's okay if she has a glass of water from my kitchen faucet.

"Fine," I say.

Folsom produces her own notepad and a pen. She clicks the pen with her thumb.

Saavedra turns on the recorder. "This is Special Agent Saavedra speaking at the residence of Elisabeth Ross." She gives the date and time, then says, "I am speaking to Elisabeth Ross. Elisabeth, you said you're her. Who?"

"Lilith."

"Lilith who?"

"Just Lilith. The woman who killed Maximillian Akers and the others. That's what you want to hear, isn't it?"

"Only if it's true."

"It is."

"Tell me about it. Why and how."

"I think you know why."

"I'd like to hear it in your own words. We've had countless women 'confess.' Ninety-three women, to be precise. And fifteen men. And of course, not one has proved to be her, have they?"

"Why would anyone confess if they didn't do it?"

"You'd be surprised. Some have genuine mental health issues. Some want attention. Glory. Fame. Infamy. Drama. There are as many reasons for false confessions as there are those who make them. So. You'll have to convince me it's you. That you are Lilith."

"You don't need convincing. That's why you came to my house the first time."

"You're mistaken about that," Saavedra says.

I'm not mistaken.

"So," Saavedra says. "Why?"

"Because of what happened after that day."

"What day?"

"That morning at school."

"What school is that?"

"Franklin Elementary."

"The shooting."

"Yes," I say, "*the shooting.*"

"So you did it because of what happened to you and your son and the others that day?"

"Not exactly."

"What then, exactly?"

"It was a couple weeks after that. Maybe more? I was in Lydan's ICU. And I saw, on TV, that *man.*"

"Man?"

"You know who. Don't play dumb. Akers. Maximillian Akers. I saw him giving an interview, going on about how more guns equals less crime, about how the only way to stop a bad guy with a gun was a good guy with a gun, and it made me sick, in my soul, each word a corrosive toxin in my veins, to hear that. And it sickened my mind to hear him suggest so very carefully and vaguely that just perhaps, *who is he to say,* some victims weren't even real, people like me and my son and all those kids and teachers that day were not real people, and the evil we endured was a staged stunt. It was evil, madness, feeding some deeply sick and greedy societal psychosis to blame everything except the gun and men. Him and his ilk, anyway."

Folsom is writing with fury, and when I pause, she keeps writing to catch up.

"He was a fiend beneath the human flesh, like so many through the ages. He wasn't fooling me. I knew he'd want to buy the LAR, could not help himself. He degraded dead children with sick jokes. Fomented chaos, and I saw it, right then on TV, that he and his 'war' have never been about the right to bear arms; it is about his perceived right to violence, his privilege of violence. A man's privilege to enact violence on others as he sees fit, and what more expedient way than by the gun to enforce oppression and submission and fear, to lord over others, to dominate. All *men* are created equal, so it says. All *men*. Not all people. Not all humans. Not all individuals. Not all citizens. All *men*. You get the intent. I don't need to tell you.

"I saw what he was. What they were. Despite their cloaks of being good men, family men, community men, they are, at heart, men of violence. Toxic men who profit off fear and death instead of love and peace. Men whose wet dream is to be able to use the gun against another human being, to kill another human being, one they consider lesser than them, and to have that killing justified, to stand their ground against the hooded teen, to defend, to get away with it. And they love these gunmen, they do. They love them because they live out some foul, primal acts they do not dare to live out themselves. These shooters are avatars for the Akerses of this world. But Akers didn't count on one thing."

"What is that?" Saavedra says.

"The good woman with a gun."

Saavedra stares at me, but I see nothing in her eyes at all. Nothing human.

"I'm not making excuses," I say. "Just giving context. I'd been through what I'd been through, and I'd been sleepless for weeks, sitting in that chair next to Lydan's ICU bed, he in a coma, and I didn't more than doze for a blink here or there, couldn't sleep, haven't slept except fitfully, exhausted beyond exhaustion. Numb. Hollow. Except when I watched my boy in his bed. Then I was lit with rage at the unholiness of it all and my absolute impotence to stop any of this, to do anything. I thought, How can this be? How can this Akers not just get away with spewing such filth but get a platform to vomit his filth to millions? I had a student ask earlier that day, before we had our lockdown drill, if I had to practice for shootings when I was a kid—because that's what we do now, *practice* for shootings, practice for being slaughtered—and I said no, things were different back then, we were different, and she asked why, and I said I guess we were kinder back then, and I don't know if that's true or not, but something has gone wrong with us, terribly, terribly wrong; some poison has seeped into our collective blood, soiled our souls and spoiled our minds. Can you tell me when it all changed? When we went from collectively, truly, *truly* mourning our murdered schoolchildren together and sharing a national outrage and grief to now allowing people to profiteer off them, to people voting in so-called politicians who mock and attack high school shooting victims on the street? Can you tell me where we started to become so diseased? There is evil at work here, true, timeless evil as old as *man*kind."

Saavedra stares at me.

"They're not rhetorical questions," I say. "They're real questions I can't answer. Can you?"

I await her answer.

None comes.

"Even if you can't answer why or how or when," I say, "you can answer who these profane people are, can't you?"

She does not answer.

"Bullies," I say. "Men. Bullying, weak, violent men. Almost always without exception."

After several minutes of what seems true contemplation, Saavedra says, "I think above all, we're traumatized in the extreme. As a people. And traumatized people act in extremes."

"The Akerses of the world," I say, "need people outraged and afraid so they will buy new guns and keep him in business; they need the perpetual bogeyman outside the house at night, ready to invade your home and kill your family. The other. The man who once exclaimed 'Damn you all to hell,' now paid to exclaim you'll take his gun from his cold, dead hands. Akers loved these shooters because he banked on them. And he got his wet dream. He got the showdown he dreamed of his whole life, a chance to defend himself with his gun, to be the good guy. It just didn't end the way he thought it would. I fear it will never end. It is fate."

"None of this proves you're Lilith," Saavedra says.

She is right, I realize. None of it does. Is she skeptical of me? Perhaps.

"How did you go about it?" Folsom says.

"You know how, I'm sure. I got into his chat rooms and found his email and dangled the carrot of the illegal LAR."

She makes a note on her tablet. "The LAR." She glances up at me. "How did you come to acquire it? From whom? You're a teacher. One wouldn't think you'd ever have access to such a rifle, such a world, or the means, the money, to get it if you did."

"You're wrong, clearly."

"So. Explain it to me. Who did you get the rifle from, and how did you get the money?"

"I can't say."

"Is there someone or some organization behind it? Someone you fear? Because even if you have committed this crime and will face prison for it, we will still protect you from—"

"I don't need protection. I'm not afraid of anyone or anything."

"Who did you get the LAR from?"

"You don't need to know."

"We *do*," Folsom says, and her voice is like a gunshot to me. I flinch.

"You're not going to know," I say. "Not from me."

"You don't need to protect anyone else," Saavedra says.

"I do what I need to do. I explain what I want to explain."

"Where is it then? The LAR? Even better, the forty-five that was used to kill Akers and his colleagues."

"Not far," I say.

"Don't play coy."

"I'm not."

"Where are they? If they are in this house, we will find them in short order. We will strip this house to its studs and then turn the studs to sawdust if we have to. And dig a pit where the house stands, then fill it in with concrete. Is that what you want your boy to experience? We will find them."

They will. Easily.

In minutes.

"Are they here?" Saavedra says.

"In the basement," I whisper.

"Of this house?" Folsom says.

"I don't know any other basement I'd put them in," I say.

"Where in the basement?" Saavedra says.

"Underneath the workbench, in the far corner, behind the wall paneling."

Saavedra eyes Folsom. "Stay with her."

Saavedra reaches into her pocket and produces a pair of blue latex gloves, stretches them onto her fingers.

Folsom places her handgun on the table, leaves a hand resting on it.

"Through the door there." I point to the basement door.

When I make the motion, Folsom's fingers tighten on her handgun's grip.

Saavedra opens the basement door and peers down the stairs.

"Light switch is on the left wall," I say as if I am directing an electrician who needs to check the circuit breaker.

Saavedra flicks the light switch on and proceeds down the stairs, out of sight.

When I hear the bottom stair squeak, I steel myself. I must remain resolute. I must show strength in front of my son. I must adapt.

Folsom's handgun is within my reach. If I fought her for it, I might get it. I might be able to use it against her. Against Saavedra. But even if I killed them and fled with Lydan, we would not get far. Perhaps I would be shot to death in front of my son. I cannot expose him to that. Will not.

I'm sitting at my kitchen table with an FBI agent who holds a gun on me, another FBI agent about to return with the two guns.

I hear Saavedra on the stairs.

I close my eyes and hold my breath.

This is how it ends.

And begins.

"What game are you playing?"

Saavedra's voice is sharp.

I open my eyes.

She is standing there, her eyes hot. "What game are you playing?" she says.

Her hands are empty. I expect her to be holding the LAR case or the .45. Then I understand she must have had to leave them down there, in place as she found them, so experts can take photographs of them, obey some protocol for evidence.

"What is it?" Folsom says.

"There's no guns down there. Something was hidden there, but it wasn't guns."

My head hums with white noise.

Saavedra is the one playing some game. Not me.

She takes an object from a pocket.

"What is that?" my voice says, even though I know what it is.

Lydan's tiny Pikachu stuffie.

"Call your son out here," Saavedra says.

"No."

"Call him out, or I will go get him."

"No you won't," I say.

"She will," Folsom says.

"Call him out here," Saavedra says. She steps toward the hall.

I make a move to stop her, but Folsom says, "Don't." She's holding the handgun now.

"Liie-dun," I say. My voice is shrapnel.

I swallow. Try again. "Lie-a-dun!"

"Yes, Mama." His voice floats down the hall.

"Come out here."

He enters the kitchen on his crutches. I see in his eyes he knows why he's been called out here. I wonder if Saavedra and Folsom can see it too. I don't think so. He is not their son.

"Lydan," Saavedra says. "Is this yours?" She holds up the Pikachu.

"You found my hiding spot." He looks astonished and confused. "How'd you find my hiding spot?"

"You hid this?" Saavedra says.

"I hide all kinds of stuff in my hiding spot. Candy and toys. Pokémon cards. How'd you find my spot?"

"Why do you hide stuff?" Saavedra says.

"For fun. For secret treasure."

"It's a great hiding spot," Saavedra says and squats in front of him, her hands planted on her knees. "Have you gone down there recently?"

"Uh-huh."

"When?"

"Yesterday."

"You can go down with those crutches?" Saavedra says.

"Not with them."

"How?" Folsom says.

"I hold the rail real tight, and I go real slow and careful."

"You're not supposed to do that," I say. "You're not stable enough."

"I can't always do nothing, Mama," he says.

"Let me see you do it," Saavedra says.

"No," I say.

"Show me," Saavedra says to Lydan. "I'd love to see how good you are at going up and down stairs on your own. See how much you've recovered."

"Okay," Lydan says.

Lydan crutches over to the open stairway door. He leans his crutches against the kitchen wall and takes hold of the handrail and takes a first ginger step down. Pauses. Takes another step as we watch.

Each step he takes is placed with care, as if the stairs are made of wet ice. He makes certain he is stable between each step. When he makes it to the bottom, he looks back over his shoulder and grins.

Saavedra goes down the steps behind Lydan before I can stop her.

"Show me how you get under the bench," she says.

I take the steps down to see Lydan reach out for the edge of the workbench and use it for support. He picks his way along it to the corner. Before Saavedra can ask him, he eases himself down to his knees with a grimace and a loud exhale. His recovery has been miraculous, but I know his pain is real. It must be gargantuan. But he manages to crawl under the workbench and move the panel aside. He backs out. When he stands, his face is pale and damp. His lips blue.

He limps along the workbench to Saavedra. He hands her two brownies in a Ziploc bag. She squeezes them. They squish beneath her fingers and thumb. They are fresh. The ones I made last night. I don't know how he got down here without my knowing. But there are no guns behind the panels.

I don't know what is happening, where the guns have gone.

I would not think it possible that Lydan carried the LAR out of the basement. The .45 and the ammo box, maybe. They're smaller, the box lighter than it was, being empty. But there is no other explanation.

I try to rid my mind of the image of him with the loaded .45 in his hands.

Lydan takes the rail and ascends the stairs, pausing and sweating between each step.

In the kitchen, Lydan takes up his crutches again. He looks as if he might be sick.

Saavedra asks him, "A lot of work to hide stuff. Why not hide it upstairs?"

"Then it wouldn't be a secret spot. And I'm not a baby."

"How often do you go down there?" Saavedra asks.

"Most days. For the exercise. To get better. Stronger. And for balance."

"I see," Saavedra says. "And have you ever found anything down there, in your hiding spot, that you didn't put there?"

He seems genuinely confused and distressed. "It's *my* secret spot."

"You haven't seen other things down there?" Saavedra says.

"No." He meets her eyes. Not to challenge. Or defy. He's just a boy answering a curious question with a soft yet assertive no and an honest gaze. He has nothing to hide.

"That's good exercise," Saavedra says. "You should be proud. Thanks for showing me."

"I'll have to find a new secret hiding spot now," he says.

"No secret stays secret forever," Saavedra says.

"But," he says and again meets Saavedra's eyes, "why were you down there?"

Saavedra has no answer.

"We were playing a game," I say.

"What kinda game?" he says.

"One where no one wins," Saavedra says.

Lydan shrugs and navigates his way back to his room with his crutches.

"Where are they?" Saavedra says to me.

"I don't know," I say, and I know I will never confess again. Never. If they are to catch me, they will have to do it on their own, without my help.

"You're a liar."

"I never had them," I say.

I don't know what is happening, but I am seizing this second chance. Adapting.

"You did have them. You killed those men," Saavedra says.

"Turn your recorder back on, and I'll tell you the truth."

"You told the truth the first time. We're going to search this place."

"Take your phone out," I say, my voice cold. "And record what *I have to say*."

Saavedra takes out her phone and starts to record.

"I'm not Lilith. And I didn't kill those men."

"Why did you say you're her and you did do it?" Saavedra says. Her jaw is tight. Her entire body rigid with resentment and contempt.

"Because," I say, "I wish to God I *had* killed them. I wish I had pulled the trigger and had the imagination and the guts to do it. The means and ability. But I don't. I could never do it. I wouldn't know how to get hold of a rifle like that. I don't know anything about guns. I didn't have a father who hunted or was into them. I didn't have a father at all. I wouldn't know the first thing. And as you said yourself, I don't have the means to buy a gun like that. And I'd never know how to shoot a revolver," I say, knowing the .45 isn't a revolver but a semiautomatic, feigning casual ignorance. "I wouldn't know how to load one or shoot one. I wanted to take credit for Akers because it would feel good to be brave enough to do it. I suppose I've lost my mind since that day at school. I can understand why this Lilith did what she did. I guess I am like all the others who 'confessed,' for my own reasons. But I am not her. I could never be her."

Saavedra steps so close to me I can smell the wintergreen gum she snaps between her back molars, see crow's-feet splinter at the corners of her eyes.

"I don't believe you," she says.

Folsom's look reveals she does not believe me either.

"And," I say, "I would never leave my son alone at night. All night. He wakes up most nights, crying out for me, and there is no way I could stand the thought of having him wake up alone, find me gone. I could never live with myself over that, never mind losing him over killing those worthless men."

Saavedra snaps her gum.

"You killed them," she says.

"I didn't," I say.

"You've made a mistake. And I will find it. You were right. That's why I was here the first time. You slipped up. Enough for a warrant.

And what works to my advantage is you don't know what the slipup is. You won't get away with it. I don't care how ugly the people you killed were. How monstrous. Justice will find you."

"Maybe justice already found who it needed to find," I say.

Saavedra swipes at the screen of her phone and speaks into it. "Bring them in," she says.

For hours, Lydan and I sit in the kitchen at the table and play checkers and go through his Pokémon trading cards, organizing them in binders as Saavedra and Folsom and the two other agents hunt through our home with meticulous attention, leaving no stone unturned. They open and search every drawer and closet and cupboard. They enter every room, and I can hear them in each, drawers opening and closing. Agents file in and out with no regard to our presence, taking out clear plastic bags with contents in them, everything from an old watch of mine to Lydan's plastic walkie-talkie set. The two agents go out to the garage. I try to breathe, try to remain calm. My heart hammers. Saavedra seizes my laptop and my phone. I know my phone had the search for Akers on it from when I was outside the hospital, but I was on his site for all of a couple of minutes, and I have not deleted it. I've left it there in my history, because I have nothing to hide. I've told Saavedra about seeing him on TV and loathing him, so it's not so suspicious that I visited his site out of curiosity. There is no law against that. And there is not a trace of me doing anything else on my phone in regard to him. The burner phones have been obliterated and will never be found. I do have a couple of calls from Homer but no texts from him. There is no evidence of what we talked about, and if they find their way to interviewing him, I trust he will not betray me. My laptop is clean, with no connection whatsoever to Akers.

"What are they doing?" Lydan said at the outset as the agents buzzed around him.

"Playing the game," I said, "sort of like a treasure hunt."

"Why are they wearing those gloves?"

"It's all part of the game," I said.

"Are we in trouble?"

The agents do not find a gun or an ammo box.

But they leave the place in disarray, without any plan to put things back in order. The car is left with its doors and trunk open, seats pushed all the way back, mats left on the garage floor along with the contents of the glove box, console, and door pockets. A patch of vinyl has been cut out from the driver's seat.

"You'll see me again," Saavedra says, her voice ice.

When the agents are gone, I count to ten and breathe. I must galvanize myself.

I must fight the urge to collapse.

I lean into Lydan's ear and whisper, "What did you do? Whisper it to me."

He smiles. He's delighted by the secrecy. The game. "Nothing," he whispers.

"You did. It had to be you."

"Let's play checkers," he whispers.

"We can't be playing checkers. You need to tell me what you did."

"I don't know what you mean."

"They're dangerous. Very, very dangerous and can get you in big, big trouble."

"What can?"

He starts to set up the checkerboard.

"Lydan. This is serious."

He looks up at me, his eyes clear and bright.

"You go first." He nods at the checkerboard.

"Lydan, I don't want to play checkers."

"Play," he says.

I slide a checker toward him at an angle.

"What did you do?" I whisper.

He places a fingertip on a checker and pushes it.

"Nothing."

I move a checker.

He pushes his checker without hesitation, hemming in my checkers so with my next move I will lose a checker to him.

I cup his ear with my hand and whisper even more quietly. "You're not in trouble. You're a brave boy. But I need to know where they are, and I need to know you won't handle them. They are dangerous. And if those two ladies find them somewhere else, nearby, they will know they were here. And I will be in big trouble. I will have to go away. We will have to be apart."

I slide a checker, and he starts to jump it before I even have my finger off it.

He takes my checker off the board.

"Your move, Mama."

I place a hand on his, give it a soft squeeze. "I'll buy you a Pokémon Vmax booster box," I whisper.

His eyes glimmer.

"Two boxes," he says.

"Two," I say.

He smiles, gleeful.

"No one will find them," he whispers. He moves a checker without looking at me.

He did move them. They must be close by.

"How did you find them?" I whisper.

"Playing hide-and-seek. With Wendy. I knew she would never guess I could go up and down the stairs. I'd been practicing. I wanted to do it. Be normal. I wanted to surprise you with how good I got, how normal."

"Okay," I say.

"I sneaked under the workbench."

"Don't tell me any more."

"I saw the panel was loose," he says. "I knew they shouldn't be there.

I saw them on TV when you were watching the news, and I knew they were bad."

"Lydan," I say.

"I know it wasn't you who put them there. I know it was that lady in the doorway that night. She was here. And you were asleep. You just never woke up 'cause she was so quiet. But it must have been her. I think she did something bad with them."

"You did the right thing," I say. "Let's not talk about that lady anymore. Ever again, especially if those two ladies who were here or anyone else asks about her."

"I'd never say anything to those ladies. I'd be scared they wouldn't believe me about the lady, like you didn't, and they'd think the guns were yours. And they're not. Are they, Mama?"

"No," I say, "they're not." He believes me because it is the truth. They are not mine. They are Homer's. And I have to contact him, tell him I want to go fishing. But I can't. Not yet.

"Now," I say, "you need to tell me exactly where they are."

The guns are at the jobsite down at the end of the cul-de-sac.

The night I caught him in the kitchen with the cat, I thought his pants and hands and face were muddied from crawling around after it. They weren't.

He'd seen the guns, and he looked for the right time to get rid of them. He knew they were bad and he needed to get them out. Just like, I suppose, he knew something bad was going to happen that morning at Franklin.

He did know. I know he did.

I don't know if the FBI is watching me. But I know it is only a matter of time before they get a warrant to search the surrounding area.

The dots will be connected.

I cannot do nothing.

I cannot wait.

I must act.

I know one place that has a landline phone I can use. I call Dr. Downing for an emergency appointment.

I take Lydan with me to the hospital. I tell him I have to go there for an appointment, and he has to come with me. He does not argue.

On the drive there, I check the rearview mirror every couple of seconds. I don't see any cars following me. A blue Toyota Tacoma is behind me for a few blocks but gets on the interstate, leaving a motorcycle behind me. The motorcycle follows me for less than a block before turning in to a liquor store. There is a school bus behind that.

When I turn in to the destination, no vehicle turns in behind me, and the car that continues on is driven by a teenage boy with a dog in his lap.

When I park and step out of the car, I see a mother with a baby in a sling getting into a car where a middle-aged man waits at the wheel. No one else.

"Follow me," I say to Lydan, and we enter.

The hospital smells of disinfectant and bleach.

No one except a nurse in scrubs is on the elevator with us as it rises.

While we wait for my appointment, Lydan and I play games in the back of the *Highlights* magazine. When I am called, Lydan joins me.

My appointment is brief.

"I'm glad you've decided to try the prescriptions," Dr. Downing says. "You'll find they help. And I am glad to see you doing so very well, Lydan."

Before I leave for the registration desk in the doctor's office, I ask a nurse in the back office if I could please possibly use her phone to make a quick call. "My cell phone is dead," I say. "It will only take a minute."

"Of course," she says. "Dial nine to get out."

I dial nine. Then the number.

"Hi," I say. "I'd love it if you could take us fishing. Lydan is so stir crazy."

I listen carefully to what Homer says.

"We can do that," I say and hang up.

From the garage, I take out our fishing rods and tackle boxes and set them out on the lawn. I do this in broad daylight. I have nothing to hide. I wear sunglasses so I can look around more freely to see if we are being observed, without any potential observer being able to tell I am scanning my surroundings. I see no one. No vehicle I do not recognize. No stranger walking a strange dog. No unknown joggers or cable-company vans. Nothing. No one I do not recognize. Just Claire. Yet even she pays me no mind. She's in her yard and, to my surprise, putting up a FOR SALE BY OWNER sign.

For a second she looks my way. I know she sees me, but she turns away and promptly heads back into the house.

"Where are we going fishing?" Lydan says as he opens the tackle boxes and peruses the choices of shining and colorful metallic lures.

"A secret spot."

"Put this one on mine," he says, animated as he lifts out a red-and-white Dardevle.

I want to hurry to get this done, yet it also serves us if I take my time, naturally.

"That's a good one."

"I've had good luck on it. Remember?"

I do remember: last summer on the dock at the local state park's pond. He caught big bass while the other kids caught perch.

Ages ago.

"What do we have to tie on first?" I say and glance up and down the street.

"The barrel swivel, so it won't get all twisted," he says.

I tie on a swivel and then let him work the Dardevle on it.

"Careful," I say, "that treble hook is sharp."

"I got it," Lydan says, earnest.

"We'll bring the big cooler," I say, "and make a big lunch, make a day of it."

He helps me wheel the cooler out and hose the inside out, clean it up.

"When are we going?" he says.

"Dawn."

Two thirteen a.m.

Dark. Black night. Good.

I sneak out the back basement window wearing black sweatpants and a black hoodie. I crawl into the screen of trees at the edge of the backyard and pick my way behind the houses.

The jobsite is dark, and it takes me a while to find the pile of scrap wood and metal, even longer to dig around and move pieces of lumber and siding and corrugated roofing. The long dumpster nearby is loaded to the top, and I'm sure it's due to be swapped out any day and these scraps to be thrown in the new one. Lydan's hiding spot would be found in minutes.

The .45 is just lying there on the ground beneath the metal roofing pieces. The LAR case is wedged farther under. The ammo box is all but sitting in the open, save for one piece of plywood atop it.

I grab the .45 and tuck it into my waistband.

I pick up the LAR case and ammo box by their handles and work my way back home. I sneak in the back door this time and put the guns and ammo box at the bottom of the long camping cooler. The LAR case doesn't quite fit flat at the bottom. It's too long, but it will have to do. I cover them with ice until they can't be seen, then put hot dogs, sandwiches, potato and macaroni salads, and bottled drinks on top of them.

I load the cooler into the trunk of the car. The fishing rods and tackle box are in the back seat.

Now, much as I don't want to, I wait till dawn.

As we drive toward our rendezvous spot, Lydan is a chatterbox, talking about the fish he hopes to catch, the lures he plans to use. "Can we keep some fish to eat?" he says. I tell him we can.

It is all I can do to behave in a natural way, to hear his words and respond to them. Every vehicle behind us might be the end of us. There is no way to know.

Homer's boat, an old Boston Whaler V hull he uses to troll for lake trout and coho salmon, is backed up, still trailered to his truck, at the bottom of the ramp. Homer is standing beside it, waving at us as if there is not a worry in the world.

There are several other pickup trucks and SUVs parked in the gravel lot, but they and their boat trailers sit empty. The real anglers were out on the lake before light.

It's nearly noon now.

"Who's that man?" Lydan says as we get out of the car and Homer ambles up the ramp toward us, saying hello.

"It's your great-great-uncle."

"Are we going out on a boat?" Lydan says.

"We are indeed," Homer says as he approaches and sloshes his remaining coffee from his travel mug onto the ground. He takes the two fishing rods and the tackle box out and hands them to Lydan, then points at the boat and tells him to put them in it.

Lydan does so.

"Cooler in the back?" he says.

I tell him it is.

"Pop the trunk and I'll grab it."

Homer is reaching into the trunk when a green SUV pulls into the lot.

A police SUV.

Its tires crunch on the gravel as it stops at the top of the ramp, blocking us.

"Homer," I say. "Homer."

Homer straightens up and shuts the trunk.

A cop gets out of the SUV and zips up a green jacket. He's a large man, early middle age, with a black mustache. He adjusts his gun belt and strides toward us down the ramp. I glance at Homer. He's not looking at me; he's watching the cop advance on us. He reaches a hand deep inside his jacket.

He's going for a handgun.

He's stepping toward the officer now with his slow but determined gait, to meet him.

I am riveted in place, unable to stop this.

Lydan is at my side. "Are we going now? Are we ready? Where's the cooler?"

Homer's hand is coming out from inside his jacket now as the officer reaches a hand down toward his gun belt.

"Officer," I say and lunge past Homer in a few quick strides, putting myself between Homer and the officer. "Officer."

The officer smiles. His mustache quivers.

"Miss," he says.

"I've got all my paperwork and license here," Homer says.

The officer's hand brings out a notepad from his pocket.

I look at the officer again, at his SUV.

He's not a police officer; he's a game warden.

"There's a man who is prepared," the warden says and reaches out for the papers that Homer hands to him. I note his brass name tag: Bruce Parks.

The warden eyes the paperwork, eyes Homer as he walks past me and Lydan, down to the boat. He checks the outside of the hull. He's looking at the registration sticker.

He hands the paperwork back to Homer and looks in over the side of the boat, inspecting it. He walks to the rear of the boat and examines the down riggers.

"You're just heading out?" the warden says and walks back up to Homer.

"Yup," Homer says.

"Late start," the warden says.

"My days of getting up at the ass crack of dawn to catch a few togue are long gone."

"It's a long way past the crack of dawn," the warden says. "Fish aren't that likely to be agreeable by now."

"I'm not so agreeable anymore, period, so I guess that evens it out. I fish when I can. This is more a pleasure cruise anyhow. And some fun for my niece's boy."

"Going to get after 'em?" the warden says to Lydan.

"I hope so," Lydan says.

The warden addresses me. "You fishing?"

I sense a glance from Homer and realize I forgot to buy my license.

"Not today, just the boy," Homer says.

"So no need for me to ask you for your license then," the warden says to me.

"You can ask," I say. "But I don't have one because I don't plan to fish."

A truck pulls into the lot, its stack pipe just behind the cab thunderous.

"We all set to shove off here?" Homer says.

"Not quite," the warden says. "I don't see any life vests in the boat. You need to have one per person on any craft."

"I do," Homer says.

The warden walks back to the boat and looks in over the side. "I don't see any."

"They're in the back of the truck," Homer says.

"They're no good to you there." The warden looks into the truck's bed. "Don't see any."

"In the tool vault. It's locked."

I chew my bottom lip. I'm not sure Homer has the life vests, or enough of them for all three of us. If he doesn't, the warden won't let us on the water.

The warden clasps his hands in front of him.

"Go ahead and grab them," he says and nods at me.

I want to peek over at Homer to see if his face gives away anything. But I don't.

"She'll need the key for the padlock."

Homer gives me the key, and I climb into the back of the truck. I fumble with the key, trembling.

I finally seat the key and pop the lock and lift the tool vault's lid. I don't see any life vests.

"Move the ropes and the toolbox," Homer says.

I move them out of the way.

The vests are there.

"Look at that," Homer says.

I hear the warden's boots shift in the gravel.

I snatch the vests out of the vault.

The warden is looking at Homer, who is pointing up into the sky at a bald eagle.

The warden shrugs. "We got a lot of them around."

"I know it," Homer says. "I can't get used to it, though. Each one I see is a marvel. What a success story."

"A lot of fishermen hate 'em," the warden says. "Think they're no more than glorified seagulls."

"Here they are," I say and climb out of the bed with the vests. "One for each of us." I drop them over the side of the boat.

"Doesn't look like those have been used in some time," the warden says. "Good thing I was here to remind you."

"I wouldn't have forgotten," Homer says.

"Well," the warden says, "I'll leave you to it." He looks at me. "You'll want to get your car parked and out of the way."

A red truck that pulled in is idling at the top of the ramp, behind the warden's SUV, leaving little room for even the warden to back up past it.

"Will do," I say, forcing a smile. "I have to get other stuff out of it first."

The warden taps his notepad against his hip.

"You can put them through the routine while she's doing it," Homer says, referring to the boaters in the red truck.

"Guess I could," the warden says.

He lumbers up the boat ramp. He has the red truck back up some, then backs up his SUV to make room for my car.

Out of his truck, the warden looks back once at me, then addresses the driver of the red truck as the truck's window powers down.

I exhale a long breath.

"Can we go now?" Lydan asks, impatient.

I pop the trunk, and Homer seizes the cooler and lifts it out while the warden is engaged with the driver of the red truck.

"Go park," Homer says.

I back the car slowly up the ramp. The warden stands close to the idling truck's door as I squeeze my car past him.

The driver ogles me.

I park the car and walk back down the ramp, the warden nodding as I go past.

"Quite the big lunch," the warden says. "I hope it's not liquid."

I stop. "Excuse me?"

"Your cooler. It's a big cooler."

"It is."

"I hope it's not full of booze," he says. He holds up a finger for the driver of the red truck to wait a moment, then walks down the ramp behind me toward the boat. "Drinking and boating is illegal."

I feel a rush of blood come to my face. "The cooler is for the fish," I say.

"An optimist, eh?" The warden leans over the side of the boat and looks at the cooler.

"There's no booze in there," Homer says. "And if there was, it's not illegal unless the pilot is drinking."

"You won't mind opening it then?" the warden says. "Just to humor me."

Homer reaches over the side and lifts the cooler's lid, backs away, his hand going inside his coat.

The warden looks into the cooler. On top of the ice sit the sandwiches and hot dogs and bottles of iced tea and water.

The driver in the red truck is watching intently. I feel his eyes on me. He's waiting for me to make eye contact so he can give me his big winning smile, the one he thinks is so mesmerizing, so hypnotizing and charming, the one he thinks I don't get from every other chump I encounter all day long when I'm out running errands.

I glance at the driver. He offers a big grin: *Look at me, look at me, notice me. Respond to me.* I respond, with a smirk that is unmistakable, one that says, *Fuck off.*

Rankled and impatient, the driver honks his horn.

"All right," the warden says and closes the cooler lid.

I lift Lydan up at the edge of the boat. "Here we go," I say and place him in it. The motor is already running, its prop churning the water with a froth and burble.

Lydan sits up in the front, holding his rod. "When do we fish? Can I cast now?"

"In a while," Homer says.

Homer backs the boat out into the water and steers it in a wide arc until the bow is facing out toward the broad lake. He pushes the shift forward and the boat surges, accelerating, its prow lifting as if it is weightless, then finally lowering again as the boat reaches speed and smooths out to plane through the water.

"I need you to take some Dramamine," I say. "This lake can make you feel seasick."

I give him two pills.

"I thought Dramamine was orange?" he says.

"Some are orange, some purple, some white. These are white," I say. "Here."

I take a bottle of water from my handbag.

"Aren't they chewable?" Lydan says.

"Not these, not for the water."

He swallows the pills down.

Twenty minutes out on the lake, Lydan is dozing.

I close my eyes as the wind rakes back my hair and the lake water sprays my face. It's cold. It feels good on my skin, which is hot from the stress of the encounter with the warden.

"I didn't like him," I say, raising my voice over the drone of the boat motor. "I think he sensed something."

"There's nothing to sense," Homer says, his voice raw when he raises it. His eyes are watering from the wind. "We're a niece and her son and uncle out on a nice day of boating, maybe a little fishing. That's it."

"I thought he was going to push his hands down in the ice in the cooler. If he had—"

"He didn't."

"But if he had."

"Don't 'if.' He was just a game warden going through the motions. I've dealt with dozens over the years. They spend their days making sure boats are registered and anglers have their licenses and life vests and nobody is drunk. He didn't sense a thing."

For the next hour and a half, we ride in silence, Lydan asleep against me. It is too difficult with the wind and spray and the need to yell over the sound of the motor to bother to talk. So we ride in silence.

The boat's speedometer reads thirty-two miles per hour, so we have to be at least fifty miles out into the lake by now. Fifty miles. That's a long way. I lost sight of land a long time ago. We might as well be out on the ocean. Just black water and blue sky. There is a good swell out here, but the boat chops right through it. We've not seen another boat in an hour.

The boat is slowing now, Homer easing up on the throttle, the boat settling in the waves and rising and falling with them.

I stand and fall back in my seat, legs unsteady.

I grab hold of the seat beside me and stand again, feet wide apart.

Homer adjusts a knob on his depth finder.

"This is it," he says. "It's not the deepest part of the lake, but it'll do."

"How deep is it?"

"Nine hundred feet. Nine hundred and thirteen, actually."

I knew the lake was deep but somehow never knew it was this deep.

"Deepest part is another hour out, thirteen hundred feet. But we're not out here for a geology lesson."

He takes hold of the cooler and looks inside it.

I take out the food and drinks, and he scoops out the ice with his hands.

Without ceremony he places a ten-pound dumbbell inside the ammo box, latches the box, locks it up, and drops it into the lake. It disappears in a trail of tiny silver bubbles.

He picks the .45 out of the cooler by slipping a screwdriver shaft into its trigger guard. He drops it into the lake. He puts on a pair of rubber gloves that fishmongers might use and lifts the LAR case out. Opens it. He takes the LAR out as a huge swell of a wave knocks the boat sideways. Lydan stirs, mumbles.

"Shhhh," I say, stroking his hair.

He settles.

Homer takes out a tool kit.

With expertise, Homer takes the LAR apart, breaks it down into pieces. Stock, forearm, barrel, action. He drops one piece in at a time as we drift along. In seconds the gun is gone. He places three ten-pound dumbbells in the case, aligning them in a row. They just fit. He has to force the lid to close and latch. He locks it.

I look over the side and watch it sink.

I feel sick and lightheaded.

"Sit," Homer says. "Get off your feet. Take some Dramamine yourself."

"I'm not seasick," I say. The sun is too bright and too fierce. I close my eyes against it. "They'll find it. They'll find it all, somehow. Someone will."

Homer rests a hand on mine.

"They won't. Not out here. Nine hundred feet below the surface. No one fishes out here. No one comes out here at all. No reason to do it. It might as well be on the moon. We're so far out there's no cell service; we have to use radios for contact. People have gotten turned around out here, lost, and never seen again, even with modern equipment. Swells can rival those of an ocean during a storm. Enormous waves that sink cargo ships." Homer points to his depth finder. "It's far too deep for an anchor. In the short time we've drifted, we've covered nearly a mile.

"A mile. We've only been idling fifteen minutes.

"So no one is going to find them. The rifle is gone. The forty-five. All of it. Gone. Forever."

Lydan stirs. Blinks. "Where are we?" he says, rubbing his eyes, yawning.

"On the lake."

"I fell asleep," he says.

"Yes," I say, "you did."

We sit on the couch watching *Bob's Burgers*, Lydan and I, Lydan with his Pokémon cards spread out on the coffee table, forever organizing and reorganizing.

He takes a break and tucks in close to me, hugging his Pikachu stuffie.

I haven't watched the news or been online in days.

It doesn't help, knowing.

I was offered the chance to return to work, but I declined. I took a severance. I cannot go back. Lamb and Mitchel have been suspended, but it doesn't matter. It doesn't help. It doesn't help that Claire has a for-sale sign in the yard, and that soon she'll be gone and won't be watching us anymore. Causing worry. Knowing this doesn't help.

I live knowing any moment I might be caught.

If I am caught, I must make the most of it. Adapt. I will speak out. There isn't a media outlet on the globe that will not want to interview me. Lilith.

If I wanted, I could choose to try to tamp down the firestorm of violence that rages now across the land, or I could give orders to never retreat, to fight.

I could do this.

I have this power.

I can choose to do whatever I feel is just, as Lilith.

I am prepared.

I did not start this.

I saved my son and I saved those children that day.

And if we had not been attacked, I would not have done what I'd done; that which needed to be done long ago, in an ancient time.

It is not for me to say if I've made things better or worse.

I honestly do not know.

But I know this:

I owe nothing to anyone, except to my son.

And all I want to do is spend whatever time I have left with him.

Maybe one day I will tell him what I've done.

Maybe one day I will have to tell him who I am, besides his mother.

For now, I will sit on the couch beside him and laugh, hug him at my side, and never let him go as I wait for the knock on the door, and the world outside hurtles toward oblivion.

Acknowledgments

My continued thanks to my lovely and loving wife and to my daughter and son, for their smiles, hugs, and joy and for their love of books and stories.

My thanks to everyone at Blackstone Publishing, especially to Josh Stanton, for having enough faith in my writing to take on several books and for making my inaugural novel with Blackstone, *I Am Not Who You Think I Am*, a huge success. Thanks to Stephanie Stanton and her genius as an art director that assures that all the artwork associated with my books stands out from the crowd with striking and original designs. It is an immense pleasure to know my books have the backing of such a committed and gifted team. Thank you to executive editor Josie Woodbridge for leading the way and shepherding this book through the editing process.

Special thanks to my editor for this book, Michael Signorelli. I've looked forward to working with Michael for a long time, and his keen eye and professional input helped shape and improve this book in ways I never could have achieved otherwise. I hope this is just the start of working with him.

There are so many tiny yet supremely critical problems and incongruities to account for in a novel, too many for an author to ever find on one's own. I thank Riam Griswold for that special copy editor's eye that discovers countless such aspects throughout to make this a much better novel.

For insight into challenges I faced with law enforcement matters such as warrants and searches for evidence, I am fortunate to have befriended my fellow Little League coach, Detective Sergeant Tyson Kinney of the Vermont State Police Major Crime Unit. Tyson is kind enough to tolerate and answer my questions. If there are any errors in the novel, they are on me, or done for the sake of a fictional narrative. Thanks again, Tyson.

A big thanks again must go to Ryan C. Coleman at the Story Factory, who is always there, along with Shane, to talk me off the edge of the ever-present cliff I seemingly live on. Your direction and support and good humor are invaluable in the process.

Of course, none of this would be possible without my agent, Shane Salerno of the Story Factory, who dedicates immense time and energy and talent into championing my work and finding the perfect publisher. Shane never seems to sleep and is constantly at work for myself and other TSF writers. My continued gratitude for all you've accomplished on behalf of my novels and my family.

Among the many friends and family members who've supported me are Beth and Judy Rickstad; Gary Martineau; Bryanna, Eric, and Willa; Boone, Hailey, and Poppy; Ben, Bill, and Mary Wilson; Libby, Herb, and Todd Levinson; Allyson Miller; John Mero and Ali Sieglitz; Steve and Carole Phillips; Mike and Janice Quartararo; Dave Stanilonis; Roger and Susan Bora; Dan Orseck; Dave and Heidi Bouchard; Dan and Stacey Myers; Rob O'Donovan; Jon Frederick and Jill Durocher; John Arlotta; Bill and Bebe Bullock; Jim Lepage; Greg Cutler; Rona Long; Stephen Foreman; and many others. My ongoing thanks to each of you.